IF NOT FOR
THE KNIGHT

Knights are Forever Series
Book # 1

DEBBIE BOEK

ALSO BY DEBBIE BOEK

Sommers' Folly

THE DEVEREAUX CHRONICLES

Devil's Bait

Devil's Retribution

Devil's Gathering

Visit the author at:
debbieboek.com
debbieboek.blog

CHAPTER 1

Northern England 1067

Regan walked slowly back toward the village, admiring the flowers in her basket, pleased at how the yellow primroses complimented the blue of the wild hyacinth that she had finally been able to locate. She had wandered far while collecting them and would surely be punished for being away from the cottage for the whole day and neglecting her chores. She was confident though, that she would be able to convince her father to be lenient. After all, the flowers were for her bridal headpiece; she had wanted to find the prettiest, freshest flowers possible. Surely, he would not be angry about that.

She sighed deeply, unable to hide, even from herself, the heaviness in her heart. She had been promised to Edgar when they were but children. Both had known that they would be married one day. It was just hard to accept that the day had finally arrived.

Edgar was a good man and had pleasing features. He was well respected and worked hard in the Lord's stables. The cottage that he built for them was not large, but it had room enough. He would be able to care well for her and the children that they would one day have together.

The reason for her melancholy eluded Regan. After all, it should be the happiest time of her life. She knew that she had no choice in the matter; it was the way that things were done. There was nothing wrong with Edgar and she was very fond of him, but she could not help but feel sad that this was how it had to be.

In her daydreams, Regan always envisioned being swept away by passion and love, but try as she might, she could not make herself feel anything more for Edgar than friendship and affection. She had gone to pick the flowers hoping that it would help settle the matter in her own mind, but she was not sure if it had.

Smiling wistfully as she made her way through the field of wildflowers, she decided that perhaps she was just being silly and childish to expect to feel differently about her future husband.

Maybe love was not important to a good marriage. Or, perhaps her mother was right and love was something that developed and grew between two married people as they carried on their lives together.

Lost in her musings about the impending wedding, Regan did not at first register the noises she was hearing, screaming and crying, sounds of distress that were coming from the direction of her village.

She climbed atop a knoll, where she could look down into the valley and see the village below. To her wide-eyed disbelief, great plumes of dark smoke billowed from some of the cottages and people, her people, were fighting with, or running from, men on horseback.

Momentarily stunned and frozen to the spot where she stood, Regan watched in horror as her fellow villagers were struck down one after the other, their handmade weapons ineffectual against the attacking army.

Normans, her brain screamed, as her mind and body began to function again. Regan felt her heart begin to race and ran as fast as her slippered feet would carry her down the slope toward the village.

"Please let mother and father be alright," she prayed as she flew down the hill. The circlet fell from her hair, the plait loosening enough that her long, copper-colored curls blew around her face as she ran. Unable to see clearly, her foot caught in the skirt of her long, linen kirtle. She pitched forward and her temple collided with a large rock. The basket of flowers flew from her hand and the screams faded as the world around her went black.

* * *

"Draco," Calder's voice boomed across the courtyard, "are all of the men accounted for?"

"They are, Milord," he responded.

The males of the village huddled, unarmed, in a large group in the center of the courtyard. Mingled among the soldiers who sought to defend their Lord's lands were farmers and craftsmen, who had also taken up arms against the Normans.

The knights were awe-inspiring on their large destriers, both men and horses covered in protective armor from head to toe. Most of the knights had removed the conical helmets that they wore during the battle, but their armor and weaponry still clattered forbiddingly as they held the villagers at bay.

Calder rode his large black warhorse around the circle of men, each of whom watched him with a mixture of hatred and distrust in their eyes. He had seen that look many times before and refused to let himself be bothered by it. Some of the men showed fear; but not all, despite the knowledge that he could slay them at that very moment should he choose to.

"You men," he called to the captives, his voice loud and strong, "I am Calder Wyndym. These lands, and you with them, now belong to my brother, Aric, Earl Of Marlboro, by order of King William. Aric will be here within the week, and you will then swear your fealty to him. Should you not, you will immediately be hung for treason. Should any of you take up arms against my men, or my brother and his men, I will personally see to it that you die slowly and painfully."

"Do you understand me?" His voice was surprisingly level and matter-of-fact, but the promise it held was unmistakable, none of the men doubted his words. The thin, moon-shaped scar that ran from his right eye down to his jawbone was a livid red against his white skin, making him look even more fearsome.

He continuously circled the group of men, his horse's enormous hooves coming within inches of the prisoners' feet. Some nodded in response to his question, their heads hung in shame and fear. Even with Calder in full battle dress, however, and broadsword and axe hanging within hand's reach, some of the captives refused to look away from his formidable visage or back away from his mighty horse.

Whether due to empty bravado or true courage, Calder could not be sure, but it was time to separate the true rebels from those who were just putting on a show for him and his men. Raising his voice so all would be sure to hear him clearly, he called out. "You will kneel on the ground now, in acknowledgement of your surrender and your acquiescence to your new Lord. When you have done so, and my men have finished searching your homes for weapons, you will be released and no further harm will come to you. Should you refuse to submit, you will stand as you are, under the guard of my men, for as long as it takes for you to comply."

He made one more circle around them, trying to make eye contact with each one as he passed. Then he directed his steed back toward Draco.

The two knights looked unyielding and fear inspiring as they sat side by side on their war horses. One light, one dark, both large and powerful, their faces set and implacable. The way they held their bodies, taut and alert, was a sure indication that any slight move against them would be dealt with in a swift and deadly manner.

Slowly, one by one, men started to kneel in the dirt. The older men first, then others followed their example. The angry, frustrated looks on their faces showed that they complied, not out of loyalty or respect for their captors, but rather because they knew they had no other choice.

Finally, all knelt save for a dozen men, most of them soldiers. Calder closely studied the faces of those still standing. He saw stubbornness and defiance and knew he would do well to remember these men.

"Draco, have all of the cottages been searched?"

"Graeham is approaching, Milord. He will tell us." His voice, low and gravelly, came from deep down in his barrel chest, the result of too many battle cries and overseeing the training of too many young, green recruits.

Calder waved Graeham over, then paused to look up toward the sky. Clouds were blowing closer, blotting out the sun and darkening the day. He was pleased to see it.

"The cottages that survived the flames have all been cleaned out, Milord," Graeham called as he approached. "We found a few poorly made swords and knives and added them to the pile of weapons we took off these curs." He added the last as he nodded toward the circle of captives.

"You didn't harm the women, did you?" Calder asked curtly.

Graeham looked quickly up into Calder's face. "We all understood your orders, M'lord, and none of the women were touched. A few jumped on the men and screamed at us when we entered their homes, but we did as you instructed, one held them back while the other searched."

Calder nodded, realizing that he had insulted Graeham by asking such a question. "Thank you for handling it so well. We must try to be as gentle with these people as possible. They do not want us here to begin with, and I do not want to antagonize them anymore than need be. It would serve only to set things even more awry for my brother."

"As long as we are not so gentle that we allow the pigs to stab us in our sleep," Graeham replied, his tone clearly indicating his disdain and distrust of their captives.

"Those of you on your knees," Calder's deep voice carried easily across the courtyard "go back to your cottages now." The men scrambled up and raced back toward their homes, or what was left of them, without a backward glance.

His voice lowered as he glared at the men still standing within the circle, their arms crossed in front of them, their legs spread wide and their eyes focused solely on Calder.

"You men who have refused to kneel before me will stand as you are until you submit." As Calder spoke, it started to drizzle; a stroke of good fortune in the knight's opinion, though the men standing in front of him might not agree. It would make them even more miserable in the coming hours and, Calder hoped, might get this over with more quickly.

"Graeham, set three men to watch over this group," he said, nodding to the dozen or so men still standing. "If they kneel, let them return to their homes, once they have spent enough time in the mud."

Lowering his voice so that only Graeham could hear him, Calder added, "Make sure that our men are out of the rain while they watch, but are readily visible to these simpkins."

"Garrick," he continued, "get some of the other men together and take these bodies farther away from the Manor. Cover them and let the relatives collect them in the morning for burial."

Removing his armor and handing it to his squire, the knight turned toward Draco. "Would you come with me? I need to get away from the stench of death for a bit."

Draco nodded his assent and the two men rode away from the village, the hooves of their great beasts thundering as they spurred them on to greater speeds. The drizzle changed to a light, but steady, rainfall. Calder basked in the cleanliness of it, lifting his face toward the sky and allowing the fresh, clean water to wash the stink of blood, fear and death from him.

They had ridden their horses hard that day, so they slowed to a walk as soon as they were away from the village.

"Come, Draco, we will see what lies atop this hill. It might be a good place for Aric to build his castle."

"Would be easy enough to protect," Draco returned, as he glanced up the slope. "Good view of the surrounding valley."

Calder nodded his agreement as they made their way up the steep incline. Halfway to the top, he spotted something lying in the grass. Reining in his mount, he rode slowly toward the object, his hand on the hilt of his sword.

He quickly dismounted as his gaze fell on a young woman. He put one hand to the pulse on her throat and the other on her wrist. Looking at her pale, waxen face, he could not be sure if she was dead or alive, but the slow beating of her pulse confirmed that she was still among the living.

Lifting her off the sodden ground and cradling her in his arms, he breathed a sigh of relief. He had been responsible for enough deaths that day and did not want this woman's blood on his hands, as well.

She had high cheekbones and her skin felt like silk as he brushed the long, wet strands of hair away from her face. A thin stream of blood trickled from a cut on her temple and he tenderly wiped it away.

Laying her gently back down onto the ground, Calder hastily removed his chainmail hauberk. Pulling off his aketon, the heavy, padded tunic that he wore underneath it, he wrapped it gently around her cold, damp body. Her wet clothes clung to her body and he knew they had to get her warm soon, or she may still die.

Draco sat quietly astride his horse, watching in bemusement as Calder ministered to the wench. He found his leader's gentleness quite out of character, particularly since the woman was a Saxon, but kept his thoughts to himself.

"Help me put her on my horse," Calder ordered.

Draco dismounted and lifted the waif up into the knight's arms.

"We must get her back to the Manor quickly," Calder said, his voice tense as he kicked his horse's flanks and headed back toward the village.

Calder's horse had barely come to a stop when he jumped off its back and caught Regan as she slid toward him. Kicking open the front door of the Manor and carrying his burden upstairs to one of the bedchambers, he never noticed the furious glare directed at him by one of the Saxon men still standing in the courtyard.

Draco followed him inside after bellowing to Calder's squire, Skeet, to wipe down and feed the horses. His voice boomed throughout the building as he yelled orders to have a fire lit and food and ale provided as soon as possible for the Lord and his guest, leaving the servants quaking in their shoes as they hurried to respond.

Draco stopped at the entrance to the bedchamber, watching quietly as Calder gently removed the girl's sodden clothing. He moved from the doorway only when a servant brought in an armload of wood and hurried to place it in the fireplace, then set it ablaze. The servant carefully kept his eyes averted from the bed as he scurried back out of the room.

Two women arrived, carrying trays filled with ale and food. Calder had removed all of the girl's clothing by then and had covered her with a heavy blanket.

"I've a broth here, M'lord, for the lass. There are special herbs in it that will help her sleep restfully."

The servant's eyes traveled furtively between Calder and the unconscious woman on the bed.

"Out, hags!" Draco roared, noting the curious looks. The women stumbled over themselves as they tried to escape from the room.

Draco strode over to the fire and stretched out his hands toward its warmth, trying to get the chill out of his bones. "What will you do with her?" he rumbled.

"See if she lives," Calder replied softly, as he stared down at her.

He shook his head, pulling his eyes away from her angelic face and trying to forget the satiny feel of her skin as he undressed her.

"I'm starving." He grabbed a drumstick and took a large bite out of it. "Join me, Draco. There is much here and it does not appear that she will be sharing in it."

After they finished eating, Draco went downstairs to check on their own men, as well as the stubborn Saxons still left in the courtyard. He shook his head in disgust at the few who remained. Drenched to the skin and standing in mud up to their ankles, still they stood defiantly, their faces set with a stubbornness born of disgrace and contempt.

"You are fools," he told them dryly, "and you will learn respect, later rather than sooner, it seems."

The prisoners watched him closely, fear mingling with their hatred as they took his full measure. He stood a head taller than any of them and, even in the cold rain, wore only a Jack over his leggings. The leather tunic was reinforced with metal plates and, unlike some of the other knights', it had no sleeves. With his cloak thrown over one shoulder, it was difficult for the village men to look at his thick, muscular arms and not envision them effortlessly swinging the great broadsword that hung in its scabbard at his side.

Grunting at them in disgust, he walked away. After changing the guards, he returned to the Manor and took up his position at the bottom of the stairs. His large body blocked most of the bottom step; no one would be able to get past him to approach his Lord's bedchamber.

*   *   *

Calder stood next to the bed, once again staring down at the young woman. He was able to get her to swallow most of the broth the old woman brought, but she had not yet come back to full consciousness.

Something about her tugged at his heart and it surprised him to find that he still had one. Perhaps it was the innocence that he saw in her face as she slept, he mused, bringing to mind all the days he had spent amidst nothing but blood and death, dealing with treachery and deceit from all sides.

Even at Court, one could not let down their guard. All was intrigue and betrayal there, everyone looking to gain the King's favor in any way they could, men and women alike. He rarely, if ever, spent time with anyone other than Draco and his men, unless forced to do so.

Unable to tear his eyes away from her, he watched as the firelight cast a rosy glow to her cheeks and made the red highlights in her hair dance. Reaching down and touching her face, he gently caressed her cheek as she slept. She moaned, but did not awaken.

His brow creased in concern when she started to shiver, and his anxious gaze searched the room, looking for something, anything, he could use to help her. The Manor was a large, drafty building and even the brightly burning fire could not keep the room warm during such a damp, spring night. Calder decided that the best he could do was to give her the warmth of his own body. Removing his own wet clothing, he slid into the feather bed next to her.

Though he had not been with a woman for a long time, it was his warmth that he wanted to give her, not his body. He held her close, feeling the smoothness of her skin and smelling her sweet flowery scent, as the shivering quieted and she began to rest easier.

Regan drifted in and out of vivid dreams and nightmares due to the herbs contained in the broth she had been given. Deep in the night, she slowly began to rise to the surface of consciousness but found herself unable to get there completely. Her head was fuzzy and her thoughts disjointed.

At one point, she felt a hard body pressed against hers and long, supple fingers stroking her. Still not completely coherent or awake, she believed she must be in the midst of yet another dream.

Enjoying the feel of the hands that caressed her, she turned into equally strong arms, eagerly responding as lips swept down onto her own. She pressed her lips tighter against the specter's, then gasped in surprise at the warmth and passion that coursed from one end of her body to the other.

Large hands traveled all over her skin, leaving a warm, shimmering trail behind. Lips were molded to hers and she hoped never to be released by them.

She found her own hands exploring a hard, firm body, playing across wide, smooth shoulders and a long back. She gripped a firm buttock and was rewarded by a sharp intake of breath.

With her eyes still tightly closed, she struggled to understand what was happening. It all felt so real, but there was no question that it was a dream. What else could it be?

The mouth ravaged hers again, harder and more demanding this time, a man's mouth. He rolled her over onto her back then. The fire was behind him when she finally managed to pry open her eyes. Her dream lover's face was hidden in shadow as he lowered his head to kiss her neck, then her breasts, and then lower still. Her body took over and responded to each kiss and caress. She felt like she was on fire, burning from the inside out. His lips and hands continued their gentle assault, seeming to touch every inch of her body as she writhed underneath him.

She was suddenly and rudely jolted into complete awareness when he nudged her legs apart and thrust deep inside her. She froze, every muscle taut, as the pain of his entry seared her to the core.

"Good God," he whispered, in a low, hoarse voice, "you're a damn virgin." She had turned to him, she had wrapped herself in his arms. Her response to his kiss was so passionate that he had no doubt she had experience. What the hell was this about? He would have stopped it before it ever started had he suspected she was a virgin, no matter how much his body yearned for her.

Regan began to struggle. She had no idea who he was. She had no idea where she was. In truth, she knew only one thing for sure at the moment, this was not a dream.

Calder grabbed her hands and held them tightly over her head. "Lay still," he commanded. With the weight of his body on hers and her hands held in his strong grip above her head, there was little else she could do.

He spoke slowly and softly, his words interrupted by the light kisses that covered her face. "I did not know you were an innocent, but I cannot stop now. It has been too long a time and we've gone too far. I will try not to hurt you anymore."

Capturing her lips again, he kissed her with such sweet and all-consuming passion that it took her breath away and made her body ache for whatever would come next.

He took her gently and thoroughly, showing even her virgin's body the heights of fulfillment. Afterward, he continued to hold her trembling frame tightly in his arms as their pounding hearts quieted and they slowly made their way back to reality.

Calder breathed in the scent of her, enjoying the feel of her satiny skin against his own. He was not able to see the tears of shame that slipped quietly down her cheeks, as she prayed for sleep to come and release her from the disgrace of what she had done on this night.

Regan woke the next morning to the pale, gray light of the early dawn. Her head was heavy, her brain muddled with dizziness, until the memory of the night before flooded her mind, filling her with embarrassment. Her entire body blushed a furious shade of pink.

She looked around the bedchamber and, thankfully, found it to be empty. Breathing a sigh of relief, she cautiously got up from the bed and found her undertunic and kirtle near the fire. She donned them quickly, carrying the hose over her arm rather than risking the time it would take to put them on. The fire had just recently been stoked, and she could not help but fear that whoever had been with her would soon return.

Her faced burned with shame as she recalled the events of the night before. How could she have let this happen? She remembered hearing the screams and realizing that the Normans were attacking the village, but she had no idea of how she came to be in this bedchamber, sleeping naked next to a stranger.

"God's Wounds," she thought in horror, *"have I given my body to a Norman?"* She did not even know what the man looked like.

Well, that was not entirely true. Although she might not recognize his face, Regan was sure she would know him on sight. She blushed again at the memory of his hard, muscular limbs as he wrapped himself around her, and the feel of his smooth, wide shoulders and back under her hands. Yes, she was sure she would know him when she saw him again.

She crept stealthily down the staircase toward the front door. Norman soldiers slept on pallets on the floor throughout the Hall. She hoped that their noisy snores would keep them from hearing the soft creaks of the old steps as she descended, not knowing that they had heard her as soon as she reached the landing. Realizing immediately that she posed no threat, the men pretended to sleep rather than let on that they were aware of their Lord's dalliance of the night before.

Regan had heard the gruesome tales of what these Norman bastards did to York and some of the other areas they had overtaken. Men, women and children were murdered, burned out of their homes, left to die from starvation and disease. Fear replaced her embarrassment now, as she tiptoed nervously around the knights' sleeping bodies.

Panic rose when she realized that she had no idea what had become of her parents. Or of Edgar. Had he survived the battle? she wondered anxiously.

Her thoughts of Edgar were answered the moment she opened the front door. He stood in the courtyard beside two other men. All of them were wet, shivering and covered with mud, their exhaustion making them sway on their feet. A few other men lay in the mud nearby, dead or just sleeping, she could not be sure.

"Edgar," she yelled as she ran down the stairs. He looked up her with dull, brown eyes, having difficulty focusing on her. His long brown hair was matted to his head and beads of water dripped from his beard and down the front of his mud stained tunic.

Before she could reach him, she was intercepted by one of the Norman guards who were standing watch. She stomped on his foot and, catching him by surprise, was able to wrench her arm free and release his grip. She slid in the mud, but still managed to reach Edgar before the knight could grab her again.

"Edgar, are you all right?" she asked, as she wiped the mud from his face.

Using what little strength he still possessed, he swatted her hand away. "Leave me be, you Norman whore."

Regan stumbled backward as if she had been slapped in the face. Edgar's words stung far worse than the burning pain in her wrist, and the hatred and fury in his eyes as he stared at the hose draped over her arm chilled her to the bone.

She had only a second to recover before thundering hooves approached. Turning in that direction, she saw two mighty warriors riding toward them. Unlike the Saxon men, who preferred long hair and full beards, these men were clean shaven.

The larger man had short dark hair and, as he dismounted, she could see that the back of his head was cut close to his scalp, maybe even shaved. His face was broad, his nose bent at an irregular angle, apparently having been broken more than once. His eyes were narrow slits as he stared hard at Edgar. Regan found his visage so frightening, that she felt compelled to look away.

It was the other knight who caught her attention completely. Not as big as the barbarian who accompanied him, he was nonetheless large and powerfully built. His golden brown hair was also cut short, but not shaved in the back as the other's had been. His face was intense. His deep blue eyes fixed steadily on Regan.

She felt herself blushing as she watched him. She knew those broad shoulders, remembered the feel of those strong, supple fingers caressing her so tenderly. Regan knew who he was.

Calder stopped his horse and dismounted. His eyes never left Regan's as he walked toward her. A long, thin scar marred the right side of his face. For some reason she could not fathom, it made him even more ruggedly handsome than he would have been without it.

"Can you not even take your eyes off him in my presence, slut?" Edgar hissed.

Before Regan had even comprehended what he said, Calder struck out with a large fist, hitting Edgar square in the jaw and knocking him down into the mud.

"The girl was hurt, you insolent cur. We tended her wounds. Now, show her the respect that is her due."

Edgar just lay in the mud, glaring scornfully up at Calder as he rubbed his jaw.

"Show her the respect that she is due." Calder demanded again, in a low, threatening tone.

Edgar glanced at Regan and she flushed in response, knowing she was no longer worthy of anyone's respect. She reached out and placed a hand on Calder's arm as he took another step toward Edgar.

"Please," she whispered, her eyes wide and pleading as she looked up at him. She was not sure what she was pleading for, no more humiliation for Edgar, perhaps. No more undeserved gallantry on her behalf, maybe.

Calder simply stared down at her for a moment, mesmerized by the endless depths of her brilliant green eyes, caught up in the memory of how she had felt in his arms, and knowing that, given half a chance, he would take her again, right here and now.

Sanity returned to him once more when he heard Draco loudly clear his throat.

"What is your name?" Calder asked softly.

"I am Regan," she answered a little shakily, finally removing her hand from his arm. He stood so close to her that she could feel the warmth of his breath on her cheek. His nearness, and the intensity of his gaze, caused her heart to pound furiously and she found it difficult to breathe normally.

"And what is this man to you?" He indicated Edgar with a nod.

"He is my betrothed. We were to be wed in two days' time." Tears filled her eyes as she spoke and only Calder knew the true reason for them.

He felt no shame or regret for what had happened between them, but he did feel sorry for the position he had placed her in. If the villagers found out what they had shared, she would be ostracized by them, particularly if he had gotten her with child. He accepted his responsibility for her predicament and decided he must do what he could to help her.

He turned back toward Edgar, who was still lying in the mud. "You have my permission to marry this girl two days hence."

Edgar continued to glare at him. "Will you be done with her by then, Milord?" he asked, his voice thick with sarcasm.

He doubled up in pain when Draco kicked him in the ribs. "Watch your tongue, Saxon cur, or you won't live long enough to see your wedding night."

All of Calder's men had come out of the Manor by then. They stood nearby, watching the exchange, their hands never far from the hilt of their swords.

"Graeham," Calder said, "take these three and lock them up in the stables. I'll decide what to do with them later."

Edgar and the others were dragged, none too gently, toward the stables. Calder remounted and prepared to leave, but stopped when Regan called out to him.

"Milord," her voice was soft, with a musical lilt to it, but he could hear the fear in it as well "what if Edgar chooses not to marry me?"

"He does not have a choice in the matter," Calder replied firmly, reining his horse about and galloping away without a backward glance.

CHAPTER 2

Regan hung her head as she slowly made her way back to her parents' cottage. Rancid smoke still filled the air around the smoldering cottages, or what was left of them. She picked her way around the personal items people had been able to save from the flames that were laying on the ground. Men stood alongside their ruined homes, their faces filled with defeat and hatred. Women cried, hugging themselves; scared, angry and confused.

She was relieved to see that her parents' cottage had survived and hurried towards it.

"Filbert, come quickly," her mother called when she entered the cottage, easing Regan's mind as to their fate.

Filbert was quite elderly and did not move quickly, no matter what the circumstances. Her mother had already poured her a cup of tea before he reached the room.

Giving Regan a heartfelt hug, he sat down beside her and vainly tried to hold back his tears. "I was so worried about you."

His first wife had borne him four sons, none living to see adulthood. When she died, he had married Gayle, a much younger woman, hoping she would bear him many children. Instead, she was only able to produce one beautiful little daughter, whom he doted on as if such a child had never before graced a man's life.

"I'm fine, Father," Regan said, unable to stop the trickle of tears escaping down her cheeks. "I heard the fighting and saw some of the cottages burning. I was running home when I tripped and hit my head." Her hand, involuntarily, went up to her temple which had developed a deep, ugly bruise around the cut.

She had never lied to her father before, but certainly could not tell him all of what had happened after that.

"One of the Normans must have found me when I was unconscious and took me to the Manor. I woke there this morning and found Edgar and some of the other men standing in the Courtyard. I fear Edgar thinks I went to the Manor on my own. He seemed quite angry with me."

"No, dear one, he is angry with the Normans, not you. It is just easier to express his anger at you. We lost many friends in yesterday's battle. And Heaven only knows what evil will befall us now that we are under the rule of these barbarians."

He shook his head in anger and sorrow, then gave Regan a sad smile. "Do not worry, my child. Edgar will come to his senses and realize it is not you that he should be angry with. But, perhaps we should postpone the wedding for awhile, until we see how we fare with our new rulers. Mayhap, they will not be ruling us for long, after all."

Regan looked at him in surprise, wondering if it was wishful thinking on his part, or if there would be more fighting soon. Remembering how fearsome the Normans had looked that morning, she shuddered at the thought of it.

"But, Father, the scarred warrior has already told us the wedding will take place in two days."

"That is Calder," her father spat, "the leader of this gang of brigands. It is his brother t'will be our new Lord."

Then he looked over at Regan in confusion. "How did he know you were to be married?"

She blushed. "I told him this morning when we were in the courtyard with Edgar. He says that he will insist that Edgar go through with the marriage."

"Why would that matter to a Norman dog like him?" Filbert wondered aloud, staring thoughtfully at his daughter.

"Enough already, Filbert, the girl is hurt and needs her rest. Leave her be." Gayle hustled Regan over to her pallet and made sure she was warmly covered before kissing her on the cheek. Returning to the kitchen, she began to heat a large stone in the fire. When it was hot enough she tossed it in water and then bathed Regan's bruise. Once that was done, she made a balm of the whites of new eggs and rubbed it over the cut to help it heal quickly.

In the meantime, Filbert made his way back outside to finish the repairs on his fishing net and to ruminate about what would become of them under Norman rule.

*   *   *

Later, the entire village, except the men still locked in the stables, turned out for a mass burial of family and friends killed in the battle the day before. The Norman warriors kept a respectful distance away, but sat strong and proud on their destriers, ready in case the high emotions of the day should cause trouble to begin.

That evening, Calder had all of the men in the stable returned to their homes, except Edgar. He was given a loaf of bread and a flask of water, nothing else. Calder had him brought before him in the Great Hall the following morning.

Edgar was cold and hungry and miserable. The presence of the huge warriors standing on all sides of him did not make him feel any more comfortable, but he tried not to show his fear.

The aroma from the food on the trencher in front of Calder caused his empty stomach to roil and growl, his embarrassment at it fueling his anger. Calder appeared not to notice and casually popped a piece of cheese into his mouth. He chewed it slowly and washed it down with a large draught of ale. Then he raised his head slowly and stared into Edgar's eyes.

"My brother will be here shortly. If you do not swear fealty to him, you will be executed immediately. I assume you know that?"

Edgar just stared back at him, wishing he had a knife with which to cut Calder's throat at that moment.

Calder shrugged. "It's your choice. My brother is a good man and will do much to help you and your people, if you give him the chance."

"Like the chance you gave my father and brother and the others when you cut them down?" Edgar spat.

Calder looked intently at Edgar, wishing this one was not the betrothed of Regan. Given the choice, he would put this man to death immediately. Edgar was young and impulsive. The hatred inside of him would just continue to grow and fester until he finally did something stupid, causing his own, and perhaps others', deaths. But Calder could not leave Regan to fend for herself. Because of what had happened between them, he would have to let this man live, so that she could be properly wed and cared for. Calder hoped he would not end up regretting his decision.

Edgar felt a tremor of fear go through him as Calder continued to study him. His face was still as stone, his expression giving away nothing. Most disconcerting were his eyes, so blue that they appeared almost black, piercing into his very soul it seemed. Edgar could see death in them, and feared it might be his own.

"Grow up, boy," Calder said in a low, cold tone. "The only men killed were those that fought against us. If a man takes up a weapon, he must be prepared to die. Those men fought with courage and died with honor. They would not want a sniveling coward like you crying on their behalf."

"You bastard," Edgar yelled, as he lunged toward Calder. He stopped abruptly as Draco's enormous war axe struck the table with a loud thud, vibrating where it was buried, just inches from his extended hands.

He backed away, his face pale and his hands trembling. He wanted to weep with frustration and anger but would never allow himself to do so in front of these men.

"You will be released to return to your home now." Draco looked over at Calder in surprise. "And tomorrow you will wed Regan."

Edgar narrowed his eyes at Calder. "You cannot force me to take your seconds."

Calder vaulted over the table and, in the blink of an eye, had his large hand wrapped around Edgar's neck.

"Your woman was hurt and unconscious." His voice was so low that none but the two of them could hear. "She was not responsible for being here, nor for anything that occurred while she was under this roof. Do you understand that?"

Edgar's face turned a bright red and the pressure being exerted on his throat made it difficult to breathe. He barely managed to squeak out a 'yes' in response to Calder's question.

Leaning his face even closer, but not yet releasing his grip on Edgar's throat, Calder said quietly, "Whatever anger or hatred you bear toward me, you will not take out on her. Do you understand that? Not tomorrow, not next week, not next year. For I will never be far away and for every harm that you do to her, I will revisit it on you tenfold."

Calder threw Edgar away from him and returned to the table. Edgar lay on the floor, coughing and gasping for breath.

"Take him to his home, Kenny, and see that he stays there. He has a wedding to prepare for and the sight of him disagrees with me."

After Edgar was taken from the Hall, the rest of Calder's men sat down to eat.

"I want all of you to keep a close eye on that man," Calder advised them. "I will warn Aric about him, as well, but do not allow him to start any trouble while we are here."

His men all nodded their heads as they shoveled food into their mouths. "Shall we knock him around a bit, if it's called for?" Garrick asked eagerly.

"No," Calder said, "if anything is called for, bring him to me. I want to take care of him personally."

He could feel Draco's questioning gaze on him, but when he turned to challenge him with a stare, Draco just shrugged his shoulders and grabbed another piece of venison.

"We will let the wedding festivities take place as they would normally. You men will keep your distance and not interfere unless you have to. There could be some trouble if they bury their heads in those kegs of ale I saw. Let them have their fun, just don't let it get out of hand."

"No drinking and dancing for us then, eh, M'lord?" Holt yelled from the end of the table.

"That's right," Calder answered.

"Damn, I haven't held a woman in my arms in a month of Sundays." He shook his massive head in disappointment.

The men all laughed. Holt was a formidable warrior, but in no way could he be termed a ladies' man. With his bald head and what looked like one long, bushy, black eyebrow across his face, combined with a large, bulbous nose and a loud booming voice, he frightened women away more often than naught.

"We'll be back in London by month's end, Holt. You can make up for lost time then."

The conversation turned ribald as the men took turns describing the looks of the women Holt might encounter once they reached London, and the rest of their morning meal passed quickly.

Calder did not join in the conversation, his mind instead filled with thoughts of Regan and Edgar; frowning as he worried about what might happen to her once she was married to Edgar and he was gone.

*   *   *

That afternoon, after a rigorous practice with his men, which was meant more to instill fear in the villagers than because it was necessary, Calder decided to take a ride and maybe do some hunting. He set out alone on his great steed, Alerio.

Draco wanted to come with him, but he needed to be alone. It was a beautiful spring day and he felt himself relaxing for the first time since he had arrived as they slowly wandered through the fields and then the woods. The sun was shining brightly and the cool breeze blew pleasantly across his face as he rode.

He enjoyed the freedom of the outdoors and dreaded the trip to London. He hated the pomp and ceremony of Court. His older brother, Aric, loved it, had been born to it as the first son. When their father passed away, Aric became The Earl of Marlboro, as was his due.

As the second son, Calder was not entitled to inherit his father's land. His only options were to become a soldier or join the clergy. Envisioning himself as a clergyman made him smile, knowing the vow of celibacy would have proven very difficult, more likely impossible, to keep.

That, in turn, led his thoughts to Regan as he let Alerio carry him along a meandering trail near the river. She was a pretty young thing, with long copper curls and deep green eyes. Like a wood nymph, he thought fancifully, glancing around at the canopy created by the large fir trees above him.

Why had she turned to him that night? He would have expected a shy, young virgin to scream and leap from the bed when she found herself lying next to a naked stranger.

Why had she turned in his arms and offered herself to him? He was not able to come up with a reasonable explanation, so instead, dwelt on the more intimate details of that evening; her soft moans and sighs, her sweet, full lips and smooth, silky skin. The feel of her body pressed against his.

Alerio stopped suddenly and Calder roused himself from his thoughts. Looking up, he saw her sleeping under a tree. He blinked and looked again, to make sure that it wasn't some vision he had conjured up with his thoughts.

He dismounted and slapped Alerio on the rump, sending him off to graze as he walked over to her sleeping figure. Regan lay on her side, long tresses partially covering her face. He knew it was her though, that particular shade of reddish-gold hair could belong to no other.

He squatted down next to her and gently moved the hair from her face. There were stains on her cheeks from the tears she had been crying before she fell asleep. Calder frowned, feeling the weight of his responsibility for them. Tomorrow was her wedding day and, because of him, she would have to explain to her new husband why she was no longer a virgin.

He did not regret the time they had shared together, in fact, he had found it to be one of his more pleasurable experiences. But he did feel guilty for the position it had left her in. For a Saxon woman to have relations with a man out of wedlock was sin enough, but when that man was a Norman, Calder couldn't even imagine the extent of ridicule and scorn that she might have to bear.

It was not fair to her and he would do all he could to see her properly wed, so that she would not have to face any disgrace or embarrassment.

Marrying her himself was not something that occurred to him. He was a knight, one who could not, and would not, even try to see himself as a husband or a father. It was not a part of who he was.

He watched as she slowly opened her eyes and gazed into his. She did not seem at all scared, or even surprised, to see him as she sat up and leaned against the trunk of the tree.

"I was dreaming of you," she said softly, raising her hand to touch his face. Running her finger along the scar on his cheek, making sure, this time, that she was awake and that he was really here with her.

He smiled at her with wide, full lips. 'Was the dream as good as what we shared together the other night?"

She blushed and lowered her eyes without answering him.

He took a long, tapered finger and placed it under her chin, forcing her to look back up at him.

"Why did you turn and give yourself to me?"

"I thought I was dreaming," she said hesitantly, her face flaming bright red now, afraid he wouldn't believe her and would think she had just thrown herself at him like a common trollop. "When I finally realized I wasn't, it was too late."

"Do you make love with strangers often in your dreams?" he asked in a low, smooth voice. His lips were curved in a slight smile and she could see the devilish twinkle in his eyes.

"Of course not," she responded. "I don't understand it myself."

He was unable to look away from her face, her eyes appeared almost luminous and her soft lips were slightly parted, begging to be kissed. "Do you mind if I sit here with you for a few minutes?"

"As you wish, Milord," she answered primly, when he leaned back against the same tree. His arm grazed hers and his long legs ran the length of her own and beyond. She could not help noticing how heavily muscled his thighs and calves were under his hose as his leg rested against her own.

She found it a little easier to breathe normally when he was sitting next to her and she did not have to look into his piercing blue eyes, but it was still discomfiting to be so close to him.

"What are you doing out here?" he asked. "It could be dangerous for a woman alone."

"Oh, no, Milord, I love the forest and come here often when I want some time to myself. It is a good place to collect one's thoughts."

"Yes, I feel the same way myself," he said honestly. "But men prey on women they find alone."

"No one bothers me." She hesitated, afraid to tell him her thoughts, but feeling the need to do so. "Or at least they never have. I do worry what could happen now that you Normans are here."

She looked at him out of the corner of her eye to see if she had made him angry. He had his head back against the tree with his eyes closed and a lazy grin on his face.

"Why are you afraid of the Normans? We are decent people, here to take back lands that rightfully belong to King William."

"Well, that is a question for some debate, I would say."

He opened his eyes and raised an eyebrow at her. "You would debate me on my right to claim this land for the King?" he asked dryly.

"Oh, no," she said hastily, realizing how dangerous it was for her to have made such a comment. "I only meant that I've heard stories, you know, about the evil that the Normans have done. I've heard you are a very violent people. We are just peace-loving farmers here and are not used to such things."

"Why then, were there enough weapons, and men to use them, to fight against us when we arrived? What would peace loving men need with all those weapons?"

She had laid her own trap with her words and he had been quick to pounce on them, but she was not willing to give up so easily. Considering for a moment, she turned toward him, trying not to get flustered as his brilliant blue eyes fixed on her.

"Even a peace-loving man must take up arms when the situation calls for it, else how could he protect his home and family from rabble? How can a man keep his peaceful existence, if he is not willing to fight for it? A peaceful man does not go looking for a fight, he just does not back down when he is threatened."

She felt very pleased with her explanation and had started to relax, until Calder spoke. "So now you call me and my knights rabble? You should tread lightly with your insults, Regan."

She flushed and began to make a nervous apology until she saw one corner of his mouth lift into a roguish smile.

"Are you teasing me, Milord? Or do the words of an innocent young woman cause your blood to run hot with the need for vengeance?"

Their eyes met and held. "A little of both, I think, but my blood is not running hot because of any need for vengeance."

She finally managed to look away from his magnetic eyes and fumbled nervously with her tunic, trying to keep her hands from shaking. She stared at his chest, so that she would not become immersed in his gaze again.

"With your leave, Milord, I should go now. I am supposed to be picking flowers for my bridal headpiece and have not yet begun."

He grabbed her hand as she started to rise, forcing her back to the ground beside him.

"You may go, but not yet," Calder said gruffly, irritated for some reason at the mention of her impending wedding. Finally releasing her hand, he removed a gold medallion from around his neck.

"I want you to take this."

"It's beautiful." Regan admired the face of it, which depicted a rising sun with a rainbow above it.

"But, I cannot accept it," she stated quietly but firmly, handing it back over to him.

He took it from her hand and placed the heavy gold chain around her neck. The medallion nestled snugly between her breasts. He picked it up and rubbed it with his thumb. His voice was very soft as he spoke.

"My father gave this to me when I was young. It is a symbol of hope and rising good fortune. He told me it would bring me luck and that, if ever I was away from home and found myself in trouble, I could send this to him and he would come to help." He lifted his eyes to hers, not releasing the medallion from his hold on it. She could see the sorrow in his eyes.

"This medallion means a great deal to you, Milord. I could not possibly accept it."

"My father is dead now and I have no further need for his assistance. I want you to keep it. These are troubled times and there is much to fear. If you find yourself in danger, or need protection, from anyone, give this to my brother and ask him to see that I get it. I will come to your aid, no matter where I am."

He felt unsure about forcing this marriage between Edgar and Regan. Even after he had been threatened, Edgar may still feel the need to vent his anger on someone. If he chose to make that someone Regan, Calder hoped she would have the courage to ask for his help in the matter. It was the best he could do for her.

Not knowing the true reason for the gift, tears swam in her eyes at his thoughtfulness. "Thank you, I will treasure it always."

Again she started to get up to leave and he held her back. "Before you go, you must answer me a question."

"Yes?"

"Why were you out here crying today?"

She looked at him in confusion. How could he know she had been crying?

As if reading her thoughts, he trailed a finger down her cheek. "I saw the dried tears on your face while you slept."

"Oh," she said, relieved that he had not been in the woods spying on her. She looked down at his strong hand, browned by the sun, his long fingers entwined with hers, wondering whether or not she could be honest with this unusual man. Perhaps, if she was, he would not force Edgar to marry her against his will.

"I was crying about everything and about nothing," she began hesitantly, then winced in pain as he squeezed her hand.

"No riddles, girl, I want the truth."

"The truth is that I'm not sure. I'm not sure if I want to marry Edgar. I'm not sure if Edgar wants to marry me anymore. I'm not sure how I will explain to him why I am no longer a virgin, and," she said, raising her tear-filled eyes and staring directly into the endless depths of his, "I am not sure that he will ever be able to make me feel like I did when I was with you."

With a sob she pulled her hand out of his grasp, jumped up and ran away into the forest.

Calder sat alone for a while longer, focusing on his hatred of Edgar, the man who would get this exceptional woman as a bride, when all he deserved was a sharp dagger through his heart.

CHAPTER 3

Calder and Draco went hunting while the wedding festivities took place the following day. Calder knew that he should stay, in the event there was any trouble, but could not bring himself to witness the ceremony.

He had not been able to get Regan out of his mind since they met the day before, and the thought of her marrying Edgar caused him great consternation. He was afraid that he may not let the wedding proceed if he had to stay and watch.

Not, of course, because he wanted her for himself, but because he worried for her safety and did not want Edgar to have her.

Draco laughed loudly as Calder's arrow flew high, missing the running buck completely. "I think maybe your thoughts are elsewhere, Milord," he said, still grinning.

"I worry that things might get out of hand back at the village, is all," Calder replied defensively.

Draco kept the smile on his face. "You slept with the wench, didn't you?" Calder did not answer him for a moment, looking down and playing with the string on his bow.

"I did not mean for it to happen, but it did." He shrugged his shoulders as if it was of no consequence.

"If you want her for yourself, why did you push for this marriage to go forward so quickly?" Draco was not a very talkative man but, when he chose to converse, he always came straight to the point.

"I don't want her for myself!" Calder almost yelled. "Her life and family are here. We leave soon and I would not have her alone. There will be many others to replace her in my bed soon enough."

Draco kept his thoughts to himself but knew there was more to this than Calder was willing to admit.

"Shall we sit here and yell at each other all afternoon, or shall we go after the buck that you weren't able to shoot straight at?"

"Let's go," Calder said, relieved that the conversation was over.

They hunted for the rest of the afternoon, bagging enough game to last the men for several days. They did not return to the Manor until well after the village was quiet and enveloped in darkness.

*   *   *

The wedding took place as planned, although the festivities were subdued in light of the recent events with the Normans. It was difficult to celebrate when family and friends had been buried just days before, and Norman knights closely watched over the gathering.

Regan walked slowly toward the river with her empty buckets, trying to remember the good parts of the day. She was acutely aware that Calder had been nowhere to be seen.

She and Edgar said their vows, though woodenly and without much joy. He would not look her in the eye, neither during the ceremony, nor at the celebration afterward.

They had lain together that night and he took her in the dark, roughly and with no love.

"There," he said when he finished, "that should help take away your lust for that Norman bastard."

She did not respond, just curled up on her side and quietly cried herself to sleep. He knew that she was not a virgin, and he knew why. But it was the only comment he made about it, and for that she was grateful to him.

Regan continued along the stony trail, swinging the buckets to and fro, enjoying the spring breeze blowing through her hair. She watched the birds flit from branch to branch, but in her mind's eye all she could see were deep blue eyes and soft, full lips.

Somehow, between the morning she awoke to find the proof of her lost virginity in Calder's bed and now, she had lost the shame for what happened.

Regan tried to feel bad about it. She tried to be repentant, but found she could not. The big, mighty warrior had taken his large, strong hands and used them for nothing but tenderness on her, as Edgar had not. Calder had caused her body to respond, even when her mind did not want to, He had loved her well, as Edgar had not.

If I must spend the rest of my life with Edgar, she thought, I am glad to have the memory of one night with a man such as Calder.

Like the rest of her village, Regan feared the large, Norman knights and worried about what would become of them now, but she did not fear Calder. Both during the night she spent with him and the afternoon in the forest, he had shone her a side of himself that she was sure none of the other villagers would ever see.

As fierce a warrior as he was, he could be extremely gentle when the occasion called for it. He was not as fearsome as he would like to have the villagers think. But, soon he would be gone and her mundane life would continue as before, albeit under the rule of his brother.

She had caught glimpses of Calder over the past few days, practicing with his men or riding his great steed through the village. When she saw him, a blush would instantly cover her cheeks and her heart would begin to beat wildly in her chest. She found it hard to look away from him and knew others in the village would start to take notice if she was not careful.

He must leave soon and not ever come back, she thought sadly, else I will never be able to find peace of mind again.

She filled her water buckets and was on her way back home. Nearing the edge of the forest, she stifled a shriek as someone jumped out, grabbing her around the waist with one hand while putting the other across her mouth.

"Hey, lass, we hear the Norman bastards took yer village, is that so?" His rancid breath almost made her retch as she nodded her head.

He took his dirty, smelly hand away from her mouth and she gasped in deep breaths of fresh air.

There were two of them, both dirty and unkempt, and they greedily looked her up and down, lecherous grins exploding on their faces.

"Mayhap we best have a piece o' ye afore the Normans slit yer throat, eh, Miss?"

She tried to back away from them, but the tall, skinny one held tight to her waist.

"Don't be runnin' now, lass. We've a need fer some infermation. There's some what would pay in gold fer it."

The shorter man, with the wide, stupid, gap-toothed grin said, "But, there's no reason we can't be havin' a little fun wit ye first."

Regan screamed then, as loud and as long as she could before the tall one slapped her hard across the face, knocking her to the ground.

"Don't be tellin' me ye've turned into a Norman lover, lass," the tall one growled, his small, pig like eyes devouring her.

He reached down to take her arm, then whirled at the sound of thundering hooves approaching.

"Damn!" the short one exclaimed. "Grab the girl. We best get out o' here fast." The tall one bent to seize her. She kicked him between the legs as hard as she could and he doubled over in pain. With a venomous glare at Regan, he turned and began to limp slowly away. Just a few feet from where Regan lay, he came to a stumbling halt when an arrow flew through the air and struck him in the back of the neck. Pitching forward onto the ground, he died instantly.

Calder and four of his men arrived seconds later.

"How many?" he yelled down to her.

"Just one more. He ran that way." she answered, pointing toward the river. Calder reined in his mount and nodded in the direction she indicated. His men took off after the vagabond.

Gracefully sliding off his horse, Calder knelt beside her. "How badly are you hurt?" he asked, seeing the red welt on her face.

"I'm fine," she said shakily. "You arrived before they could do anything."

"Who were they?" he asked, helping her up.

"I've never seen them before. They wanted information about you and your men. They said someone was willing to pay them gold for it."

He looked at her sharply. "Did they say who, or for what reason?"

"No," she replied, shaking her head.

He saw her tremble and put his arms around her, enveloping her completely. "Looks like you were right, after all," he said softly, resting his chin on the top of her head. "We Normans have made the woods more dangerous for you."

She stepped out of his embrace, fearing her own response to his nearness. The scent of him, sweat, horses and pure maleness, was filling her senses, making her feel almost dizzy. And the safety and comfort she found in his arms was too dangerous to become accustomed to. She needed to get away from him as quickly as possible.

But Calder was not willing to let her escape so easily. He gently grabbed her arm, pulling her back close to him, lifting her chin so that she would have to look him in the eye. "Do not come back into the forest for awhile, Regan. The next time my men and I may not be close enough to hear you scream."

She lost herself completely in his sapphire eyes; they had some sort of magnetic pull that she was helpless to resist. Taking a step closer and raising herself on her toes, she gently kissed his lips.

The spark she ignited by doing so quickly turned into a raging fire and she found herself being held tightly against his hard, unyielding body as his mouth took possession of hers.

Of their own volition, her hands found their way around his neck and entwined themselves in his thick, soft hair. Regan moaned aloud then, as the onslaught of his kisses continued. She wished they could stay like this forever, but it was not to be. Calder quickly disentangled himself from her as they heard the men returning.

"You got him?" he asked, a little hoarsely, as they approached.

"Aye, Milord," Draco replied, staring curiously at their flushed faces. "He'll do no more harm."

"Good. Have the men take the bodies back to the village. See if anyone knows who they were."

Draco sat on his horse, leaning forward with a slight smile on his face and many questions in his eyes, as he stared down at Calder.

"I will be along momentarily. You can go ahead with the others," Calder told him brusquely.

"I must go also, Milord," Regan said quickly, realizing what might happen if she did not. She would surely burn in hell if she acted on the thoughts and desires that were threatening to overpower her.

"No," Calder said sharply. "Skeet, take her buckets and refill them. See that they get to her cottage."

"Yes, M'lord," the young man called, grabbing the buckets and riding back toward the river.

"You men, get back to the village and find out who they were." He nodded his head toward the bodies that lay over their horses' backs.

As the men rode off, Calder helped Regan onto his saddle and swung up behind her. "I will see you home. I want to be sure that you get there safely."

In truth, he did not want her away from him so soon. He craved the feel of her against him, wanted to crush her lips with his own, wanted to feel himself inside of her again.

Calder knew that could not be, but at least he could hold her against him while they rode. It was not enough, but it would have to do.

Regan sat sidesaddle in front of him. She could not keep her body from reacting to his touch, as his arm brushed against her breast while he moved the reins to direct the horse. Keeping her eyes forward, she tried not to think about how comfortable and safe she felt nestled against his broad chest.

"Did all go well on your wedding day?" he asked.

She looked up at him in surprise. "As well as could be expected, Milord. After so many recent deaths, it was difficult to find joy in the occasion."

"That's not what I meant," he said, catching her gaze with his own. She lowered her eyes. "As I said, Milord, all went as well as could be expected."

Calder reined in his horse and lifted her chin. "Did he hurt you?" The coldness of his voice caused a shiver of fear to race down her spine.

"No, he did not."

"But he knows?"

"He knew even before our wedding night, as Milord is well aware." Chagrinned, Calder smiled down at her. Its brilliance was dazzling and Regan felt as if her heart stopped beating for a moment.

Slowly, she lifted her eyes to his. Passion flared in them, and she did not try to stop him as he lowered his lips to hers.

Her body molded itself to his and he felt the flames of desire ignite once more. His kisses became harder, more insistent as his hands roamed her soft curves. He wanted more from her, but knew he could not have it. Knew he should not even be allowing this much to happen, but could not stop himself.

He had no choice a few moments later. Alerio became restless and started to prance about, and Calder had to force his attention back to the horse so that they would not be unseated and dumped onto the ground.

His voice was low, and husky with restrained desire, as he spoke. "My brother will arrive within the week, and then I will be returning to London."

She nodded and lowered her eyes, not wanting him to see the tears collecting in them.

"I think it would be best for you to avoid me as much as possible until then, and I you. You make me forget myself and where I am."

He drew his finger slowly down the satiny skin of her face, feeling the tears that slipped down her cheeks. "It would be best for you. I fear I could cause much trouble between you and your husband, and that is not my intention."

"I know," she whispered tearfully. The thought of never seeing him again gripped her heart so tightly that she felt as if all of the blood were being squeezed from it, leaving her to die a slow, lonely death.

He ran his hand through her long, coppery tresses, knowing he would never have a chance to do so again. "May I have one more kiss, Milady?" he asked, feeling a heaviness in his own heart.

She did not answer, simply turned her face up to him, needing to feel his lips on hers one last time.

*   *   *

Aric arrived early the following week and, shortly thereafter, Calder and his men left the village. As Regan watched them depart, she was filled with a sadness so profound that she was not sure she would survive it.

Staring wistfully at Calder's broad back as he rode out of her life, Regan placed a trembling hand over her stomach.

"Please, Lord," she prayed, *"let me be with child. And let it be Calder's. Let me keep a piece of him with me always. For, right or wrong, he's taken my heart, and I do not know if I'll be able to endure the pain without at least a small part of him to hold onto."*

CHAPTER 4

London, England 1071

Calder saw King William nod to him and made his way among the throng of people to the monarch's side. Shouldering his way through, he tried not to show his frustration and impatience with them.

"Walk with me, Calder," the King said, after his subject had executed a courtly bow.

They walked slowly toward the veranda, where they could breathe in some fresh air and be alone without the curious stares of the crowd.

Calder had recently returned to London after putting down a revolt led by Hereward The Wake. There had been many such rebellions since William was crowned as the rightful King of England that Christmas Day in 1066, and all had been successfully quashed.

"It went well?" the King asked. "I understand that your success was due in part to some monks?"

"Yes," Calder replied with a slight smile. "The monks from Ely showed us a secret route to the rebels' hideout, which enabled us to crush them sooner than we had anticipated."

"So, we weren't the only ones that wanted Hereward stopped," the King replied thoughtfully.

"Apparently not," Calder agreed. "We did lose a few men, but the battle was over quickly. I believe we have most of the countryside under control now and don't foresee any more problems in that area, for the time being at least."

William nodded. Calder was one of his favorite and most dependable knights. He and his men fought fiercely and with more courage than most. There were few others that he trusted or respected as much, and he disliked having to have this conversation with him.

"I have been getting a lot of pressure from Roderick lately."

"The Earl of Newport?" Calder asked in a tone that showed just how little respect he had for the man.

"Yes," the King replied, staring out into the dark streets of London. "He feels slighted by me. He and his men fought valiantly when we arrived on these shores, and his knights have also come to my assistance during these revolts over the last few years."

Calder remained silent, wondering where this was leading.

"He feels I have not compensated him sufficiently and wants more lands. All that I had were given to my supporters, except the few who refused them, such as you, my friend." He turned to look directly at Calder. "He wants the lands I gave to your brother."

"Why?" Calder asked, half-knowing the answer already.

"The man has a very intense dislike of you, Calder," the King returned with a smile. "Apparently due to some problem that occurred back in Normandy involving his sister."

"Sire," Calder began to explain, but was quieted by a wave of the King's hand. "It is of no consequence, Calder, just my interpretation as to the core of this problem."

"Surely, you would not consider taking back the lands that you gave Aric? He has given you much financial support, as well as providing myself and my men as his vassals all this time. He deserves the lands that you granted him."

"Yes, he does, Calder, and probably more. But being the man that he is, he would not ask for it. The services of you and your knights alone were sufficient for what he was granted."

"Then why do you tell me of Roderick's request?"

"When he first came to me, I decided to send Osbern to your brother's estate to look into any possible problems there." Calder was well aware that the King's most trusted comrade was William Fitz Osbern. The King relied heavily on his opinions and Calder, himself, had much respect for the man.

"He spent a reasonable amount of time with your brother," the King continued, "and was dismayed by what he saw."

"In what way?" Calder had not spoken to his brother since he left the estate and had no idea of its condition.

"I directed my Barons to build castles on the lands which I granted to them." With the continuing revolts by the Saxons, the fortification of the castles had been the telling factor in defeating them since William became king. "Your brother has made a half-hearted attempt, but has not even completed the ground floor yet. I find that unacceptable.

Owning properties in Normandy, he has sufficient knowledge, and is capable of enlightening his people as to better and more productive ways to farm the lands. But, the vassals do well, while your brother does not."

Calder looked at him in confusion, so the King continued. "He is not used to governing a defeated people. He is too lenient with them, Calder. He does not dictate to them with a strong hand. They do not pay the required levies to him, but he must still pay me and has not the gold to complete the castle.

He has allowed his lands to be overrun by vagabonds and thieves, who steal his cattle and livestock and trample the fields. It is an unacceptable state of affairs."

Calder knew that the King's strength depended on the strength of his Castellans. Aric was creating a weak spot for the King. He could not dispute what William was saying.

"What is it that you need me to do?" That was one of the reasons the King admired Calder so much. He was quick to see a problem and quicker yet to try and resolve it.

"I wish you to take over as the Baron of your brother's lands."

Calder took a deep breath, knowing he was about to tread a very thin line. One did not usually defy the King and live to tell of it. "Sire, your confidence in me is gratifying and I am humbled that you would feel I am fit to take my brother's place, but I must decline."

Keeping his voice firm, even after seeing the King's eyes narrow at him, he continued. "I fear that the time my men and I spent away from my brother may have contributed to his problems. Although I have no wish to be a Castellan, a keeper of farmers and their farms, I would request that you allow my men and me to return to my brother's estate. We can stop the raiding and thievery. I will help him get the castle completed with due haste. I have been his vassal, Sire, and could not now make him mine."

The King appreciated Calder's loyalty to his brother but could not allow a weakness in such a volatile part of the country.

He turned back to the dark streets once again. Being a fair man, he did not feel comfortable turning the two brothers, whom had each shown their loyalty to him time and again, against one another.

"I will allow you to return to Aric's estate," he replied at long last. "But, Calder," William looked him straight in the eye, wanting no misunderstanding "if you cannot assist your brother in making the necessary adjustments, I cannot guarantee that Roderick will not eventually acquire those lands. By taking them yourself, you could ensure that they at least remain in your family."

"Thank you, My Liege," Calder said solemnly and with all due respect, "but I could not do that to my brother."

The king smiled at him and clapped him on the back. "You are a good and loyal man, Calder. I will miss you."

"It has been my pleasure to follow so brave and noble a leader such as yourself, Sire. I am always at your disposal, should you have further need of my services." He spoke the words with the utmost sincerity and, with a low bow, left the King and the festivities.

*   *   *

The long ride to his brother's estate gave Calder plenty of time to think. His brother was five years older than he. Aric had always been a nobleman, never a fighter. How would he react when Calder tried to tell him how to run his properties? Would he welcome the help, or banish him for overstepping his bounds? Would the fear of losing his lands be incentive enough for him to give Calder a free hand? There was much work to do and little time to squabble over it.

Try as he might, he was unable to keep his thoughts from turning then to a certain green-eyed Saxon wench. One who had given her virginity to him in the deep recesses of the night and had taken a piece of his soul along with her in doing so.

Since leaving the village, he had returned to Normandy with the King for a short while, fought battles for William in Southern Italy, and had then returned to England, where he and his knights spent their time putting down insurrections throughout the country.

Most nights he was so sore and exhausted that he slept as soon as he lay down, but on some of those cold, lonely nights, he would watch the stars overhead and remember Regan. The look of her, the smell of her, the sound of her voice, the feel of her body against his. All were so vivid in his mind that it was as if she were there beside him. In particular, he liked to recall the details of the night they had spent in each other's arms.

Perhaps the memory grows sweeter as time goes by for lack of a better one to replace it, he thought with a rueful smile. Or, perhaps she is one different than all the others I've had been with, both before and since.

He shook his head, trying to clear his thoughts of her. After all, she would be married now almost four years. Probably fat and carrying yet another babe. Even so, he spurred his horse on faster as they neared the village.

Not because of his need to see her, of course, but because there was so much work to be done.

*   *   *

It was a bright, sunny day as Regan carried her basket of wash back from the river. Radolf ran ahead of her, his reddish-gold curls bouncing as he went. He tripped frequently, usually over his own feet. He had lost most all of his baby fat now and was fast becoming a little man.

Her heart swelled whenever she looked at him and the love she felt for the boy threatened to burst out of her at times. Life was not easy for either of them. *Poor Radolf*, she thought, as she watched him try in vain to catch a butterfly, *I wish you could know your father*.

From the day Edgar saw those deep blue eyes staring up at him from the cradle that he carved with his own two hands, he had known the baby was not his son. Regan could not fault him for the way he had acted since then, some men in his circumstances would have treated her and Radolf much worse. She felt sorry for Edgar. He was never the same after the Normans came. In his youth, he was a good man, eager to do what he could to help people. Now he was bitter and resentful, always plotting for the revenge he would have one day.

He had never forgiven Regan for her night with Calder. He was cold and distant and rarely came home anymore, which Regan found to be a blessing. If he spoke to the boy at all, it was only to find fault with him.

She tried to love Radolf even harder, to make up for the lack of love he got from Edgar. A sharp pain pierced her heart, however, as she watched the boy cringe and cower each time Edgar walked through their door.

She never allowed Edgar an opportunity to be alone with the boy since the time he tried to beat the child for some inconsequential deed. Edgar had delivered only one blow before Regan had her dirk at his throat.

"Touch the boy again and I will slit your throat before his eyes," she had threatened softly.

Edgar backed away from her, daggers of his own shooting from his eyes. "One day, whore, you and I will have this out, and it will not be my throat that ends up being slit."

She did not answer as he walked out the door and slammed it behind him, but her entire body trembled uncontrollably for quite some time afterward. There were few times that he came home after that. On those rare occasions when he did, it was usually late and he was very drunk. Sometimes, when he was able, he would take her, as roughly as he possibly could. She never fought him. This was her penance for what she had done with Calder. But, never would she let him touch the boy.

Edgar was the Avener now, his job was to oversee the grooms and stables. Lord Aric was completely fooled by Edgar and did not realize his true feelings toward the Normans.

Edgar spent most of his time with Maida, a pretty, young widow. Her husband was killed during the battle with the Normans and their mutual hatred fueled their passion. Their relationship didn't matter a whit to Regan, as long as Edgar continued to provide her and Radolf with enough food to eat and wood to keep warm.

Maida initiated the rumors that were circulated about Radolf being Calder's son. Word spread quickly, and it was soon after Maida and Edgar started to spend time together that the villagers attitude towards Regan changed. Their comments became rude and hurtful, if they spoke to her at all. The anti-Norman feelings still ran strong and the fact that she had slept with one made her no longer one of them.

Regan still occasionally spent time with her parents, who doted on Radolf, but even they felt the scorn of the villagers after her visits. Consequently, she did not see them often. Her father was an old man and there was nothing he could do to help her, although she knew that it broke his heart to see his daughter treated with such cruelty.

She and Radolf spent most of their time out of doors and away from the village. It was a lonely life, but at least they had each other.

Sometimes, when he looked at her through Calder's eyes, Regan would forget herself and drift back to the short time they spent together. She could not forget how it felt to be with him and clung to the memory. It was her only consolation in this hell that had become her life.

A sudden, loud thundering roused her from her reverie. She looked up and her gaze fell upon an army of mounted knights, approaching at a breakneck speed. Regan's eyes darted around the clearing in search of Radolf. He had tripped again and was laying in the path of the fast-moving steeds, unseen by the charging knights.

Regan broke into a run. She screamed and waved her arms, spooking the horses in the front and causing them to rear back as she dove on top of her son. One large, deadly hoof landed within inches of her head.

She heard the clink of steel and the creak of leather as they drew their swords and dismounted. Grabbed roughly by the arm, Regan was pulled to her feet. Her eyes blazed with fury as she whirled to stare into Calder's face. His eyes rounded with surprise, and something else that she could not fathom. Regan wrenched her arm free of his grip and knelt beside her sobbing son.

"Radolf, love," she whispered, "are you hurt?"

"No, Momma," he said, crying even harder and hugging her close.

She sighed in relief, knowing it was just fear that made him cry. Picking him up and hugging him tightly in return, she turned back to Calder. Her emotions ran high and she let them explode on him.

"You almost killed my son, you Norman bastard." She spoke softly, but with such intense fury that Calder's surprise kept him speechless for a moment.

One of his men, Davis, used the moment to lay the flat side of his sword against her back. The blow, combined with the weight of her son, brought Regan to her knees.

Calder was beside the knight in seconds. He struck the man with such force that Davis flew backward onto the ground. "Do not ever touch this woman again or, I swear, you will not live to regret it."

"But, M'lord, the wench had no right to talk to you like that," he replied nervously, from where he still lay on the ground.

"I have no need for you to defend me against a helpless woman," he gritted through clenched teeth, trying to restrain his anger. "Draco, take the men to the Manor. I will be right along."

"Yes, Milord," Draco replied, waving his arm and spurring his horse forward. Calder turned back to Regan and helped her to her feet.

"Are you badly hurt?"

She shook her head, afraid to trust her voice for fear the sobs that clogged her throat would escape with the words. It was not the sting of the sword that nearly reduced her to tears, but rather the realization of who stood before her.

"I do apologize, Mistress, for my man, but for the past several years we have done naught but fight Saxon rebels who had but one desire, and that was to see us dead. I fear he overreacted and I beg your pardon."

Taking a deep breath, she was finally able to speak in a fairly steady voice. "I am glad to see that the rebels were not successful, Milord. And I must apologize, as well, for I should not have spoken as I did. I was just so frightened for my son."

"Tis of no account," he said, with a dismissive wave of his hand. "You look well."

He was unable to take his eyes off of her. She was even lovelier than he remembered, possessing a face and body that would rival any woman he had seen. Her deep green eyes were open wide, her copper curls blew softly in the breeze, and her skin was like porcelain with a slight pink blush to her cheeks.

"Thank you," she answered shyly, nervously patting Radolf's back as he continued to cling to her. "What brings you back here?"

"I am vassal to Aric, here to do as he bids," Calder replied.

"Will you be with us for long?" she asked, wanting to prolong the conversation and gaze at him for a few moments longer. He was as strong and handsome as she remembered. The lines on his face were deeper now, not so much from age, she surmised, as from what he had witnessed and experienced since she had last seen him. The scar seemed less noticeable on his tanned face, and his eyes were still such an intense blue that she had trouble tearing her gaze from them.

"I do not know exactly," he replied, staring at her lips, wanting to taste them again, as he had dreamed of doing on so many lonely nights. He quickly realized that the next weeks and months would not be easy, to be so near to her and not be able to touch her. Time had not diminished his desire in the least.

Radolf started to squirm, and Regan did her best to keep the boy from turning around. Surely, Calder would see himself in the child's eyes. He could not know that Radolf was his son, only trouble could come from the knowledge.

"I'm pleased to see you again, Milord," she said quickly, "but, I must get my son home now."

She put Radolf on the ground and took his hand, leading him away from the knight as she picked up her clothes basket and headed toward their cottage.

Calder stood and watched the gentle sway of her hips as she walked away, feeling a stirring inside of himself the likes of which he had never known before.

*   *   *

"Caldor, what a great surprise," Aric said, as Calder approached his bedside.

"But, I fear I am unable to give you a proper reception," he added shamefacedly. Calder shook his brother's hand, felt the weakness in it and looked at the other man in concern.

"What is it, Aric?"

Aric had never been as physically strong as his brother, but now his face looked sallow and ill. His body appeared to have shriveled beneath the blankets, except for his left leg, which was swollen to twice the size of the right one.

"It's silly, really," he said with a weak laugh. "it started when I swung myself up onto my horse. There was some sort of thorn or pin protruding from the saddle. The stable hands were never able to find out exactly what it was, but it scratched along the inside of my left leg. Just a little scratch, mind you." The fear showed in his eyes as he spoke. "That was three weeks ago. Each day it grows worse and I become weaker and more ill."

"Poison?" Calder asked, his heart gripped by an icy chill.

"I see nothing else that it could be, Brother. They have bled me and drained the leg many times, but whatever pricked me got the poison in deep. I can feel it spreading through my body as we speak." He raised his cold, pale hand to Calder, who took it in both of his own.

"Do you know who is responsible for this?"

"No. There are many here who continue to hate and mistrust us. The hills are overrun with Saxon outlaws who plot against me continuously. I am glad you are here." His voice faltered and his eyelids sagged with fatigue.

"Talk to my master stableman, maybe he will know." Aric closed his eyes, as if the lids were too heavy to hold open any longer.

"I will, Brother, and don't worry. I will set all to the right." Calder's brow furrowed in worry and in anger as he swiftly left the room.

CHAPTER 5

He passed his sister-in-law, Devona, as he left the room. She was barely recognizable, having aged a great deal since he had seen her last. Her brown hair was streaked with gray, there were tight lines surrounding her mouth, and her brown eyes seemed dull with the overwhelming fear and grief that she felt. "Calder," she cried, her high, mousy voice as annoying as always, "I am so glad you are here. What will we do? Whatever will we do?"

He hugged her tightly, loving her only because his brother did. "I will make things right, Devona. I will write to the King and have him send his best surgeon. I will take care of things until Aric is better."

"Thank you, Calder," she said in a high whisper, tears forming in her eyes.

"How are your children?" Calder asked.

"They are as worried as I am," she said, shaking her head in despair. Her son, Harlan, would be about twelve now, Calder thought, and the girl, Eadda, several years younger than that.

As was the custom of noblemen, once their children reached five or six years of age, they were sometimes sent to either a monastery or another nobleman's home to stay. Both of Aric's children had been sent to live with their cousin, Wallace, The Earl of Monterey, for their schooling and preparation for adulthood. There, Harlan would learn what he needed so that he could take over his father's lands and possessions one day.

With their being so young at the time, Devona had not wanted to bring them to this country, which she considered barbaric and unsophisticated, and Calder had not seen them in many years.

"Have faith, Devona, all will be well," he said, with a confidence that he did not feel. Walking hurriedly down the to the Great Hall, he called for paper, ink and quill, which were promptly brought to him by one of the servants.

He wrote a note and sealed it, then called Draco over. He explained what had happened to his brother and asked Draco to take his missive to London.

"I fear you will get no sleep for awhile longer, my friend. I need this to get to the King as quickly as possible. Hopefully, he will allow his surgeon to return with you. I fear my brother does not have long to live, and I do not think you will let any of the King's minions prevent you from getting an audience with him."

"That I won't, Milord." He placed his hand on Calder's arm. "I will ride as if all the devils of hell are on my tail. I will get the surgeon back here in time to help your brother."

"Thank you, Draco, Godspeed."

Draco gave him a quick nod and left to remount his horse, which had not even been unsaddled yet.

Calder and his men rode over to the stables to unsaddle and feed their own mounts. Loosening the girth on Alerio, he asked one of the stable hands to fetch the Avener.

"Yes, Milord," the pock-faced, young man stuttered, as he ran toward the back of the building.

He had Alerio unsaddled and in a stall and was throwing him some hay when he heard the man approaching. Turning to find Edgar standing in front of him, Calder's body tensed and he felt tight as a coil ready to spring.

"Milord," Edgar said respectfully, although he could not keep the hatred from showing in his eyes, "can I be of assistance?"

"I need to know where my brother's saddle is and how he came to be poisoned by something stuck in it. Have you any knowledge of it?" He watched as Edgar's face flushed in anger.

Looking defiantly at Calder, he replied, "My men and I went over the saddle, but could find nothing. I fear your brother was mistaken and was cut somewhere else."

Calder stared thoughtfully at Edgar, the only evidence of his own anger was the narrowing of his eyes and the whiteness of the scar against his tan face. "Bring me my brother's saddle."

"Alan, bring the Lord's saddle here," Edgar called to a young stable hand.

"No," Calder's voice was low and firm, "I told you to bring it to me."

Edgar stood stock still, his hands clenched in fists at his side, his eyes glaring into Calder's. Without a word, he turned abruptly and walked into the stall containing the tack.

He returned with a large, ornate saddle and thrust it toward Calder. Taking it from Edgar, he carefully examined every inch of it, but was unable to find anything to indicate what might have cut his brother.

"Who has access to the tack?"

"Myself, the three stable hands and anyone else who wanders in here," Edgar replied smugly.

"My men and I will saddle and feed our own horses." Calder's tone was brusque as he looked suspiciously at Edgar. "No one else touches them, or the tack, understood?"

"Yes, Milord," he responded, his voice laced with sarcasm. Calder hesitated, then determined that now was not the time to teach Edgar a lesson in respect. Soon, he promised himself, very soon.

With one last scathing look at Edgar, Calder and his men returned to the Manor. After they had a chance to refresh themselves with food and ale, he stood to address them.

"We have a great responsibility here and dangerous conditions under which to accomplish what needs to be done."

All of his men were quiet and attentive as they listened to their leader.

"My brother was poisoned by a thorn or pin which was stuck in his saddle. We must inspect all of our clothing and tack carefully, to ensure the same does not happen to us. These people wish us as much harm as those we have been fighting since we landed on these shores. Have a care when dealing with them.

I will be riding out tomorrow to look over the lands and decide where best to build the castle. What Aric has begun is useless and will be dismantled.

We will split into groups of four. One group will ride the fields and forest to rout out the thieves and renegades that are stealing the livestock. The others will stay in the village and make sure that the necessary work is done and punishment rendered when it is not."

"Will we determine the punishments, Milord?" Garrick asked eagerly.

"For the time being, I will try to be here in the village as much as possible. I will make those determinations and I will need you men to assist me in carrying them out. Initially, we cannot be lenient with these people. They must learn to obey us. I am hopeful that the lessons will be learned quickly, so that we can relax the severity of the punishments imposed."

The men shook their heads in silent disagreement, knowing how stubborn and inflexible these Saxons could be, and that things seldom resolved themselves quickly where they were concerned.

"At dawn tomorrow, have the entire village brought to the Courtyard, I will give my terms to them then. Rest well tonight men, tomorrow begins a new kind of battle for us. One I will not lose."

*   *   *

Regan hummed softly as she boiled the mutton and turnips that she and Radolf would have for dinner. Her heart felt lighter than it had in a long time.

She knew it was because Calder had returned. She also knew nothing could, or would, happen between them again. But, just the knowledge that he was here and she would be able to see him from time to time, even if from a distance, filled her heart with a quiet peace, something she had not felt in a very long time.

She noticed then that Radolf, who had been running around the kitchen playing with a small, wooden figurine his grandfather had whittled for him, suddenly quieted. Her heart jumped in her throat as she turned and saw Edgar standing in the doorway.

"Good evening, Edgar," she said, nervous at his unexpected arrival. "Is there something you need?"

"This is my home, is it not? I am here to enjoy my family." His voice was pleasant enough, but Regan did not care for the look in his eye. Radolf ran over and clung to the back of her skirts.

"Of course, Edgar," she replied at last, "will you be joining us for dinner?"

"Yes, I would like that," he said, pulling a chair from the table and sitting down. "More Normans arrived today and I fear for your safety. I think it best that, for now, I stay nearby to watch over the two of you."

So that was it, she realized. He plays games with Calder, trying to make it seem as if all was well between the two of them, and Calder's son. Her stomach twisted with fear as she worried how Edgar might try to use Radolf to get even with Calder. Of all the Normans, it was Calder that he hated most. Edgar would not rest until he had his revenge on him.

The three spent an awkward and uncomfortable evening together. Edgar tried to be pleasant, to her and Radolf, but neither of them trusted him enough to relax when he was around. She slept with Radolf in her bed that night, while Edgar chose to sleep in a chair by the fire, much to her relief.

*   *   *

The following morning, the entire village was gathered in the Courtyard. Calder stood on the top step of the Manor, so that he could look down on them. He let his eyes drift over the crowd until he found the one he was looking for.

His eyes met Regan's and he felt a small jolt of excitement run through him. She stood with her young son, back away from the rest of the crowd. She had no other children with her, so he had to assume the boy was her only one, and for some reason that pleased him.

He studied her face, which looked pale and haggard, and wondered what could have happened since he had seen her the day before to distress her so.

Of their own volition, his eyes then sought out Edgar, knowing he was the reason that Regan looked so scared and unhappy. He found him standing with a small group of men and a short, buxom, blonde woman.

"I am Calder Wyndym, vassal to Lord Aric," he spoke in a voice loud enough that all could hear him well. "During his illness, I will take his place as Lord and Castellan of these lands. You will serve me as you would serve him."

He paused, watching the crowd as they whispered nervously amongst themselves.

"There is a castle to be built," he continued, "and your labor is required to complete it. You have sworn fealty to my brother and, as his vassals, you owe him your services in return for the use of his lands."

The whispers turned to disgruntled murmurs throughout the crowd now. His men had taken up positions every few feet along the outside perimeter of the group. They were looking tense and uneasy and Calder worried that there might be trouble.

"You will be divided into groups and every third day you will work for me, all of you, even the women."

"And our children, as well?" came a loud, brash voice from the crowd.

"If you cannot handle the job, then yes, your children also." He tried not to smile as he watched mothers grabbing their small children and hiding them behind their skirts, as if to protect them from him.

He saw that Regan did not feel the need to do that. She stood, head high, listening to his every word. Her tow-headed, little boy was holding her hand and watching him intently, as well.

"Who is your village elder?" he asked.

A slight old man, with flowing, white hair and a beard to match, stepped forward. "I am Filbert, the Elder," he called, his voice strong despite the fragile appearance of his body.

"For now, you will act as my Steward and will assign these men and women into three groups. Put the men and women of the same households into different groups. Each will work one day for me, and the next group the following day, and so on."

"How long do you intend to keep us from our fields, by having to do your work?" one of the men near Edgar called out.

"For as long as it takes to accomplish what needs to be done," Calder replied. To the elder, he said, "It will be your responsibility to meet with me each evening to report on the progress made that day, and to get instructions for the workers for the following day."

"Aye, Milord." Filbert did not much enjoy the thought of spending so much time with this large, fearsome man.

Calder raised his voice again, although he continued speaking directly to the elder, "And you will also report to me the names of the people who did not fulfill their obligations to me that day, so that they may be properly punished for their dereliction."

Loud comments and complaints now came from the entire group and he saw his men shuffling uneasily, their hands near the hilt of their swords. He knew that he must finish quickly and get the crowd broken up before trouble started.

"Are there any of you that can read, write and do figures?" he asked.

Their response was to stare woodenly back at him, as if they did not understand the question. The buxom, young blonde with Edgar's group stepped forward.

"Regan is able to do all that, Milord," she said, with a sweet smile that belied the maliciousness in her eyes.

Calder watched as Edgar glared at the girl, then turned his eyes toward Regan. She shook her head and looked even paler than before.

"Is that true?" he called over to her. She did not answer, but her distress was evident on her face.

"It is, Milord," the elder answered with resignation. "My daughter was taught to read, write and cipher."

"Regan is your daughter?" he asked curiously, noticing for the first time how the green eyes in Filbert's old, wrinkled face matched the color of the wide, luminous ones which graced Regan's visage.

"Yes, Milord, she is," the old man answered proudly, ignoring the disgruntled muttering of the crowd.

"I must inspect the lands today. Bring yourself and your daughter to the Hall tonight. Have your groups chosen and I will give you their duties for the morrow."

"What is my daughter needed for, Milord?"

"We must be sure everyone is being properly taxed. I need one of your people to assist me in obtaining the necessary information, so that it can be done correctly."

"We ain't paying yer damn taxes," a loud, belligerent voice called out. Others yelled their agreement and began pushing forward toward him. The two knights on the bottom step had to draw their swords to stop the momentum of the crowd.

"Then you will not live on these lands," Calder said firmly, not raising his voice, but speaking in such a tone that they all heard him.

"Now get to your fields, or your homes, and do what needs to be done. Tomorrow your time belongs to me."

Still mumbling and grumbling, the crowd began to drift apart and Calder sighed in relief. Although there were probably fifty or sixty villagers in the Courtyard, he was not worried for the safety of himself or his men, but he did not want this to start out as a bloodbath. He needed these people's cooperation to accomplish what had to be done.

Turning back to the Hall, he was stopped cold when called out to by a sweet, familiar voice.

"Milord," Regan was standing at the bottom of the steps, nervously twisting her hands together. She no longer had her son with her and looked quite upset.

"Yes?"

"May I speak with you in private?" Regan asked, glancing around at the villagers still in the courtyard, all watching her with open hostility.

Calder saw the looks, as well, and bid her come into the Hall, where they sat on opposite sides of a long, wooden table.

"What is it, Regan?" he asked.

"It is just that, I do not believe I should be the person to help you. There are others that can read and write. They were just too frightened to let you know."

He watched her face as she spoke, but she would not raise her eyes to meet his.

"Look at me, Regan," he demanded, and when she finally did as he asked, Calder was surprised to see the unshed tears in her eyes. He reached across the table without thinking and took her hands in his.

"What is this all about?" he asked tenderly. "Are you afraid the villagers will hate you because I am making you help me?"

"No, Milord, it's just that," she was embarrassed to tell him what her true situation was and did not know how to explain, "well, most of the villagers want nothing to do with me."

Regan saw his eyes narrow and decided to finish quickly and remove herself from his presence. "You should choose someone else, they will get more cooperation from the villagers. I fear that if I do it, they will be less inclined to give me the information that you require."

Calder sat quietly for a moment, holding tightly to her hands when she tried to slide them out of his grasp. Sadly, he realized that even though he had managed to marry her off to Edgar, it had not helped her after all. He wondered if Edgar tried to ease her situation, or if he was the cause of it to begin with. Looking at her strained, white face, he feared it was the latter.

"I am sorry for what has happened to you," he said quietly, his long, tanned thumb gently stroking the silky skin on the back of her hand.

"Please, Milord, I am not here for your pity," she snapped, unnerved at the emotions coursing through her at his nearness and his touch. "I simply want you to know that it would be in your best interest to have someone else do this for you."

He gave her a lazy smile. "I have chosen you, and the villagers will give you the information and the respect required, or they will answer to me."

"Milord," she began, but he stopped her with a shake of his head. He never anticipated that she would be the villager whose help he needed to levy the required taxes, but now considered it his own good fortune. It would give him an excuse to spend time with her. There was no way he would let her out of it now.

"We will start this together. It is time your people learned they are no longer free to do as they please. They will respect my wishes, or they will be dealt with severely."

Regan listened to him with trepidation. These were people she had known all her life and, although they had not treated her well in the last few years, she feared for them. She could see that Calder would not yield if they disobeyed him. Knowing the way Edgar, and most of the others, felt about the Normans, she could see only trouble for the future.

Noting how distraught she looked, Calder said softly, "You will never need fear me, Regan. Only those who refuse to do as I command shall be harmed."

She nodded, not trusting herself to speak.

"Come with your father tonight and I will explain your duties and your compensation for assisting me."

"Compensation?" she asked in surprise.

He smiled at her. "Do you believe we Normans are such barbarians that we do not pay for services provided?"

"Of course not, Milord," she replied, blushing furiously. "It was just that, I did not expect it."

"I always remember a good deed done me, and I always reward the people who serve me well," he said with a soft smile. "Now go home, I have much to do. I will see you this evening?"

It was a question more than a statement and she nodded her agreement. He released her hands and walked with her to the door, unable to resist placing his hand in the small of her back, enjoying the contact and wishing the possibility existed for something more intimate between them, but knowing that it could not be.

CHAPTER 6

Calder checked in on his brother, but Aric was sleeping peacefully, so he and Graeham set out to locate the site for the new castle. After much deliberation, they chose to have it built along the river.

It would be flat, level ground once the trees around the area had been cut down, and lookouts would be able to see trouble approaching from all directions. With the proper fortifications, they would have enough water and, if properly stocked, enough food to outlast a lengthy siege.

With the river so close, they would also be able to have supplies brought in easier and it would act as a natural border along one side of the castle, leaving any assailants open to their arrows, should they try to cross on that side.

They would not be able to encircle the existing village in the bailey, which would contain the Keep and other outbuildings. It would be close enough though, that the villagers would be able to get inside the grounds and behind the protection of the walls in plenty of time, should trouble arise.

They did not return to the Manor until well after dark. Skeet was waiting for them on the steps and took their horses to feed and stable them.

When Calder came down to the Hall after checking on his brother, he saw Regan and her father sitting near the fire amidst his knights. Both looked very uncomfortable.

His brother's condition was deteriorating fast and he feared the surgeon would not arrive in time. Aric was now barely able to get words out of his dry, parched throat, as Calder tried in vain to reassure him that he would be all right. Aric fell into a deep sleep shortly after Calder got to his room. Leaving Devona to tend to Aric, weeping as she mopped her husband's fevered brow with a damp cloth, Calder returned downstairs.

The sight of Regan immediately melted some of his frustration and anger.

"Join me," he called to the two of them as he sat at the long rear table. They stood, Regan taking her father's arm to assist him, and slowly made their way around the large, bulky knights to his table.

They both refused the food that he offered. Filbert gratefully acknowledged his vast thirst, though, so Calder had the village woman bring him some ale.

In no mood for any further aggravation that evening, he watched in annoyance as she sloppily jostled the tankard of ale so that it spilled on Regan. But it was the caustic stare she threw in the younger woman's direction that pushed him over the edge.

"What is your name?" Calder snapped at the village woman.

"Iona," she answered nervously, realizing too late that she had caught his attention.

"These people are my guests and you will serve them as respectfully as you would me and my knights."

"Yes, Milord," she mumbled.

"Now, apologize and wipe up the ale you spilled all over them. Do not come to this Manor again. I will find someone else who is able to fulfill your duties properly."

"Yes, Milord," she said, trying not to cry as she darted between Regan and Filbert to clean up the mess she had made. She started to scuttle away when he bellowed at her again.

"I said to apologize to my guests."

"Please forgive my rudeness and accept my apology for makin' a mess on ye," she said, with a pleading look at Filbert.

"Your apology is accepted, Iona," Filbert replied graciously, as she scampered back to the kitchen. Regan did not respond, just stared down at her hands which were tightly folded in her lap.

Filbert got up his courage, cleared his throat and determined to speak his mind to this insolent new Lord.

"There was no need for you to treat her so harshly, Milord."

The laughter and chatter of his knights stopped abruptly when they heard Filbert's words. No vassal was allowed to speak to their Lord in such a way and they waited to see what Calder would do.

Lowering the piece of bread that he had just been preparing to bite into, Calder stared hard into Filbert's eyes. "Maybe you do not mind that these people of yours treat your own daughter as an unwanted leper, but I do. Had you been man enough to take up Regan's defense before now, perhaps they would not find it as easy to treat her so callously and, perhaps, she would not have become so used to being treated with such disrespect. I will not have it. I would be ashamed to call myself her father if I allowed others to abuse her as I have seen them do and sat idly by as they did so."

Filbert's cheeks bloomed crimson in embarrassment, knowing Calder spoke the truth. He was an old man though and felt the need to keep peace with the neighbors that he had lived with his entire life. He never came to his daughter's defense, nor did Edgar. They left her to face the ridicule of the other villagers alone.

"I am sorry, Milord. What you say is the truth and shames me greatly." He hung his head and Regan reached over to grab his hand.

"Must you bully everyone you see tonight, Milord? Is it my turn next?" she asked him sharply.

He looked at her in surprise. He had been defending her honor and, for some ungodly reason, she was now angry at him for doing so.

"I hadn't planned on it, but I can accommodate you, if that is your wish," he answered in a low, angry voice.

Filbert watched as the two of them stared at each other, sparks shooting from their eyes. He could feel the tension between them, but could not understand the reason for it, not until he realized that it was his own grandson's eyes looking out from Calder's face.

So, the malicious gossip about Radolf's parentage was true. He had refused to believe such a thing of his daughter but could not deny the truth when it was staring him in the face. He now understood what was going on and why. He could feel the charge in the air surrounding Regan and Calder and knew there was still much to be resolved between them, even if they did not realize it themselves.

"I have assigned the three groups as you requested, Milord," Filbert said loudly, breaking the strange spell that held them.

Calder took a deep breath and let it out slowly, trying to rid himself of his anger. He dragged his eyes from Regan's reluctantly and turned to her father.

"To begin with, we will have three separate operations and the men should be divided between them as needed. Some will have to tear down what my brother began, the timber and stone salvaged and brought to the new site. Another group will need to clear the forest around the area we will build on, and the wood will have to be made ready for use. The last group will need to begin digging for the foundation."

Calder looked at Filbert to be sure he was grasping what was said. He nodded in satisfaction when he saw how closely Filbert was concentrating on his words.

"What of the women?" Filbert asked. "They will not be able to do such heavy work."

"We will probably have more use for them later on, once the actual building starts. For now, find things they are able to do to keep them busy, the men will need food and drink while they work, they will need messengers sent between the groups; you will be able to find something for them."

"Yes, Milord," Filbert answered.

"Is there a place nearby where rocks can be quarried?" Calder asked.

"Yes, I know of a place not far from here."

"Good. We will not need the stone yet, but it is helpful to know it is available for our use. Stone will make a better fortress than wood." Calder smiled. "It is much more difficult to burn."

"That it is, Milord," Filbert returned. He was beginning to feel better about this job and this new Lord. Young as he was, he seemed organized and intelligent. Perhaps things would work out for the village after all.

"Graeham," Calder waved him over "this is Filbert, my steward. He will be working closely with you on the building of the castle. You and your men will go with him tomorrow to show him where the foundation is to be dug and the forest cleared."

"Yes, Milord." Graeham took the seat next to Filbert and began to speak excitedly about the plans they had for the new castle.

Calder listened for a moment, and then turned his attention back to Regan. Steepling his fingers in front of him and placing his chin upon them, he stared into her eyes.

"Are you ready to listen to me now, Mistress Regan?" He asked the question quietly, with the hint of a smile gracing his lips.

"Will you be reasonable while speaking, Milord?" she returned, her green eyes sparkling.

"I will do my best."

"Well, of course then, please enlighten me as to my new duties."

Calder's mood turned more serious. "First, I will need a complete list of the members of each and every household. Can you handle that?"

Raising a delicate eyebrow, she responded, "I believe so, Milord."

He could not help but smile at the look she gave him. "Good, then you must determine the extent of each of the household's lands, property and livestock. Can you handle that?"

"It will be a more difficult task, Milord," she responded honestly.

"Yes, but it is very important. It will be the basis of how much they are taxed. First you talk with them directly and see if they will give you the information you require." He saw the look of distress appear on her face. "I will be assigning one of my men to be with you at each stop."

Regan let out a sigh of relief, her face relaxing a little as he continued. "Then the figures will come into play. We will have to determine how much each should be levied, then compare those figures with Aric's books to see what they have actually paid and what they still owe."

"I know nothing about levying taxes, Milord."

"I will help you with that. Do you have any other questions about this for now?"

"Will I be responsible for collecting the taxes?" Regan asked nervously. With the villagers already despising her, she knew their barbs and jeers would increase tenfold if she was required to do that, as well.

"We can decide that when the time comes. It will take awhile to determine what is owed first. The job will not be as easy as it sounds, you know."

"Yes, but I do believe I can do it, Milord," she replied, gracing him with a warm smile. It was not going to make the villagers treat her any better, of that she was sure, but at least she would be able to see Calder periodically and speak with him. That would make it all worthwhile.

"I also believe that you can," Calder said, returning her smile.

"You will have a knight with me, when I have to actually go to their homes?" she asked, needing his reassurance on that part.

"You will not be allowed to go without the escort of one of my knights," he advised her sternly. He sensed that it was dealing with her own people that caused her apprehension, and it bothered him considerably that her life was so difficult because of what they had shared together. He made a promise to himself that, for as long as he was there, he would see that the villagers were no longer allowed to hurt her in any way.

"Do we have an understanding then?" he asked, after advising her of the amount of coin he would pay for her services.

"Do I have a choice?" she asked with a smile, already knowing the answer.

"No."

"Then we have an understanding," she agreed, extending her hand across the table.

He grasped it tenderly and they shook, sealing their agreement, his eyes smiling into hers.

"When shall I start?" she asked, her face flushing from the contact between them.

"Tomorrow, and Regan," he paused, wondering if his next instructions were really necessary, or if he was only serving his own purposes "I think it would be best if you did your work out of the Manor. That way your papers will remain secure when you are not working on them. And you can report to me daily on the status. Would that be agreeable to you?" He saw her hesitate and worried that she would refuse.

"My son," Regan began hesitantly, "I must be with him. Would he be allowed to come here with me?" She was not sure if it was such a good idea to have Radolf so near Calder, but with the knight away most of the day, it should be safe enough. She could send Radolf outside to play when she had to speak with him.

"Certainly, as long as he will not interrupt your work." He would have promised her anything, as long she stayed close by him.

"Oh, he won't. He's a wonderful little boy." Her face glowed with the love she felt for Radolf.

Calder had no desire to see how happy Edgar's son made her. It forced him to think of the two of them lying together and he could not bear it.

"Fine," he said brusquely, ending their conversation, "I will see the both of you tomorrow after you have fulfilled your duties." He rose from the table and left the room.

Regan's eyes clouded as she watched him leave, wondering what she said to make him so angry. She walked with her father back to his cottage, still bothered by Calder's abrupt change in mood.

"He is Radolf's father, is he not?"

Thankful for the darkness that hid her face, Regan simply replied, "Yes."

"Does he know?"

"No, Father, and he cannot know." In quiet desperation, she stopped and gently grabbed his thin, fragile arm. "Please, Father, you can't tell him."

"He's not an idiot, girl. He will learn of it sooner or later."

"Yes, I know," she said, with a disconsolate sigh. "It's just that, there is so much bad blood between him and Edgar, I fear for what would happen if he knew."

Her father continued walking in a thoughtful silence, wondering which of the men she feared for.

*   *   *

Radolf ran into her arms when they reached her parents' cottage. "You were gone so long, Momma," he stated petulantly.

"I know, sweetheart." Regan knelt down next to him and kissed his cheek. "But I have important news."

She smiled as she saw his blue eyes widen in anticipation.

"What news, Momma?" he asked excitedly.

"I will be working for Lord Calder."

He scrunched his lips and pouted his disappointment with the news.

"And you are going to be my assistant and receive one silver penny at the end of the month for all of your help."

His eyes widened again and he smiled his adorable, crooked grin. "A real penny?"

"Yes."

"Just for me?"

"Just for you, if you behave and help me out as I ask you to."

He jumped up and down. Running over to his grandmother, he asked excitedly, "Did you hear?"

"Yes, we did, love," Gayle said, unable to keep from smiling herself as she watched him. "You are getting to be quite a man, being able to earn money like that."

He puffed out his chest with pride and nodded solemnly at her. "I know," was his response.

"Thank you for watching him, Mother. We'd better be getting home now. It's late."

"You're welcome anytime," she responded, hugging them both. Radolf walked over to his grandfather and extended his pudgy, little hand. After all, men shook hands with other men, they did not hug them.

But, he was not able to keep his grandfather from rifling his reddish-gold curls affectionately as he walked away.

Radolf chattered constantly as they walked the short distance home, but Regan did not even hear him as she took notice of the light coming from their cottage. The fire would have gone out long ago and it should be dark inside. A cold fear gripped her heart as she realized that Edgar must be there. She stopped short, kneeling down in front of Radolf.

"When we go inside, I want you to go directly to bed, do you understand?" His pallet was in one corner, with a blanket hung around it to separate it from the rest of the cottage.

There was going to be trouble between her and Edgar, Regan was sure of it, and she wanted Radolf out of the way. It was bad enough that he would still be able to hear everything that went on.

"But, Momma," he whined.

She took him firmly by the arms. "Your father is home and I want you to go directly to bed."

Her heart dropped as, even in the moonlight, she was able to see his face turn pale and his eyes widen in fear.

"It will be okay, love. Just go straight to bed, alright?"

"Yes, Momma," he said through trembling lips.

She squeezed him tightly and kissed his cheek. Taking his hand in hers, she squared her shoulders and headed to the cottage. Radolf followed her instructions and ran quickly to his pallet as soon as they got inside.

"Where have you been, wife?" Edgar slurred from his chair by the fire.

She moved to the far side of the room, well away from him. "I was at the Manor, discussing my new duties with Lord Calder."

There was no sense lying about it, Iona would have told the entire village by daybreak.

"Lord Calder," he spat, getting clumsily to his feet. "Come here, woman."

Regan remained where she was. "Edgar, perhaps you should get some sleep."

"Come here," he repeatedly softly. "You know better than to make me have to go to you."

Her heart raced with fear and disgust at the knowledge of what was to come. If she fought him, Radolf would worry and come out, and she could not take the chance of Edgar doing something harmful to him.

"Yes, Edgar." Regan steeled her shoulders and slowly walked to him.

He grabbed a handful of her hair and pulled her head back, bringing tears of pain to her eyes as he lowered his mouth onto hers. He slobbered on her and plunged his thick, disgusting tongue into her mouth, leaving her feeling as if she might retch.

Releasing her, he motioned for her to sit down. "Before our fun begins, wife, we must talk." He never called her by name if he could help it. More often than not, the ones that he did use were cruel and malicious. From his lips though, "wife" was the vilest that she could imagine.

"You and I will be visiting Lord Calder at first light tomorrow," he said, his words sluggish.

"Why?" she asked nervously,

"Because, Wife," he answered, his small, bloodshot eyes boring into her, "you will not be doing any service for him."

"But, Edgar," she began.

"Don't even think to argue with me about this, Regan." His use of her name sent a chill down her spine. "I have sworn no fealty to the pig. I will not give him my time, nor my wife. He has taken enough from me already."

Regan stared down at the table, her heart beating furiously in her chest. She knew that Calder would not be denied and wondered if all of Edgar's bravado was due to the amount of ale he had drunk. She hoped that was the case and that he would forget all of this nonsense by the morning.

"You will stand by my side in front of him while I make my case."

"Yes, Edgar, as you wish."

His eyes narrowed at her. "But, before I go to him, I must know if he has bedded you since his return."

Regan flushed. "Of course not, Edgar."

He gripped her face tightly in his hand, forcing her to look at him.

"Should I find out differently, I will kill the both of you."

"I have done nothing but talk to him." The words were difficult to get out because of the pressure he was exerting on her face.

"You will show me now, how you save yourself for your husband alone," he said, dragging her toward the bed.

"Please, Edgar," she whispered frantically, "don't do this."

He ignored her plea and, instead, ordered her to remove her clothes.

"Please, Edgar, don't," she pled again, her voice barely a whisper.

"Remove them or I will tear them off of your body."

Her hands trembled as she removed her clothing. She closed her eyes as his hands fumbled roughly over her body, trying to picture in her mind a handsome, smiling face with vivid blue eyes.

As Edgar threw her onto the bed and entered her, tears of pain escaped down her cheeks. She pictured Calder's soft, full lips and heard, once again, his deep groan as he filled her with the seed that had created their son.

Holding onto the image of Calder was the only thing that kept her from such an abysmal despair, that only pulling out her dirk and plunging it into either Edgar or herself could end it.

CHAPTER 7

The following morning, Calder stopped short in surprise as he walked out of the Manor and found Edgar, Regan, and their son, waiting for him.

Edgar's eyes were bloodshot and his face bloated from the ale he had consumed the night before. His head pounded and he was ready to do battle with anything or anyone. He looked forward to this meeting with his "Lord".

Calder saw that the boy was hiding behind his mother's skirts, far away from Edgar. Regan stared at the ground. She would not meet his eyes.

He stood straight, staring directly at Edgar, his face hard and unyielding. He would not speak first, he did not initiate this confrontation.

Calder's refusal to speak disconcerted Edgar. It was not what he had expected and those damned blue eyes staring down at him, into his very soul it seemed, made the blood roar in his head.

"My wife will not be fulfilling the duties you require of her," he said, loud and firm.

"Which duties would those be?" Calder asked. His voice was calm, but the scar on his face had turned bone white and his body was tensed for battle.

The question took Edgar by surprise and infuriated him when he realized the innuendo. "She will fulfill no duties, other than those of my wife. I have sworn fealty to your brother. Until he directs me and my family otherwise, we will continue taking care of our own affairs."

He grabbed Regan's arm and began to walk away.

Calder's voice was not loud when he spoke, but the threat it contained caused Edgar to stop in his tracks. "Do not walk away from me." He waited until they turned around before addressing Edgar again. "If you continue to show me such disrespect, I will have no choice but to see that you are punished. If that doesn't help your manners, then it will give me great pleasure to beat you senseless."

Edgar's eyes were small dark holes in his face as he glared at Calder. 'You are only a vassal to Lord Aric, as am I. You have no rights or power over my family or me."

"There you are wrong, Edgar. My brother has entrusted me with the running of his estate until he is well. I will honor that obligation, and you will obey my orders."

"Your brother is dying," he spat, "and you will be nothing after he is gone. Do not think you can own us for these few days that he has left."

Edgar gasped when Calder appeared in front of him an instant later. He could not help shrinking back from him, having felt his wrath before.

Calder backhanded him, knocking him to the ground, wanting to leap on him and choke the life out of him, but not willing to do so in front of his son.

Calder stood staring down at Edgar, breathing heavily, his hands clenching and unclenching as he tried to restrain himself from doing any further harm. "You are fortunate that you are such a coward. Were your child not here to witness it, I would gladly end your life right now."

Taking a deep breath, Calder turned to Regan, who was watching him with wide, frightened eyes. "Do not fear for him, Regan," he said coldly. "I will not kill him. Not today, anyway. But his insolence makes it necessary for him to be punished; and you will honor your agreement with me."

With that Calder stalked back up the stairs to the Manor. "Kenny, tie this piece of dung up to the pole in the Courtyard so all can see what happens when my orders are questioned."

"Yes, M'lord." Kenny ran down the steps with two of the other knights and dragged the unfortunate Edgar to the pole in the center of the courtyard. His hands were bound together and his arms stretched far over his head by a long rope. He was left to hang from the pole, his feet barely touching the ground.

Calder was watching the scene when he felt a tug on his tunic. Looking down, he saw Regan's son pulling at it. "What are you doing, boy?"

"You are Lord Cawer?" he asked, having some difficulty with the name.

"Yes."

"Will I still get my silver penny? Will I still get to be the assissant?" he asked. Even his awe of this large knight would not let him forgo the possibility of getting his first coin.

Calder removed the boy's hand from his tunic and picked him up in his strong arms. "What is your name?"

"Radolf, M'lord. It means red wolf," he answered proudly, with a lop-sided grin.

"And you are to be my assistant and get a silver penny?"

"Yes, Momma told me so." Then the smile dropped from his face and Calder could see only pure misery in it. "But, Daddy came home and I din't know anymore."

Calder looked down at Regan, who was standing at the bottom of the stairs watching them nervously, unable to hear what was being said.

"Was it your Daddy who didn't want you and your Maman to help me?" he asked, needing to know if this was all Edgar's doing, or if Regan really did want no part of it.

"Yes," he answered, nodding his head, his bottom lip trembling as he looked over at Edgar. His voice dropped to a whisper, as if he were afraid Edgar would hear him. "He hurt my Momma."

"How did he hurt your Maman?" Calder asked, trying to keep his voice calm and even, although rage began to swell inside of him.

"I don't know," Radolf said firmly.

"How do you know he hurt her then?" Calder asked in confusion.

"Cause I heard her saying please no, over and over, and then later I heard her crying, when I was apposed to be asleep."

Blue eyes met blue eyes in mutual sympathy for Regan. Calder saw the tears forming in Radolf's and was touched by his concern for his mother.

He set the boy down on the ground and knelt beside him. Chucking him under the chin, he said, "No tears, boy. Only women cry."

Radolf sniffed and stifled his tears as he nodded at Calder.

"You and I," Calder whispered confidingly, "will have a secret mission together."

The boy's eyes opened wide. "What's that?"

"Our secret mission is to watch out for your Maman. To make sure no one hurts her or makes her cry. You will let me know if that happens, and I will give you two silver pennies."

The boy's eyes almost popped out of his head and he started hopping excitedly from one foot to the other.

"But, Radolf," Calder said sternly, gaining the boy's attention again, "it is a secret between you and me. You cannot tell anyone, not even your Maman." The boy frowned. He disliked keeping secrets from her.

"We are doing it for her, Radolf, to help her be happy. Do we have a deal?"

The boy's features relaxed and his lop-sided grin appeared again as he extended his hand toward Calder and said, "Deal".

Calder could not help smiling down at him as they shook their agreement. He felt better, hoping that he now had an unwitting accomplice in Radolf, who would tell him when things went wrong, as Regan would not.

Regan found that her heart actually stopped beating in her chest when she turned from watching what was happening to Edgar, only to find Calder holding Radolf in his arms and talking with him.

When it did start to beat again, it pounded so furiously in her chest that Regan feared she might pass out. Will Calder see himself in Radolf? she worried, feeling close to panic.

Seeing Radolf smile, she was able to relax a little. He had a fear of most men, no doubt due to Edgar's treatment of him. Although still nervous that Calder might realize their relationship, she could not help feeling a warmth blossom in her chest as she saw how comfortable Radolf was with him.

She watched them curiously as Calder and Radolf shook hands, then walked side by side back down the steps toward her.

"Stay away from them, you Norman bastard," Edgar screamed from the other side of the courtyard. Calder frowned when Edgar's outburst caused Radolf to run and hide behind his mother's skirts.

Calder turned toward Graeham. "Gag him," he ordered coldly.

Graeham quickly ran over and roughly tied a wad of cloth over Edgar's mouth.

Calder forced his features to relax as he turned back to Regan.

"You have quite a son, Regan," he said, smiling down at her.

"Thank you," she replied, still upset at everything that was happening, but unable to keep her face from beaming with pride as she ruffled Radolf's hair.

Radolf had also watched as Edgar was gagged and now drummed up his courage and stood proudly at his mother's side. "I'm still gonna be a assissant."

She smiled tentatively at Calder. "Is that what your conversation was about?"

"Of course," he replied, with a wink at Radolf. "There's money involved, you know. Men have to come to agreements on these things."

"I'm sorry about what happened," she began, but the shake of his head stopped her in mid-sentence.

"I need to know just one thing," he said, the humor gone from his eyes now. "Do you want me to release you from our agreement?"

She hesitated for a moment but could not deny the truth when he looked at her that way. She would pay for it once Edgar was freed, but knew that she could tolerate anything if it meant she could be near Calder.

"No, I don't want you to release me," she answered softly, wanting to touch him, to hold him, to let him keep her and Radolf safe from Edgar and the others.

It took all of his willpower to not reach out and caress her face at that moment. Instead, he looked over at Edgar, who was still glaring at them. "Come inside for a moment then, I'll show you where you can work. Then I'd best be about my own duties."

He looked down as Radolf put his tiny hand in his own large one and walked side by side with him up the stairs and into the Manor.

"I have paper and ink set up for you over here." He indicated a table in the corner. "For today, just list the different households for me. It should not take more than a day, should it?"

"Oh, not even that long," she replied confidently. "That's the easy part."

"Good. Leave your papers with one of my men when you are done." They stood awkwardly for a moment, neither sure of how to address the subject they needed to discuss.

"When will Edgar be released?" she asked hesitantly.

"I wish never, but I will have to let him go later this afternoon. Will you be all right with him?" She could hear the concern in his voice and was touched by it.

She started to nod her head, but Radolf interjected. "Can we live here with you, Lord Cawer?"

"Why would you want to do that, boy?" Calder asked curiously.

Radolf just shrugged his shoulders, but he looked upset.

"Come, Radolf," Regan said, her face flushing, "you and I are fine in our own home. We take good care of each other, don't we?"

"Yes, but Daddy might come there again," he whined tearfully.

"Shush, Radolf," she said sternly, flushing an even deeper shade of red, not wanting their secrets spilled to Calder. "It is none of Lord Calder's concern. We will be fine, Milord."

He knelt down in front of Radolf. "I am always here if either of you need me. Will you remember that?"

Radolf nodded and gave him a hug, his little body shaking as he began to sob in Calder's arms.

Calder looked at Regan worriedly, hoping she was right and that there would be no repercussions for the two of them. But, just in case, he would be sure to have a little talk with Edgar before releasing him that afternoon.

"Radolf," he called firmly, and the boy let go to look up at him, "all will be well. I have much work to do and must go now. You look out for your Maman, all right?"

Radolf wiped his nose with his sleeve as he nodded to Calder.

"Well, then," he said, reluctant to leave, "I will see you tomorrow."

"Yes, Milord," Regan answered, bowing her head to him and leading Radolf over to the table that Calder had indicated. She hoped that she was not misleading all of them by insisting that all would be well with Edgar once he was released.

*   *   *

Calder spent a busy day riding from site to site, helping to resolve problems and making sure that the work was being done according to his instructions. He was in an ugly mood due, no doubt, to the fact that little more than half the group of villagers assigned had shown up that day.

It was early afternoon when Garrick came riding pell mell toward him. "Draco and the surgeon have arrived, M'lord," he said, a little breathless from the hard ride.

"It's about time," Calder replied, turning Alerio toward the village and spurring him forward. He leapt off the horse when he reached the Manor, tossing the reins to Garrick as he bolted up the steps.

He found Draco waiting for him in the Great Hall. "The surgeon is with your brother now, Milord."

"Good. He is not doing well at all, Draco," Calder replied, the sadness evident in his voice. "Your trip was uneventful?"

"Once I made my way through His Highness' moronic aides to get to his side, all was handled quickly," he replied, his gravelly voice even deeper due to his fatigue.

"I should be with Aric."

Draco put his hand on Calder's arm as he turned to go up the stairs. "Wait, Milord. You must let the surgeon work alone for now. And I need to speak with you first."

Regan must have finished her work for the day, because the Hall was empty as the two men sat down on opposite sides of the long table. Draco handed him a missive with the King's seal affixed to it.

"What is this?"

"Read it for yourself," Draco replied, not sure how he would react to the news.

After reading the document over several times, Calder continued to stare down at it in silence. "You know what this says?" he finally asked.

"Yes, the King told me of its contents."

"So, believing that my brother is about to die, he has given these lands over to me?"

"Yes," said Draco. "He does not want to give Roderick a chance at them."

"I see," Calder murmured thoughtfully. He had never wanted to be a landowner and told the King that repeatedly when offered one of his fiefs. Apparently, his wishes were not to be taken into account, after all.

"The country is close to being at peace," Draco said quietly, knowing how Calder felt about this issue. "There is less need for men such as you and me. Perhaps it is for the best to have a place of your own to call home."

"Perhaps, Draco," Calder replied absently, "but we will keep this between us for now. I will not have Aric know of the King's insult to him."

"As you wish, Milord."

The surgeon came downstairs just then, and Calder yelled loudly for one of the servants to bring them food and ale. Once they were served, Calder addressed the surgeon.

"How is he, Gideon?"

"Not well, as I'm sure you have seen," the tall, slight man said, shaking his head sadly. "He will not last out the week, Calder. There is nothing I can do for him, save help him sleep through the pain of it."

Calder laid his hand over Gideon's. "I ask only that you do whatever you can to make his passing easier for him to bear."

"I will do that, Calder," he replied.

Calder stood then and began to turn away from them. "I am going to take a walk, Draco, to clear my head. I will return shortly. I need you to find Garrick. Have him get some men to build a dozen pilories. We will have need of them in the morning. Then get some rest and thank you for your help in this matter with my brother."

"Yes, Milord," Draco said, draining the last of his ale and wiping his mouth with the back of a hand.

"Devona will show you where you can sleep, Gideon. And thank you for coming so quickly."

"It was no trouble, Calder. I just wish there was more that I could do for Aric. He and I have been friends for a long time."

Calder gave him a sad smile and walked out into the courtyard. Seeing Edgar still hanging there fueled all of his impotent fury at the impending loss of his brother.

He strode over to Edgar and sliced through the rope with his dirk. Edgar fell to the ground, his legs unable to hold him up. With shaking hands, the prisoner unwound the ropes from his wrists and took the gag from his mouth, glaring hatefully at Calder as he did so.

"You will do as I command," the knight ordered. "For every time that you refuse, you will spend another day as you did today. Do you understand me?"

Edgar just continued to glare silently up at him. Tired of his insolence, Calder kicked him viciously in the mouth. Spitting blood, Edgar looked defiantly back up at him.

"Do you understand?"

"Yes," he replied thickly through his split lip.

Taking several deep breaths, Calder tried to calm his rage. It would take very little for him to beat Edgar senseless right now, but it would serve no good purpose.

"Once before, I warned you about hurting Regan because of your hatred for me. Do you recall that conversation?"

Silent at first, he answered quickly when Calder took another step toward him. "Yes."

"Good, then we do not need to go over it again. Against her wishes, I have ordered her to be my clerk while trying to determine the taxes owed. You will not interfere with the work she does for me, nor will you cause her to suffer, in any way, because of my orders to her. Do you understand that?"

"Yes," Edgar said again, his mind filled with visions of the revenge he would take on Calder, and on Regan, when the time was right. Edgar was confident that this arrogant bastard would pay dearly for the humiliation he had been caused to suffer, and soon.

"Go back to your home now and be prepared to give me your assistance tomorrow. If you are not here with the others at dawn, I will find you and let you spend another day hanging like the useless piece of meat that you are."

"Yes, Milord," he answered, the hatred palpable in his voice.

Calder turned and walked away from him, headed toward the woods in the opposite direction from where the men were still working. He had relieved some of his frustration on Edgar, but just a small portion of it, and needed to be alone with his thoughts.

CHAPTER 8

Calder was unable to shake the deep sorrow that consumed him. He wandered along, remembering times he and his brother had shared when they were younger, allowing the memories to soothe his mind a bit.

Rounding a bend, he saw Regan picking wildflowers and putting them in her apron. His heart began to race and he called out to her.

She looked up in surprise and smiled sweetly when she saw who it was. "Milord," she said, gracing him with a brief curtsy.

"Have you finished your work for the day, then?" he asked.

"Yes, it did not take long. Radolf and I thought we would come out and enjoy the nice weather this afternoon."

"Where is the boy?" he asked, disappointed that she was not alone.

She could not keep the grin off of her face as she answered. "He is hunting down a most fiercesome beast, Milord."

"And what type of beast would that be?" he asked, enjoying how her face lit up when she spoke of her son.

"A wicked old bunny rabbit," she said, beginning to laugh. "He started to chase it and tripped and fell three times before he even got out of my sight, the little devil. His mind knows what he wants to do, but his little legs don't always cooperate."

The gentle tinkling of her laughter lightened Calder's own heart and he determined that he was most fortunate in having run into her like this. Just the sight of her lovely face soothed his soul, even more so than the memories of his brother had just a few minutes before.

"Will you walk with me for a bit?" he asked.

"As you wish, Milord." She moved toward him, feeling light-hearted and hoping that he would not notice how happy she was just to be near him.

They walked for a while in companionable silence, listening to the twittering of the birds as they flitted from tree to tree.

"My brother is dying," Calder stated in a flat voice, catching her off guard.

She placed her hand on his arm and looked up, seeing the sorrow that filled his eyes. "I am so sorry, Milord. I heard that he had taken ill, but I had no idea it was as bad as that."

"He is ill because someone poisoned him," Calder stated bitterly.

"No," Regan whispered in horror. "Who would do such a thing?"

"I don't know yet, but I was hoping you might be able to help me find out."

"How could I help, Milord?" she asked in confusion.

"It is your village. Perhaps you know who bears him the most ill will, and who would have been able to obtain such a deadly poison." He stood perfectly still, his temper easing a bit under her gentle touch.

She looked away, thinking carefully of how she would answer.

He lifted her chin with his finger and saw the indecision in her eyes. With no conscious thought to do so, he bent down and took her half-parted lips with his own, savoring the sweet, soft feel of them as they melted against his.

He felt her lean in toward him, allowing their kiss to deepen and their tongues to dance delicately together. Her hands moved up through the hair on the back of his neck and he encircled her in his arms.

Regan relished the feel of his hard body against hers, his gentle lips drawing a helpless response from her as his hands roamed freely over her body. Regan had dreamed of this moment for so long, and the exquisite agony of it was even more breathtaking than she had imagined or remembered.

Hearing her moan softly against his lips sent a rush of passion through Calder and his body began to shake with restrained desire. He finally pulled back, reluctant to release her, but knowing that the intensity of their kisses were causing a persistent need deep inside of him. A need that would require fulfillment, regardless of the consequences, if they did not stop now.

She trembled in his arms as he lifted his head and gazed into her eyes, half-lidded with passion, sparkling like green gems in her porcelain face.

Calder trailed a finger down her flushed cheek and circled her lips, gave her one more peck on the lips and stepped back. Both of them were so caught up in the other that neither sensed Edgar watching them from behind a tree in the distance.

Calder's voice was unsteady when he spoke. "Your lips taste even sweeter than I remembered."

She lowered her eyes in embarrassment, not knowing how to respond.

"You grow lovelier each time that I lay eyes on you. I fear, I cannot keep my hands off of you when you are near, Regan."

"I fear I have the same problem when I am around you," she replied, blushing furiously.

"I'm happy to hear that," he responded smugly, taking her hand in his as they continued walking down the trail. He enjoyed the nearness of her, while at the same time had to fight to calm the fire raging within himself.

He shook his head, trying to clear his thoughts and get back to the subject at hand. "I need your help to find out who is responsible for what happened to my brother."

"Milord, I must tell you that few people in the village even speak to me anymore. They would never trust me with any information that would help you." Her voice was strong and sincere as she began but wavered a little as she continued. "And even though they do not want Radolf and I as a part of their community, I do not know if I would have it in my heart to betray one of them. They are my people and I have lived amongst them my entire life. I don't know if could do it."

"I understand your loyalty, Regan, and I admire it, particularly after how poorly they treat you. But, if I do not learn who was responsible, they may try to do harm to me or my men. I cannot allow that."

Sighing heavily, Calder continued. "I will not jeopardize your relationship with the rest of the village any more than I already have."

He looked down at her with a mixture of understanding and disappointment. "I will find the person responsible on my own."

She was ashamed that she had refused to help him but was more afraid of what would happen to her, and to Radolf, if people should find out she had betrayed one of them to the Normans. "I'm sorry, Calder," she said, her voice filled with remorse.

"You have no reason to apologize. I would feel the same in your place." He lightly brushed a damp curl away from her cheek and Regan lifted her face, leaning into his hand, grateful for his understanding.

Just as he was about to take her into his arms again, they heard a voice shrieking, "Momma, Momma," from somewhere nearby.

Calder saw the color drain from Regan's face and realized that something was terribly wrong. He turned and sped off into the woods in the direction of the voice. Ignoring the branches slapping at his face, he quickly reached a clearing where he believed the sound had come from, but little Radolf was nowhere to be seen.

Instead, he saw two large wolves circling around an old hollowed out log that lay on the ground. The wolves were whining in anticipation, one digging under the log in a frenzy, the other trying to squeeze its body through one open end.

Hearing another shriek from Radolf, coming from inside the log, Calder let out a blood-curdling battle cry, pulled out his dagger and ran straight at the wolves. His cry scared one of them off into the brush, but the large, black male turned to face him. The hair on its neck was bristling and its deadly yellow teeth gleamed as it snarled.

As Calder charged, the wolf leapt into the air toward him. The knight grabbed hold of it but was forced to drop his dagger in order to grip the beast's thick neck and keep the strong, snapping jaws away from his face.

They fell to the ground and rolled. Calder tried desperately to keep the beast's deadly teeth away his face and neck. Legs thrashing, the wolf's knifelike claws sliced through his skin as it attempted to get Calder to release his grip. The knight grimaced in pain, but, ignoring the burning sensations, rolled the wolf again. This time he brought the animal closer to where the dagger lay. Pushing the beast away from him with all his strength, Calder dove for the knife and turned just as the wolf launched itself into the air for a second time.

Calder plunged the dagger into the animal's heart. The heavy body landed full on his chest, knocking the wind out of him. Calder shoved the beast onto the ground beside him and watched as its legs continued kicking in the final throes of death, and its life's blood trickled into the earth.

Calder stood slowly, his body heaving with the exertion of the battle. The second wolf seemed to have disappeared, for now at least. Regan dashed breathlessly into the clearing just as Calder was bending over to help the sobbing Radolf out of the hollow log. Calder hugged the boy close as he cried noisily against his shoulder. The knight patted him awkwardly him on the back, trying to reassure him.

Tears began to stream down her cheeks as she paused for a moment to stare at the dead wolf. Taking Radolf into her own arms, she buried her face against his shoulder, squeezing him tightly.

"Calder," she managed shakily, "thank you. I don't know what we would have done." Her voice broke at the realization of what might have happened if he had not been there.

The adrenaline from the fight was fading now. Calder walked over and wrapped his strong arms around the two of them, holding them while they cried.

Releasing his hold as they quieted, Regan looked deeply into his eyes. "Thank you," she whispered again.

He longed to take her back into his arms again but, instead, he put his hand under Radolf's chin, forcing the boy to look up. "You're alright, son. No more need for tears," he said tenderly.

Radolf looked at Calder with a tremulous smile and adoring eyes. Regan's face blanched when she heard Calder call Radolf son, despite the fact that he did not realize the truth of what he said. That one simple word caused a sharp pain to blossom in her chest. Suddenly she felt dreadful for not telling Calder that Radolf was his son, appalled that, because of her, Radolf would never know his true father.

But what will happen with Edgar? How much more will he be able to hurt us if Calder knows the truth? Regan's head spun, filled with disjointed thoughts and questions regarding Calder and Edgar; and still trying to recover from the fear of Radolf's close call.

"I have to go," she mumbled woodenly, her emotions in turmoil.

"I'll walk back with you," Calder insisted.

Regan needed to be alone with her thoughts and doubts, but was still afraid after what had happened with the wolf, so she acquiesced. They had not gone far when Calder saw how difficult it was for her to carry the boy and offered to take him.

It was then that Regan noticed the blood seeping through his tunic and hose. "Calder, you're hurt," she said worriedly.

"Just scratches, cheri, nothing to worry about. I'll clean them up when I return to the Manor."

Holding Radolf in his arms put the thought of his injuries out of his head. Never having spent much time with children, he was pleasantly surprised at how comfortable and natural it felt carrying the boy. Radolf eventually laid his head against Calder's broad shoulder and fell asleep. Calder drew Regan close with his free hand, and they walked together back toward the village in a comfortable silence.

Though outwardly calm, Regan's mind was reeling. On top of her worries about Radolf and Edgar, she also struggled with her feelings for Calder. She was a married woman and was allowing him to be as familiar with her as her husband was. Should anyone see them, she would suffer severe repercussions at Edgar's hands, of that she was sure. But, she could not find it in herself to step away from or refuse Calder's touch. With all of her being, she wanted to be near him and to feel his strength and warmth engulfing her.

Having the presence of mind to split up as they neared the village, Regan and Radolf took a circumventive route around the Manor to get back to their cottage. But before Calder would let her go, he turned her toward him.

"You are sure the both of you will be alright with Edgar?"

With a sad smile, she nodded her head. "Yes, Milord, we'll be fine."

"Have a good evening then," he said reluctantly, lines of worry etched in his brow. He felt the need to say much more to her, but knew he could not. "Regan, you know where I am if you need me."

She touched his arm lightly. "Please don't concern yourself about us. You must tend to your brother now, and yourself. Good evening, Milord."

A heaviness returned, enveloping his heart, as he watched them walk away. It did not leave him as he made his own way back to the Manor.

*　　*　　*

Filbert arrived at the Hall after Calder and his men finished their evening meal. Garrick removed himself from the table, so that the old man could sit across from Calder while they discussed their business.

"Milord," Filbert said, nodding to him as he sat down.

"Filbert." Calder looked intently at him, wondering how honest the man would be.

"We made good headway on the foundation for the Keep, but I fear we had not enough men to accomplish as much in the woods as could have been done."

Calder nodded his agreement. "You have the names of the villagers who did not show to do their part?"

He saw the indecision on Filbert's face. The elder was torn between his newfound relationship with Calder and longstanding loyalty to his own people. "I do, Milord. I ask only that you be lenient with them."

"You have no right to ask that of me, Filbert. They must learn to obey my commands, or they could end up forfeiting their lives for their insubordination."

"Yes, Milord," he replied dejectedly, knowing it was the way that it must be, but hating his own part in it.

He listed the names for Calder and was given instructions for work to be done the following day. After Calder dismissed him, Filbert stood as if to leave, but then turned back to the table. "Tomorrow is the day we would come before the Lord of the Manor to have him settle our problems and disputes. Can I let my people know that it will proceed as usual?"

Calder was thoughtful for a moment, a frown gracing his face. He did not have the time, or the patience, to deal with these people's petty problems, but realized it was a necessary part of his new responsibilities. "We will halt work early in the afternoon and I will hear their grievances then."

"Thank you, Milord," Filbert responded and took his leave of the Manor.

"Have the pillories been completed?" Calder asked Garrick when he returned to his seat, referring to yokes of wood with indentations for a man's neck and hands. The punishment, he knew, was not especially painful, but rather very uncomfortable, particularly when a person must spend a lengthy period of time in it. They would serve their purpose without causing any serious injury to the villagers.

"Yes, Milord. They are rough, but will do fine."

Calder slid a piece of paper across the table. "Here is a list of the men that I want placed in them at first light tomorrow. Each day, when one of them ignores my commands and does not show for work as required, he will stand in the pillory the next day. Understood?"

"Yes, Milord," Garrick answered, "but what of the women?"

"They will stand in it, as well. These people must learn that I will not allow any of them to disrespect me."

"As you wish." Garrick relished the opportunity to make these Saxons pay, even if just a little, for their attitudes and actions against his own people. He only wished the punishment could be a little harsher.

"Holt, you took the patrol today. Were you able to find any evidence of where the thieves are hiding?"

"No, Milord," the bald giant answered, "and they were able to abscond with several head of cattle on the north side, while we rode to the south. There are not enough of us, M'lord, to protect all that we have to watch over."

"I know, Holt," Calder said, rubbing his brow in weariness and frustration. "But, I cannot spare any more men until we get these villagers to work as they are instructed. Once we get their cooperation, more of our men can assist you."

"And what do we do in the meantime, M'lord?"

"Herd all of the cattle and livestock into one area, where you will be better able to keep an eye on them. Kill anyone who approaches that you are not familiar with. When we are able to put more men to the task, we will find the thieves' lair and hunt them down."

"That will cause more headaches for you, M'lord," Holt replied.

"In what way?"

"These people keep their stock separate so that they know which animals belong to each of them. Mix them together and there will be no end to their squabbles over ownership."

"Better that, than to having nothing left to squabble over," Calder stated quietly.

"As you wish, M'lord," Holt responded, knowing it would be much easier for him and his patrol now, but much more difficult for Calder in the long run.

"Draco," Calder said, turning to him, "I have something that I need you to do."

"Yes, Milord?"

"I have asked Regan to go from cottage to cottage, obtaining information as to the extent of each family's holdings in order to levy the proper taxes against them."

He hesitated a moment, wondering how to phrase his request. "The villagers will not willingly give her the necessary information. I need you to go with her and lend your authority to her requests, so that they give her what she needs."

"I am to babysit, Milord?" Draco asked in a dry tone.

"No, Draco," Calder replied with a caustic smile. "I think they might try to do her harm, because she is assisting me. I need you to keep that from happening. I also need your sharp eyes, so that you can report anything she might miss."

"As you wish, Milord," Draco replied, his eyebrow raised in skepticism.

"I must see my brother now." Calder's sadness regarding Aric's impending death still weighed heavily on his mind.

He asked Devona to leave the room when he arrived to find Aric awake. "Calder," Aric said weakly, grabbing his hand.

The younger man sat beside his brother on the bed. "How do you fare today, Aric?"

"Not so well, brother. Gideon plies me with herbs that help me sleep but, I fear, I will not awake one of these times. Devona sent a messenger to bring my children to me from Normandy. I must see them before I go."

Aric's face was pale and his cheeks sunken as Calder gripped his warm, feverish hand in both of his. He wished dearly that he could give Aric his own strength to fight the battle that he waged within his body.

"I know that I do not have long, Calder," he began, but was overcome by a harsh, raspy coughing fit. Only after Calder gave him a drink of water, was he able to continue. "I ask only that you look out for Devona and my children."

"You do not have to ask that of me, Aric. You know I will see them well cared for."

"I know, brother," Aric said weakly, "but Devona can try the patience of a saint and I put the burden to you, Calder, to be sure she is all right."

Calder smiled tenderly down at him. "Have no fear for them. They are my family and will be taken care of as such."

Aric's eyes glazed over a little and he began to speak then of their childhood. "I never felt like your older brother, Calder. I always felt you were the older son."

"Why is that, Aric?"

"It was you who always protected and cared for me, when it was my responsibility to do so for you. Even as children, you protected me from others, as I could not protect you."

"I grew into a man earlier is all, Aric."

"No," he said, his voice weakening, "it is who you are, Calder. Protector of the innocent and the weak, a fearless warrior, a man of honor. I take much pride in knowing that you are my brother."

Aric's eyes closed then, before Calder could respond. His slow, even breathing indicated that he had drifted off into sleep. Calder stared fondly down at him, pulled the covers up to his shoulders and silently left the room.

CHAPTER 9

As Regan crossed the Courtyard the next morning, pulling Radolf along by the hand, she was bewildered to see all of the commotion going on. The knights were dragging some of the village men and placing them in pillories. The men were shouting obscenities at the knights and trying to fight back, but they were no match for the large, capable soldiers. Other villagers were milling about, making snide and derogatory comments about the Normans' ancestry.

"Unless you wish to join them, leave the Courtyard." Calder's voice boomed out from the top of the Manor steps. Regan saw that the boyish charm she had seen on his face the day before was completely gone from the man who stood here now. His face was hard and stern, his strong jaw set as he glared down at the villagers.

"Those of you required to work for me today, see Filbert to learn where you will be needed. And know you, if you do not fulfill your obligations to me today, it will be you standing here in this courtyard tomorrow."

There was much mumbling and grumbling, but most of the villagers began to go about their business. Regan saw Edgar on the far side of the Courtyard, glaring at her as she made her way to the Manor steps. She would not meet his eyes.

"Milord," she asked hesitantly, reaching Calder on the steps and looking down at the men in the pillories, "what is this about?"

"These men refused to do as I commanded and they must be punished. If they are not, others will follow their lead."

He looked down at Radolf, whose eyes were open wide with fear as he looked out at the men. Calder knelt down beside him.

"There is no need for you to be afraid, Radolf." His voice was quiet and gentle, not wanting to frighten the boy any more than he already was. "I am the Lord here and these people must learn to obey me. Can you understand that?"

"Yes," he answered tremulously, not understanding any of it.

"Good," Calder said, chucking him under the chin and standing up straight. He turned his attention then to Regan. "Was all well with you last night?"

"Yes, Milord, there were no problems," she answered, knowing he was referring to Edgar. She did not mention that Edgar had not returned home at all, much to her relief.

"I am glad to hear that," he said, with a pointed look in Edgar's direction. "You will begin the next phase of work this morning. Your papers are in the Hall, as is Draco. He will accompany you."

She was not sure how she felt about that. Draco scared her almost as much as the thought of confronting the villagers.

"I must go now." With a brusque nod, he turned and headed for the stables. Regan and Radolf entered the Hall to find Draco finishing his breakfast.

Radolf sat down next to him and stared enviously at the food in his trencher. "Are you hungry, boy?" Draco asked in his low, gravelly voice.

Radolf nodded.

"Here, I am done with this." Pushing the trencher, still half full, over toward Radolf, he looked curiously at Regan.

She flushed in embarrassment, but remained silent rather than let this fierce man know that Edgar had not brought food for them in sometime, and that their supplies were getting dangerously low. She planned on taking Radolf to her mother's for dinner that evening, to fill up his little belly and make up for the meager scraps she had fed him that morning.

Once Radolf cleared all the remaining food from the trencher and wiped his mouth on his sleeve, causing his mother to sigh heavily, the odd trio began about their duties.

At the very first cottage, Regan realized what a blessing it was to have Draco along. She insisted that Radolf stay outside and play as she went to the door and knocked at the cottage of Seaton. His wife, Rowena, answered the door and, seeing who stood there, slammed it in Regan's face.

"Stand aside," Draco growled, as he kicked the flimsy door open and strode inside.

"Get out of my home," Rowena started to screech, stopping only when she saw Draco's massive frame filling her doorway.

"Sit," he commanded the woman, who promptly fell back into a chair, her face blanching. "Now, you will answer Mistress Regan's questions, honestly and completely, understood?"

The woman nodded fearfully at him. She answered Regan's questions reluctantly, her eyes continuously darting over to the fearsome warrior, who stood with his massive arms crossed and an intimidating frown on his face, watching them from the doorway.

It was a similar situation with the other cottages they visited. Without Draco's presence, she would not have been allowed to even get through the door, let alone obtain the information that she needed. Regan tried to concentrate on the questions that she needed to ask, rather than on the cold, hateful looks they all bestowed upon her.

The last visit of the day was the most difficult. Alden was an elderly man, once a close friend of her father's, but no longer, because of her.

Alden was intimated by Draco, but that did not stop him from responding to her questions in a snide and hurtful way. Draco was about to step in when he made a particularly rude comment, but realized that Regan was handling the situation in her own way and remained quiet.

She let Alden's barbs roll off of her shoulders without acknowledging them, persistently and respectfully continuing with her questions.

When she had obtained all of the information that she needed, they turned to leave the cottage. Draco walked out first and, therefore, was unable to hear what Alden hissed in her ear.

"We all know you are the Norman's whore. You will burn in hell for betraying your own people like this."

Regan had tears in her eyes as she turned back to face the old man. "I am no one's whore." Her voice was shaky, but gained strength as she continued. "And it was my people who betrayed my son and me long before Lord Calder returned. For your part in that, Alden, you should look to the salvation of your own soul. I have no fear for mine."

Draco saw the unshed tears in her eyes as she left the cottage, not knowing what the man said, but seeing how deeply he was able to cut Regan. He wanted to strike out at the man, but because of his age, just sent a threatening look in his direction and took her arm. He escorted her back toward the Manor in that way, with Radolf skipping along behind them.

Regan was grateful for his support, feeling weak and totally drained after having to keep her composure all day as she faced these people. She was not sure how she would be able to find the courage to continue doing this day after day until she met with them all. It seemed a very daunting task indeed.

Thoughts of her own troubles disappeared as Skeet ran up to them. "Draco, come to the Manor quickly. Lord Aric has died and Lord Calder needs you."

Draco released her arm and ran with Skeet toward the Manor. Regan stood still, filled with indecision for a moment. Then she grabbed Radolf's hand and led him toward her mother's home.

"Lord Aric has died," she told Gayle when they arrived. "I'm not sure if anyone else knows yet. Please tell no one but Father for now."

Her mother's face paled as a myriad of emotions crossed it, the strongest being fear. Now someone else would be Lord and none would know, until he arrived, whether he would be good or a tyrant. Their fate was once again in the hands of an unknown entity.

"Please watch Radolf for me. I must go to the Manor."

"Why?" Gayle asked nervously, always afraid when her daughter had to be around the beastly Norman warriors.

Regan paused, unable to explain that she felt she had to be there in case Calder needed her.

"I will see what information I can obtain," she lied.

"Of course, Regan," her mother said, hugging her tightly. "I'll take care of Radolf. But, don't be gone long."

"I won't, Mother," she replied, returning the hug, and giving a quick kiss to Radolf's cheek as she admonished him to behave for his grandmother. Then she hastily left the cottage and headed for the Manor.

She was filled with trepidation as she entered the Hall. All of the knights were there, scowling and looking even more fierce than normal. Making her way to the front of the room, she saw Calder sitting at a table, speaking quietly with Draco.

His face was haggard, grief deepening the lines on it and making the scar appear even whiter against his tan skin.

She stood quietly to one side, not wishing to interrupt his conversation. Some of the knights glanced curiously at her, but none spoke to or bothered her. Calder rubbed his brow and glanced up around the room, but stopped when his eyes met hers across the Hall. Giving her a sad smile, he motioned her over.

"Milord," she said, with a quick curtsey, "I am so sorry for your loss."

"Thank you, Regan. The word has spread quickly then, has it?" he asked, his voice low and filled with restrained grief.

"She was with me when Skeet gave us the news," Draco explained.

"Have you told anyone else?" he asked.

"Just my mother, and I asked that she tell no one other than my father for now."

He nodded his satisfaction at her answer. "Draco, my niece and nephew are to arrive tomorrow morning. We will have his burial ceremony in the afternoon. Will you see to it that we have a priest and a proper coffin for him?"

"Yes, Milord," Draco answered, wasting no time in seeing to his Lord's wishes.

"Is there anything that I can do to help, Milord?" Regan asked quietly.

Sorrow reflected in his dark blue eyes and she wished that she could reach over and hold him, to help somehow ease his grief.

"Yes, Regan, there is." Coming around the table and taking her arm, he directed her toward the stairs. "My sister-in-law, Devona, is quite distraught, as is to be expected." He paused, taking a deep breath before continuing. "She has no friends here and I do not know how to help her through this. Could you sit with her for awhile?"

"Of course, Milord," she answered without hesitation.

"Thank you," Calder said, brushing a curl away from her face, his voice was soft and filled with emotion. "And thank you for coming here. It is good to know we are not hated by all of your people."

She gave him a sad smile. "I have no people, Milord. I do only what any decent person would."

"Will you have dinner with me tonight?" he asked suddenly, catching her by surprise.

"I'm not sure that would be proper, Milord," Regan answered, somewhat nervously.

"I have matters I must attend to now. I was hoping you would join me for dinner, when I would have more time to hear of your progress with the tax information."

"I see," she responded thoughtfully, knowing his request was logical, but also knowing, in her heart, that it had more to do with their being together than with his interest in her progress. He needed her and she would not refuse him.

"Certainly, I will join you, Milord," she said, smiling at the look of relief on his face.

"Thank you. Devona will be upstairs in the Lord's chamber. See if you can get her away from Aric, she still refuses to leave his side. She is exhausted and needs some sleep."

"Yes, Milord," Regan replied, her head spinning from his abrupt turns in the conversation.

Garrick called to him, tearing his attention away from the sight of her hips gently swaying as she went up the stairs.

"Word must have spread, M'lord, the courtyard is filling with villagers."

Calder stood quietly for a moment and then reached a decision. "Release the men from the pillories. Have all the villagers gathered in the courtyard. I will talk with them."

"Yes, M'lord." Garrick and the other knights left quickly to do Calder's bidding.

He sat quietly in the empty Hall, his chin rested on folded hands and his eyes closed as he tried to collect his thoughts. He had seen death happen many, many times and realized that it was just another part of life, but, never had he let it cut to his heart before, as Aric's death was doing.

"Lord Cawer?" A small voice called from beside him. Calder opened his eyes and looked down at the little, red-haired imp next to him.

"What are you doing here, Radolf?" he asked gently.

"I sneaked in, my gramma don't know I'm here," he whispered, as if to keep from being discovered.

"Why are you here?"

"The man tole us your brother died."

"Yes, he did."

"I didn't want you to be sad, so I brought you this." Radolf held out his pudgy, little hand and in it was a small, carved figurine.

Calder looked at it in bewilderment. "What is this?"

"My grandpa made him for me. His name is Durwin and he is my friend. When I feel sad, I talk to him."

"Have you no other friends?" Calder asked, touched by the boy's gesture.

His eyes clouded over as he responded. "The other boys are mean, they don't like me to play with them."

Radolf did not speak with any self-pity, just a matter-of-factness that was all the more touching to Calder because he was so young. He should not be forced to mature at such an early age simply because of the cruelty of the rest of the people in this village.

"Can I be your friend, Radolf?" Calder asked, rewarded by the happiness that lit the boy's face.

"Oh, yes," he said excitedly. "I would like that."

"Good, because every man needs a close friend, someone he can depend upon, right?"

"Right," Radolf answered, not really understanding what he had just agreed to, but so happy with his new friend that it did not matter.

"But, won't you miss Durwin if you give him to me?" Calder asked, lifting Radolf into his lap.

"Maybe I can still play with him sometimes?" he asked hopefully.

"I have a better idea, my little friend. Why don't you keep Durwin for now. When I feel sad, I will come and borrow him from you for a while."

Radolf's little brows furrowed in thought and then he solemnly nodded his head.

"Then I take care of him till you need him?"

"Yes, and you and I, we'll take care of each other too, alright?"

They smiled at each other as Radolf held out his little hand. Calder engulfed it in his own and they shook on their new friendship.

Calder hugged him tightly and set him back down on the floor.

"Thank you, Radolf. Now run and find your grandmother before she boxes your ears for disobeying her."

"Yes, Lord Cawer," he said, scampering off with Durwin gripped tightly in his hand.

The warmth Calder felt at his conversation with Radolf faded rapidly as he heard the sounds of the crowd milling around outside. He took a deep breath, steeling himself for this ordeal, and walked out of the Manor.

He could see the fear on their upturned faces as they looked at him.

"My brother, Aric," he began, "was poisoned by one of you several weeks ago. I have not yet determined who is responsible for that act but have no doubt that I will do so. And, when the culprit is found, justice will be handed to him swiftly and without mercy."

"My brother died today," he continued, forcing himself to keep his voice level and calm. He watched as they turned to talk amongst themselves. He saw Edgar standing at the back of the crowd and the smug look on his face fueled Calder's anger and frustration. Taking another deep breath, he fought to regain his self-control.

"Who will replace him?" A voice called out from the crowd.

"You will know that soon enough." Devona still was not aware that the lands had been turned over to him. He certainly wasn't going to let her find out like this. "There will be no work parties tomorrow. My brother's funeral will take place in the afternoon."

"Must we attend?" Someone else cried out.

The dam burst and Calder's face became a thundercloud of rage, causing some of the people in the front to back away into the crowd.

"He was your Lord for four years. He treated you all fairly and with respect." Calder's voice was low and cold, but the strong timbre of anger in it carried to even those furthest away from him. "I will not order you to attend his funeral. Look to your own consciences for that."

"Milord," Calder heard Filbert call out to him. "will you hear our grievances today?"

Gritting his teeth, using every ounce of his willpower to keep his anger under control, he turned to Filbert.

"A good man died today. I will not disrespect his memory by pretending as if it has not happened and listen to your petty grievances. Try being men for once and work out your own problems. If you are incapable of doing that, I will hear them next week." His gaze was piercing as he looked over the crowd.

"Listen well, though. If you waste my time, the parties involved will pay serious penalties. Have no doubt of that."

He strode back into the Manor and startled one of the serving girls as he bellowed for her to bring him a tankard of ale.

CHAPTER 10

Later that evening, after a quick trip to her mother's house to explain the situation as best she could, Regan appeared once more in the Hall.

Calder gestured for her to join him at his table. The mood and conversation of all the men was somber.

"How is Devona?" Calder asked her.

"She finally cried herself to sleep a short while ago. Gideon gave me some herbs to make tea for her. I think that helped. He says that she will most likely not awaken until morning."

"Good," he answered. "Thank you for looking after her, Regan. I fear I do not do well with distraught women."

Regan smiled. "With those broad shoulders of yours, Milord, I think you could do much better than you know."

What is it about this woman, Calder wondered, *that can make me feel so relaxed and at peace, just by having her by my side?*

She flushed at the intensity with which he gazed at her. Turning her eyes down, she began picking at her food, moving pieces of cod around the beans in her trencher. She had no appetite for the food in front of her. Her whole being was focused on the man who sat so close beside her, his nearness overwhelming all of her senses.

"Did you make any progress today, Regan?" he asked.

"Not much, I'm afraid," she responded nervously. "It takes much longer than I expected it would. Draco was such a great help, though. I could not have managed half as well on my own. Will he be coming with me to each cottage?"

Turning to Draco and seeing his slight nod, he answered, "Yes, he will. I'm glad you find him useful."

This last he said with a smirk at Draco, but sensed there was more to what had happened today than she was telling him. He would get further details from Draco after she left.

Feeling self-conscious in the midst of all the large and boisterous knights, she asked Calder's permission to leave as soon as they finished eating.

She saw his frown of displeasure, but he stood and took her arm, escorting her to the door.

"I will walk with you," he said, as they left the Manor.

"There is no need, Milord," she said, worried that someone would see them together.

"I feel the need," he replied, walking so close to her that their bodies brushed against one another. There was just a sliver of a moon, but the sky was blanketed by stars, lighting their way as they walked along in silence.

Calder could not resist reaching out and grabbing her hand in his own. Regan was immediately assailed by conflicting emotions at his touch; warmth and security mixed in with a strong dose of guilt and fear.

She was a married woman and, even though she felt no love for Edgar, she had promised to be faithful to him. And here she was walking through the dark, hand in hand with a handsome stranger, craving his touch, wanting his lips on hers. Wanting him to carry her again to the heights of passion they had reached that one night.

Regan's mind reeled with confusion and uncertainty. She did not want him to think she was just a common trollop, yet she did not feel comfortable explaining how empty and lost she felt. She was unable to put into words how much she longed to be wanted and needed by a man, or more precisely, by him.

Her body seemed to respond to him on its own. The guilt over her betrayal of Edgar was not quite sufficient to overpower her desire to be held in Calder's strong arms. When she was with him, she felt like a butterfly, finally released from its cocoon to fly away into the bright new day, free to be who she was and embrace the feelings he stirred within her.

"Edgar does not stay at our cottage much." It was important that he know she was not being familiar like this with him, and then rushing home into Edgar's arms.

"Then I have given him too much credit already, for what little intelligence I thought he had," Calder replied in a soft, satisfied voice. His blood boiled with anger every time he thought of Edgar's hands on her and was relieved to hear of their situation.

"Why is your boy so frightened of him?"

She sighed. "Edgar does not know how to be a father to him. He is not gentle with Radolf."

She felt his grip tighten on her hand. "Does he hit the boy?"

"Oh no, I would never allow that. It is just that, having a hand put to you is not the only way to be cowered. Edgar is most effective at using his tongue as a lash."

"Is that how he treats you, as well?" Calder asked, his voice calm, effectively hiding the fury that coursed through his veins at the thought of such cowardice in a man.

"He used to, but we do not see him much anymore."

"You and Radolf deserve better than that."

"It was you who forced us to marry, Milord," she answered quietly.

Calder stopped abruptly and looked down at her. "I was trying to do what was best for you," he replied, anger beginning to seep through in his voice.

"Yes, I realize that. And, so we will continue to live as we did before your recent arrival." Taking a deep breath, knowing that she needed to be firm, but not sure if she could go through with it, Regan stated resolutely "I should not spend any more time alone with you, Milord. Should someone see us, they may misconstrue our intentions. It would not go well for Radolf, or myself."

"So, you will stay away from me and keep yourself at the ready for Edgar?" he asked coldly.

"I am his wife, Milord," Regan answered, her tone matching his.

"And what of your feelings toward me?"

"I cannot have feelings for you, Milord, other than the respect and loyalty that are your due." Her voice was getting louder now, and she was able to hear the waver in it as her mixed emotions made their way closer to the surface. "Aric is dead and you will leave again soon. I cannot make Radolf's life any more difficult by being weak as far as you are concerned."

"You do want me." It was a statement, not a question.

"My wants have never been a high priority to the people in my life. I see no evidence of that changing now."

He pulled her into his arms and kissed her deeply, enjoying the way she leaned into him, knowing her body could not refuse him as her mind would like to.

She pulled away from him suddenly and placed her hand on his chest. "I will not be your whore, Calder. I will not do that to my son."

With that she turned away from him and walked swiftly toward her parent's cottage, fighting back tears as she went.

Calder walked slowly back to the Manor. His anger faded as he replayed her words over in his head realized that she spoke the truth.

Regan was a married woman and he was exploiting her feelings for him. He had already placed her in a position within the village where no one, including her husband, showed her or her son any respect.

He had forced her to marry Edgar. In hindsight, the marriage was obviously a grave error on his part, although his intentions had been good. He had forced her into a cruel life, one that he could not remedy at this point. The only thing he could do for her was to stay away and not prey on her affections any longer, and avoid placing her in an even more precarious position within the community.

Calder sighed heavily, looking heavenward as if the stars in the sky could show him what to do. He already knew, in his heart, that the best thing he could do for Regan would be to stay out of her life, but that realization did not sit well with him.

He had not corrected her misconception that he would be leaving soon and did not plan to. It would be best for her if she believed that for now. In time, he prayed, they would find the fortitude within themselves to put an end to the strange attraction they held for each other.

Walking up the steps of the Manor, he decided that he would have Regan finish with the taxes, and then release her from his service. It would be too difficult to see her each day and not be able to converse with her or touch her. Entering the Hall, he joined his men and bellowed for a tankard of ale, determined to put Regan out of his head, one way or another.

*   *   *

The funeral went as well as could be expected the next day, with most of the villagers in attendance to pay their respects. During the service, Calder stood beside Devona and her children, trying to keep his gaze from straying to where Regan stood alone, off to the side of the crowd.

Afterward, he walked with Devona back to the Hall. Lifting a tankard of ale, he took a large draught, hoping it would relieve the headache still lingering from the large quantity he had consumed the night before. He looked over at his brother's children, feeling the weight of responsibility for their welfare.

"What are your plans now, Devona?" he asked.

"Calder," she said, her screechy voice shooting a bolt of pain through his skull, "you must help us. You must help with the running of these lands until Harlan is old enough to run them himself."

He looked down at the hand she placed on his arm and took it in his own. "Devona," he began reluctantly, not knowing how she would take the news he was about to give her, "when the King heard how sick Aric was, he gave the lands over to me."

Devona sat back in her chair, stunned at this news. "That is not fair, Calder. How could he take away my son's legacy?"

"Harlan will still inherit the lands in Normandy. The King was worried about a bid from Roderick to take these lands. He wanted to ensure that they remained in our family."

"Our family!" she cried shrilly. "It is not *our* family who has them in their possession now, is it, Calder? It is yours and the land will be given to *your* heir, not Aric's, as was meant to be."

Her face was pale with fury as she regarded her brother-in-law. "What promises did you make the King in order to steal these lands from my son?"

"I know your grief overwhelms you, Devona, and that is the only reason you would be foolish enough to say such a thing to me." His tone was cold as he stared fixedly at her, trying to keep foremost in his mind that she was suffering the loss of her husband.

Devona hesitated a moment, knowing Calder was not a man to take lightly, but her anger and frustration ran so high that she could not let the subject rest. "My children and I will be leaving for London in the morning. I will seek an audience with the King and straighten this matter out."

"As you wish," he answered, half-hoping she would be successful in her mission.

*   *   *

The next week passed quickly and quietly. Each day the required number of villagers showed to fulfill their duties, rather than spend the day in the pillory. No more livestock had been stolen, but many were frustrated at having them mixed in together, as Filbert never hesitated to mention in his nightly reports to Calder.

Regan, Radolf and Draco followed a set routine. Draco would just be sitting down to eat when they arrived each morning and would insist they both join him. Once he was satisfied that the two of them had eaten enough, they would begin their rounds to the rest of the cottages. There was still some difficulty in acquiring all of the information they needed, but Draco's presence loosened tongues sufficiently.

Regan was somewhat dismayed by Calder's aloof attitude toward her since the night he had walked her home. She knew it was for the best but could not help feeling a little depressed that he no longer seemed interested in her at all. With a heavy heart, she determined that, perhaps her own words had turned him away, perhaps he did just want her as his whore. It was difficult though, for her to reconcile that idea with the way that she felt about him.

Watching him, talking with him and feeling his occasional touches were the only bright spots in her life, besides Radolf, and she missed them dearly.

Edgar had not been home in some time. Although eating breakfast with Draco and dinner with her parents was the only way that they were able to survive, she was happy that she at least did not have to deal with Edgar's anger.

*   *   *

Calder pushed himself hard every day for several different reasons; to ease his grief over Aric's death, to quell his frustration at having to stay away from Regan, and most importantly, because he was filled with an insistent need to get the castle completed as soon as possible. There was a niggling fear somewhere deep inside of him that trouble was coming, and soon. He wanted to be sure they would be prepared to meet any threat.

"Milord," Filbert said one night, after they had gone over the duties to be assigned the following day. "My people are most curious at whom their new Lord will be. They are more afraid of the unknown than the known. I wish to set their minds at ease. Has there been any word?"

"Tell your people that these lands now belong to me. It is the King's wish for it to be so. Go and put their minds at ease now, Filbert." He added the last with a wry grin, knowing the villagers despised him and that their reaction would be anything but joyous.

"Yes, Milord," he said, leaving quickly to spread the word. The villagers had been cooperating only because of their fear of Calder, and because of the knowledge that he would be leaving soon. They would not be happy about the news.

Filbert ran into Edgar as he passed the stables. The news that Calder was to be their new Lord instantly turned Edgar's face beet red with fury. He would die before letting that Norman bastard govern him.

He ran to Maida's, where he consumed several large tankards of whiskey while trying to decide what he could do to change this new and unwanted turn of events. But, he eventually determined that he could do nothing. Frustrated and angry, he decided it might be a good time to visit his devoted wife and see what information she could impart on the subject.

CHAPTER 11

The following afternoon, Draco pulled Calder aside. "Milord," Draco said quietly, "I cannot be sure, but I believe something happened to Regan last night."

"What do you mean?" Calder asked sharply.

"She walks stiffly, sits down very gingerly. She denies anything is wrong, but the pain shows on her face when she is not aware someone is looking."

He stopped for a moment, his face a mask of restrained fury. "The boy wears a black eye. Says he fell and hit it, but I do not believe him."

"Edgar?" Calder asked in a cold, quiet voice.

"I could not say for sure, but I would assume so."

"Tell Regan that I require her and her son to dine with me tonight. I will see for myself and try to get the truth from one or the other of them."

"Milord," Draco was uncharacteristically hesitant as he spoke "have you not noticed the way the boy looks?"

"What do you mean?" he asked curtly.

"Take a good look at him, Calder. See if there is anything familiar about his face."

Calder's brow creased in confusion. "Familiar in what way? I have looked at the boy, Draco. Why are you speaking to me in riddles?"

"Just take a good, hard look at him, Milord," Draco answered, then turned away to find Regan.

*　　*　　*

Regan was mystified as to why Calder would insist that she and Radolf dine with him when he had barely spoken to her for over a week. But, surprisingly, the meal passed pleasantly, with Calder telling her and Radolf how the building of the castle was progressing.

He and Radolf got into a long conversation about exactly how the castle would look when it was done and, of course, where all the secret passages would be.

There was something different in his eyes when he looked at her. Not pity exactly, but something she had never seen there before.

She worried that he might suspect what Edgar had done to her, but knew that could not be the case. Edgar made sure that none of her bruises were visible; all were well hidden beneath her clothing.

When dinner was over, Calder asked Regan if he could look over her paperwork.

"I'm sorry, Milord. I left it with Garrick earlier today."

"Garrick," he called, "take Mistress Regan to collect her papers."

"Yes, M'lord," he replied, leading Regan to a different part of the Manor.

As soon as they left, Calder turned to Radolf. Knowing he would not have much time before Regan returned, he had to get right to the point.

"What happened to your face, Radolf?" he asked, trying to keep his voice as quiet and calm as possible.

Radolf looked down at the table, twisting his fingers together. "I fell," he answered reluctantly, his voice barely a whisper.

"Look at me, Radolf," Calder said quietly, so no one else could hear him.

When Radolf raised his eyes, they were swimming in unshed tears.

"Friends don't lie to their friends. You know that, don't you?"

Radolf nodded, a single tear slipping down his cheek.

"I know you promised your mother not to tell." Radolf's eyes widened in amazement that Calder somehow knew that. "I won't tell her that we talked, but I must know the truth. Did your father hit you?"

Radolf looked into Calder's eyes, wanting to trust him, wanting to tell him, but afraid to do so. He remained silent.

"Just nod your head if it was your father, then you haven't told me anything and you've kept your word to your mother."

After considering Calder's words for a moment, Radolf decided they made sense and nodded his head.

"Did he hurt your mother, as well?"

Again, Radolf tearfully nodded his head.

"You are a good boy, Radolf. Thank you." Calder wanted to hold the boy in his arms and take his fear away, but did not do so because Regan would be back any second.

"I promise you that he won't hurt either of you again, Radolf. Do you believe me?"

"Yes, Lord Cawer," he answered with a tremulous smile.

"Alright, no more tears, boy. Your mother is returning."

Radolf quickly wiped his nose and looked down at his trencher, playing with the bits of food still left in it.

"This is quite impressive," Calder told Regan after looking over her papers. "You certainly are covering all of the details. Do you have many more people to see?"

"It shouldn't take more than another week before I've met with everyone, Milord," she stated, beaming with pride at his praise.

His eyes glowed with warmth as he watched her face. "Thank you for doing this, Regan. It certainly has helped me a great deal."

"It hasn't been so bad," she answered, "especially with Draco by my side."

"And how has the assistant done so far?" he asked, smiling down at Radolf. "Is he earning his money?"

The boy looked eagerly over at his mother, excitement at the thought of receiving his penny causing him to forget all about his earlier conversation with Calder.

"Oh, yes," she said, smiling tenderly at him. "He has definitely earned his wages."

Radolf was still glowing with pleasure when Filbert arrived at the table. "Grandfather, I'm gonna get a silver penny for being the assissant," he told him excitedly.

"Good for you, son," Filbert said a little shortly. He had been caught off guard by the sight of his daughter and grandson sitting at the Lord's table and speaking so comfortably with him.

Sensing his displeasure, Regan stood and made a stiff curtsy to Calder. "If you have no more questions for me as far as the tax information," she said, hoping her father would realize that was why she was there, "Radolf and I will be on our way now."

"The information you have obtained is excellent, Regan. Let me know once you have met with everyone."

"Yes, Milord." She took Radolf's hand and they left the Manor.

"Thank you for coming, Filbert," Calder said, waving him into the now vacant seat across from him. "We will have all the men at the quarry in the morning. I want to bring as much stone to the site as can be managed."

"Yes, Milord," Filbert answered, unable to keep the hostility out of his voice, or the suspicion from his eyes, as he tried to ascertain Calder's intentions toward his daughter.

"We will hold a judicial hearing in the afternoon. Everyone will be relieved from their work and I will hear your people's complaints then."

"Thank you, Milord." Filbert's expression showed his surprise. "They will be very happy about that."

"How did they take the news of my being their new Lord?"

"Some better than others, Milord," he answered noncommittally.

Calder smiled, admiring his diplomacy. "Till the morning, then," he said, dismissing Filbert, who swiftly left the Manor.

"Men," he called to his knights, "we will hold a judicial hearing tomorrow afternoon. I want all of you armed and ready for possible trouble."

"Yes, Milord," they answered, wondering what type of trouble could arise at such a simple procedure.

"Garrick and Draco, I have special jobs for you." They each took a seat next to him in order to get their instructions.

"Draco," he began, "after Regan is released from her duties in the afternoon, come to me. I will need you to be at my side during the hearings."

"Yes, Milord," he answered, curious as to why, but patient enough to wait until the morrow to find out.

"Garrick, it will be your responsibility to see that Regan and Radolf are well away from the proceedings. I do not want them anywhere near the village."

"How shall I keep them away?" he asked with a frown.

"That, my friend, is up to you. Offer them a ride on the horses from the stable, take them berry picking, do whatever you have to, but do it in such a way that Regan does not suspect why."

"Yes, M'lord," he answered, a little dubiously.

"I know that you are curious as to my plans, but I have not worked it all out in my head yet. All that I am sure of right now, is that Regan cannot be anywhere near the hearings. You must trust me on this."

"Of course, M'lord." Garrick flushed in embarrassment that Calder may have thought he was doubting him.

"Good," Calder replied with a thoughtful smile on his face.

*   *   *

The next afternoon, Calder sat behind a table at the top of the Manor stairs. Draco stood by his side and his men were stationed around the outer perimeter of the crowd of villagers.

One by one, the complainants came forward to make their accusations against their friends and neighbors. The first several complaints had to do with people milking or butchering animals that belonged, supposedly, to someone else. After the third such complaint, Calder stood to address the crowd.

Trying to keep the irritation from his voice, he said, "For now, we must keep the livestock together to protect them. I do not have enough men to patrol all of the fields. You must learn to accept this situation for the time being."

He grew angry as the mumbling and grumbling of the crowd grew louder. "Would you prefer that I let them be stolen? I will survive the winter. If your livestock is taken from you, one by one, will you?"

His eyes were blue glaciers of ice as he stared down at them. The murmuring of the crowd quieted as they accepted the truth of what he was saying.

"It is your obligation, as men, to take only what belongs to you. The next complaint that I hear such as this, I will punish the offender as a thief and have his ear lopped off. If that does not correct the situation, we will start cutting off hands. Now, who is next?"

Several people in the front reconsidered their accusations and melted back into the crowd. A few more people came forward with some minor complaints, but most seemed to have lost their interest in the proceedings and were beginning to drift away.

"I have a complaint," Lord Calder called out, standing up behind the table. "I ask that Draco stand as judge to hear the case."

Draco looked at him in surprise, then tensed as he realized who the accused would be.

Those villagers who had been leaving stopped and returned to the circle, their interest piqued once again.

Calder walked down to the bottom step and looked up at Draco. "I accuse Edgar, the Avener, of wife beating," he stated boldly. There were gasps from the crowd, for no matter how they felt about Regan, all considered wife beating to be a heinous and cowardly act.

Edgar's face was the color of a ripe tomato as he approached Calder.

"And, if I did, how would you know of it?" he asked, his voice filled with embarrassment and rage.

"I know, Edgar," Calder replied in a low voice.

"Where is Regan?" Edgar demanded. "Have you hidden her away so she cannot deny what you accuse me of?"

"She is not my wife, Edgar. How is it that you do not know where she is?" Calder answered calmly.

Edgar's eyes narrowed as he stared at Calder. They stood toe to toe, Calder slightly taller and much broader, the look of hatred identical on their faces.

"With no other witnesses present, I request judicial combat," Calder stated, keeping his eyes on Edgar.

"What is that?" Edgar asked, suddenly looking a little nervous.

Draco answered the question. "When the truth can only be known by the accuser and the accused, they fight. The winner is the man whose position is just and true."

Edgar rubbed his sweaty hands on his tunic, eyeing Calder's massive frame tensely. "Regan can tell the truth of the matter. Why can we not wait until she returns. She will tell you that I have never beaten her."

"If you beat her once, would she not say anything that you want, to keep you from doing so again?" Calder asked.

"She will tell the truth. I have not laid a hand on her. Anyway, I do not choose this judicial combat."

"It is too late," Draco boomed from his perch on top of the stairs. "There are no witnesses present. Judicial combat has been requested. If you refuse to fight, you will be found guilty and punished accordingly."

Standing silent for a moment, staring hard into Calder's eyes, Edgar took a deep breath and turned to Draco. "So be it then."

The crowd moved back, leaving a wide circle in which the men would fight. Calder's knights stepped to the inner side of the circle in anticipation of trouble.

"No weapons," Draco called. Calder handed his dirk and sword to Skeet. None of the villagers were allowed to carry weapons, so the unarmed Edgar stood to the side, silently watching Calder, his eyes filled with fury.

The two men circled, sizing each other up. Calder was taller and more powerfully built. Edgar was thin and wiry, and quicker.

Calder stood as still as a statue. He looked at Edgar with contempt and raised his hands in a beckoning motion.

"Why don't you dance with a man for a change?" he asked scornfully.

Enraged, Edgar charged him and landed the first blow to Calder's chin. It seemed to have no effect on the larger man, as he pummeled Edgar's stomach with his large fists.

Edgar doubled over in pain and Calder's fist came up, striking him in the nose and sending him flying. A cloud of dust rose as he pitched backward to the ground, gasping for breath.

Edgar stood slowly and walked toward Calder, fists up, a small trickle of blood dripping from his nose. Catching Calder by surprise, he rushed him, grabbing his legs and knocking him backwards to the ground. Jumping atop him, Edgar was able to land several blows to his face before Calder threw him off.

Circling each other again, both panting from the exertion, they inched closer and closer to each other. Finally, within striking distance, they began to exchange blows, some to the face, others to the body. Each impact drew blood or a grunt of pain from the recipient, as they poured their rage into each punch.

Calder came around with a powerful blow to Edgar's head, knocking him to the ground once again; where he lay writhing in agony, holding his head in his hands.

The crowd yelled to him, encouraging him to get up and keep fighting.

He slowly started to rise, made it as far as his knees and fell backward again. He lay on the ground, unable, or unwilling, to get up and fight any further. The crowd roared in disappointment.

"The judicial combat is over," Draco called out. "Edgar is found guilty of being a wife beater and will be punished accordingly."

The crowd was restless, excited from the savagery of the fight and angry that one of their own had lost. Calder's men faced them down, their hands close to the hilts of their swords, ready to draw them at the first sign of an attack.

Calder wearily approached the steps of the Manor. He caught Draco's eye just as he heard a gasp from someone in the crowd. He whirled, just in time to see Edgar rushing toward him with a dirk in his hand.

Calder stepped to the side and grabbed the hand that bore the knife. He twisted it behind the other man's back. Edgar screamed as the bone in his wrist snapped and the dirk fell harmlessly to the ground beside him.

Edgar's cries continued as Calder threw him down into the dust and picked up the discarded knife.

"You are a disgusting coward," he said, looking at Edgar with revulsion. "Have the arm set and return to me. Trying to murder your Lord is not an act to be taken lightly. I will take the time before you return to determine your proper punishment."

Edgar ignored Calder's words as he continued writhe in pain. Calling two of his knights over, Calder instructed them to follow the prisoner and remain outside the healer's cottage until Edgar's wrist had been tended.

Calder strode up the steps and into the Manor, refusing to watch as the villagers crowded around Edgar and offered their assistance. It hardly seemed necessary to have the arm set. Calder knew that Edgar should be executed for his deed. But he needed some time to think it through before making a final decision.

Such an act would not only enrage the villagers, but he had to consider Regan and Radolf, as well. Did he want to be responsible for leaving them without the support of a husband and father?

Ultimately, he did not have to anguish much over the decision. When the husband and father was such a cowardly low life as Edgar, who only added misery to their lives, there was no other decision that could be made. Edgar would hang at dawn.

CHAPTER 12

When night fell and still Edgar had not shown himself at the Manor, Calder sent two of his knights to collect him.

The knights returned a short while later. "Forgive us, Milord, but he appears to have escaped. A hole was cut through the back wall of the cottage and he was able to squeeze through unseen," Bert reported, looking shame-faced at the floor. "We've searched the village but cannot locate him. There are some horses missing from the stable, as well."

Regan appeared in the Hall just then, looking shaken and upset. "Milord, I need to speak with you, if you can spare me a minute."

She saw that he was in the midst of talking to his men, but was extremely agitated by the visit from the knights who had been looking for Edgar. She had to find out what was happening.

"Find him," Calder directed sternly to Bert, taking Regan's arm and escorting her outside, where they would not be overheard.

"Milord," she asked, her green eyes wide with worry and confusion, "why were your men sent to find Edgar? What has happened?"

"Edgar tried to kill me. I should have brought him to the Manor right after it happened, but he was hurt and I allowed him to go and have his injury tended. I erred in letting him out of my sight. Now it appears he has run off and taken some of my horses with him."

She was dumbfounded at his news. "Why would he do that?"

Calder blew out a deep breath. "Regan, did he beat you?"

She did not answer him.

"I could see you were hurt and can only assume that it was Edgar who did it to you."

"He was very angry when he found out you were to be our new Lord." It was all she would say in reference to what had passed between her and Edgar.

"I accused him of wife-beating today and challenged him to judicial combat. He lost and attacked me as I turned away from him."

She sat silently, noticing for the first time the bruises on his face and the cuts and scrapes on his knuckles.

"How did you know?" Regan asked quietly, taking his hands in her own.

Calder was not given to lying, but his need to protect Radolf was stronger. "You had difficulty moving because of your pain, and I could see it in your eyes."

She considered his words, not sure if she should believe him or not. "Why would you feel it was your place to become involved in whatever happened to me?"

He looked deep into her eyes. "The night we first met, we shared an incredible experience together. To this day, I cannot get you out of my mind, the feel of you against me, the smell of you, the pure joy that I felt being inside of you. My lips long for the taste of yours every time I see you."

She looked away from him, flushing in embarrassment.

"I tried my best to do what was right for you, to make up for what I took from you that night. It seems that all I have done has been wrong and has only made your life wretched. With all my heart, I want to make things right for you again."

He stopped then, his voice thick with emotions that he was trying to control. "I cannot allow you to suffer at the hands of the man I forced you to marry."

It had been such a long time since anyone had cared about her, or about what happened to her, that she could feel tears glistening in her eyes.

Calder lifted her chin, forcing her to meet his eyes. "I would give up my life if I could take away all of the hurt you and Radolf have suffered because of me."

Not trusting herself to speak, Regan stroked his face. His words and the tenderness in his voice touched her so deeply that a tear escaped, slipping silently down her cheek.

Slowly, Calder lowered his lips onto hers. He kissed her thoroughly, his body shaking with the power of the emotions that coursed through him. Taking her into his arms, he poured those feelings out as his mouth moved sensuously against hers.

She moaned softly, fitting her body intimately to his and feeling his hard, muscular body yielding to her own. Regan lost herself in the feel of him, the touch of him, the taste of him. She needed him more than she had ever needed anyone before.

He slowly withdrew his lips from hers and, in an uncharacteristically shaky voice, said, "I want you, Regan, so badly that it hurts. Come inside and let me show you how much I need you."

She hesitated, a million thoughts running through her head, telling her how wrong it would be for her to do such a thing. But her body trembled with a desire for him that was so strong, it could not be denied. Even if she burned in hell for all eternity, it would be worth it if she could be with him this night.

"Calder," she answered softly, her eyes glistening, "I will go with you but, before I do, you must know something."

"Yes?" His voice was hoarse, and his heart beat frantically in anticipation of what was to come.

"Whatever grief or sorrow I have had to sustain was not because of you. We did share something special that night. I have not been able to forget it myself. If it were not for that memory, I may not have been able to get through my days. I know you have tried to protect me. It is my own people who have caused any hurt, not you. I cherish my memories of you." She spoke the last so softly that he could barely hear her.

He took her hand, kissed the palm and, holding it securely in his own, headed inside the Manor. They went up the stairs quietly, looking surreptitiously around to see if there was anyone about. They did not see the eyes watching them from the curtained alcove.

Regan stood shyly by the bed when they reached his chamber, suddenly unsure of herself and what she was doing. Calder stood before her, his gaze so intense that she blushed and looked away.

He stroked her face, running a finger around her lips until they parted slightly of their own volition. Burying his hand in her thick copper curls, he pulled her head toward his own and leaned down eagerly to meet her lips.

Slowly, and with exquisite tenderness, his lips devoured hers. Regan wrapped her hands around his neck, trying to pull him even closer as she leaned against him.

As their tongues entwined, his hands moved lower and started to remove her clothing. Her skin, so sensitive to his touch, seemed almost alive. All of the nerve endings were at the surface, waiting impatiently for his caress.

When all of her clothing had been removed, he laid her gently on the bed, his gaze wandering greedily over her naked body.

Her eyes were glittering pieces of jade in her pale face as she watched him slowly remove his own clothing one piece at a time. Her gaze feasted on his broad, sculpted chest with its furring of dark hair, his smooth, firm hips and long, muscular legs. His member was erect and ready, leaving no doubt as to the extent of his passion.

Calder lay beside her, throwing his long leg over her hip, as he turned her toward him so that he could more fully enjoy the touch of her lips and the feel of her body against his own. He ran his hands over her silken skin, unable to get enough of her as he kissed her long and hard.

Regan felt him throbbing against her thigh and the blood surged through her body as all of her senses came alive. His mouth slashed down on hers time and again, his fingers leaving trails of searing heat along her skin.

Skillfully using his hands and lips, he moved along her body, exploring every inch until she writhed mindlessly beneath him. Calder had waited so long for this moment and wished he could prolong it, but the need building inside of him would not allow further exploration. Slowly he entered her, watching her green eyes widen as he filled her and gently began to move.

Their bodies met in silent rhythm, a slow wonderful agony at first, and then faster and faster until they lost themselves completely in the intensity of their release. Both were left trembling, neither willing to relinquish the other until the shattered pieces of their minds and bodies had come together again.

Later, Regan lay quietly in the dark, listening to Calder's deep, even breathing. She did not want to leave the warmth of his embrace, but knew she must before she fell asleep. She could not risk being caught in his bedchamber.

Slipping quietly out of the bed and into her clothing, she walked cautiously down the stairs. She was relieved to find that the knights were still out hunting for Edgar, and no one was in the Hall to witness her surreptitious departure.

She carried Radolf from her parent's house without waking them. Laying him on his pallet, she pulled the blanket up over his still sleeping body, then gently brushed the curls away from his face.

"What do I do, Radolf?" she asked silently. *"Do I tell Calder about you? Is it fair to either of you if I don't? And what about me? And Edgar? How do I face you, or my parents, or myself after my adulterous behavior this night? And how do I keep myself from wanting Calder as badly as I do, or from loving him so much that I am willing to risk losing what's left of the respect of those I care most about?"*

*   *   *

Regan was relieved when she did not see Calder at all the following week. Surely, her embarrassment over what happened between them would show if she was near him. It was but a temporary respite, as her visits to all of the cottages were now finished and she would have to give him her report, but it gave her some time to collect herself.

"Draco," she asked, as they parted that afternoon, "will you tell Lord Calder that our visits have been completed and that I am ready to meet with him whenever he has the time?"

"Yes, Milady, I will," he replied in his low, gravelly voice while offering her a slight bow. Draco did not speak much, but his respect for her was always evident and she appreciated it deeply. Even Radolf had grown more relaxed around the huge warrior.

Draco began to walk away, but hesitated, then turned back and glanced around to make sure that no one, particularly Radolf, was close enough to hear him. "Calder is apparently too blind to see himself in the boy. Why do you not tell him of his son?"

Regan said nothing at first, caught off guard by his question.

"Do you realize that these lands would belong to your son one day, should Calder choose to accept him as his heir? Will you deny Radolf that right?"

"I had not thought of that, Draco," she replied honestly. "I thought only of what more hurt Edgar could do to both of them, if Calder knew the truth."

Draco was impressed with her ability to hold her tongue for a reason so selfless; something most women, in his opinion, would not be able to do.

"Edgar is gone now. Perhaps it is time for you to give Calder a chance to prove himself to you."

"Mayhap," she answered thoughtfully, not exactly sure of what he was implying, or how much he knew of her relationship with Calder.

"I will advise him that you are ready with your report." With a nod in her direction, he turned toward the Manor and walked away.

Her summons for dinner with the Lord arrived by way of Skeet, the squire, a short time later. She was so nervous that she could barely dress her hair, or herself, properly as she got ready to meet Calder. Nor could she help noticing her father's sullen look when she dropped Radolf off at their cottage and kissed him goodnight before she left.

"Why do you leave him for the night, when you only go to the Manor for your evening meal, girl?" he asked her suspiciously.

She flushed, afraid that he had realized that her true desire for this evening was to spend it in Calder's arms. How could she ever explain to anyone, particularly her father, how she felt, the sadness that enveloped her every time she had looked at Edgar and realized that she felt nothing but loathing and disrespect for the man that he had become.

Grief bit deep into her soul at the thought that this was the man she had willingly wed and must now spend the rest of her life with. How could she tell her father about the piercingly sharp pain that twisted in her heart each time she saw Calder and knew that he could never be hers?

Calder was a man that any woman would gladly take into her heart, and her bed, she thought wistfully. A man that made every nerve in her body tingle when she saw him, even if at a distance. A man whose strength and compassion battled within himself to always do what was right. A man who could make her feel beautiful and wanted and needed with only a single glance. How could she explain these things to her father?

"I have no knowledge as to how long it will take us to go over the information that I have accumulated. I do not want to disturb Radolf's sleep if it takes until a late hour. Is there a problem with his staying here?"

Her voice was sad, resigned to the fact that her relationship with her father had changed. For Regan, there were now lies and deceit where there had been none before. For Filbert, disappointment and embarrassment over the behavior of the daughter he had once felt could do no wrong.

"Of course not, Regan," he said, reaching out and burying his hand in her rich curls. "I fear for you, lass. Do not get yourself into a position where you have only disgrace and heartache to show for it."

Her face turned a deeper shade of red, knowing what he meant, and also knowing that it was exactly what she intended to do.

"I know what I am doing, Father. Please don't worry about me."

"But, I must worry. I love you, Regan," he said sadly.

"I love you also, Father," she responded, hugging him fiercely before turning toward the Manor, her back straight and proud as she walked.

She first spotted Calder across the room, lifting a tankard of ale with one of his men. He was so handsome that just looking at him from a distance took her breath away. It was impossible not to see those strong fingers holding the tankard and remember their gentleness as they had roamed her body. Watching his quick smile in response to Garrick's jest, she could envision his full lips taking her own until she lost herself to him completely.

"Milady." Draco's deep voice came from close beside her, startling her from her thoughts and causing her to blush.

"Hello, Draco," she said, trying to keep her voice steady.

"Shall I escort you over to Lord Calder?"

"Yes, thank you," she replied, placing her hand on his arm, which felt more like the trunk of a tree than flesh and blood.

Calder turned toward them as they approached and his face lit up at the sight of her. "Milady," he said graciously, giving her a low bow. "I swear, you look lovelier this evening than any woman I have had the pleasure to lay eyes on."

"Thank you, Milord." Blushing with the compliment and feeling self-conscious in the presence of others, she smoothed the frayed fabric of her well-worn kirtle. "You look quite dashing yourself."

"Oh, please," Draco grumbled, as he walked away to find a tankard for himself. Calder smiled tenderly down at Regan, but she frowned when she saw the dark circles under his eyes and the fatigue lining his face.

"Is all not well, Milord?" she asked with concern, as he took her arm and escorted her to his table.

"The castle is coming along well." Settling in close beside her, he continued. "But the thieves are stealing our cattle at night now. We've been taking turns patrolling, but in the darkness we have not yet been able to catch them. They seem to have grown much bolder of late."

Calder rubbed his brow in fatigue, then looked deeply into her eyes as if searching her very soul for something. "I've missed you," he said softly, so that no one else could hear.

"You've oft been on my mind, as well, Milord," she answered, lowering her eyes to the table.

Sensing her discomfort, he decided to move on to safer subjects. They had a lengthy discussion as to the information she had obtained while they enjoyed their meal. Once they finished and his men moved away, to play games or converse in groups, he took her hand in his.

"Will you be able to stay here with me tonight? I was most distressed when I woke to find myself alone last week."

Her heart began to beat wildly in her chest and, unable to keep from blushing, she answered shyly, "I can stay for awhile, Milord, but not the entire night. I must be gone before anyone sees me leave here."

"Someday soon, I promise you," he said tenderly, stroking the back of her hand with his finger, "we will be able to spend the entire night in each other's arms and watch the sun come up together."

Knowing it was a promise that could never be fulfilled, Regan simply nodded. Dropping her gaze towards the table again, she hesitated, then asked, "Has there been any word of Edgar?"

When he did not answer, she looked up and saw the troubled expression on his face.

"We got close enough to the thieves last night to shoot one of their horses out from under them." Calder paused, his eyes cold. "It was one of our own horses, one that Edgar had stolen. It appears he may be behind this recent bit of thievery."

"Oh, no," she said regretfully.

"Yes, Regan, and when we catch him, which we will do, he will be put to death. You understand that, don't you?" His jaw clenched in anger at the tears he saw forming in her eyes. "Why do you care after all he has done to you?"

"He is my husband and Radolf's father," she answered simply. "How do I explain to Radolf that his father is a thief and an attempted murderer?"

Unless I tell him the truth of who his father is, she thought miserably, knowing it was something that must be done, but not knowing the right way, or the right time to tell Calder. It seemed the longer she waited, the more difficult it became.

"You tell him that a man does not have to become what his father was and let him live a life of his own. Radolf has much courage and character already for one so young. He could only be hurt by having Edgar as his father." Calder's voice was soft and cold as he spoke, an ice wedge pounding into Regan's heart as she listened to his words.

"I know," she whispered softly, trying not to cry at the thought of what she might be doing to her own son.

"Come with me," Calder said, taking her hand and leading her through the hallway to a back staircase and up to his room. His knights all pretended not to notice, but the servant girls were not so polite as they ogled the couple and whispered amongst themselves.

Once they entered the bedchamber, he had Regan sit on the bed as he knelt before her. "Regan," he whispered urgently, taking her hand in his, "do you believe, by my bringing you here, that I am making you my whore? Or do you believe that I want you with all my heart and soul and cannot live another moment without you in my arms? Answer me the truth, for I will not take advantage of you."

"What if I believe both, Milord? For surely, if anyone knows I am here, it is as your whore that I will be branded."

"In your heart, where it matters most, do you believe that?" he asked, his blue eyes penetrating into the deepest recesses of her soul.

"No," she said softly, "I believe you care for me as strongly as I do for you."

"Will you have me tonight?" he asked in a hoarse whisper.

"Aye, Milord, I will have you anytime that you want me." Regan realized that, with those words, she sealed her own fate. It was inevitable that others would learn of her relationship with Calder and she prayed that Radolf would not have to suffer the consequences of her actions. She gave herself, now and forever, to Calder, and could only hope that he truly was the person that she believed him to be, and that he would do all in his power to protect them.

No more words were necessary as he leaned in to take her lips against his own. Their hearts beat rapidly in anticipation, as he slid onto the bed beside her and engulfed her in his warm embrace. Holding one another close, they knew, as no one else could, how right it was for them to be in each other's arms.

Later that night, with their passion spent and Calder still holding her tight, Regan turned in his arms to watch him sleep. The moonlight coming in through the open window cast its glow on his strong, proud face, relaxed now in sleep. His thick lashes lay against his cheek, his broad chest rose and fell in a regular rhythm.

"Calder," she whispered softly, wishing she had the courage to say these words to him when he was awake, "I love you and would suffer anything to be with you. I wish I could tell you the truth of Radolf, that it was your seed which created such a wonderful child. I wish I could tell him that he has a father that he can be proud of. A strong and courageous knight who can be as tender and loving as any man God set down on this earth. But, I don't know how."

She watched him for a few more minutes, wishing she could stay with him, but knowing she could not.

Consumed with her own thoughts, she did not notice when Calder opened his eyes and followed her movements as she dressed, reveling in the knowledge that Radolf was his son.

CHAPTER 13

Draco noticed how quiet Calder was as they rode slowly toward the site of the new castle the next morning.

"It's coming along well," he said.

"What?" Calder asked, shaking himself from his reverie.

"The castle is coming along well," he repeated, gazing at Calder curiously.

"Yes," Calder replied, "but, although the Keep is almost complete, it will take quite a bit more time before the outbuildings and wall are finished."

They stopped their horses so that they could look down at the site. Calder turned to Draco. "How long have you known that Radolf was my son?"

"Since the first time I saw his face up close. Remember that I knew you as a child. It was obvious who his father is. I'm surprised you could not see it yourself."

"I don't have a lot of time to study myself in a mirror, Draco," Calder replied dryly.

"Did she tell you, then?"

"Yes, without realizing that she did so. She is not aware that I know."

"She keeps her silence, thinking to protect you."

"In what way?" Calder asked curiously. He was not angry at Regan for keeping the boy's true parentage from him. He was still too awed at the thought that it was his seed that had created a boy such as Radolf.

"She worries that Edgar will use your knowledge to hurt you, or the boy, in some way."

"He would have tried, I'm sure of that. Which reminds me, how did the patrol do last night?"

"They saw no one, but several more head of cattle were missing this morning."

"Tonight, we will come up with a plan to deal with this. I am tired of playing these games with him."

"Yes, Milord," Draco replied. "What will you do about the boy?"

"Nothing for now. Once Edgar has been dealt with, I will see what Regan does."

"There is another problem with her."

"What?" Calder asked, surprised at the extent of concern that flooded through him.

"I do not believe she has food. I've been having them eat with me at the Manor in the morning, but her work for you is finished and I can do so no longer."

"How can they have no food? There is plenty for everyone in the village."

"Edgar has not provided for her in some time. They have no fields, own no livestock and, I imagine, any money that they had disappeared with Edgar. Her parents do feed them every night, so they are not starving."

"Damn," Calder said softly, "I never considered that Edgar could be that much of a bastard. I'll make sure that she gets the wages I owe her tonight." He looked appraisingly over at Draco. "You have some free time on your hands now that Regan has completed her tasks, don't you?"

"Yes, Milord."

"Feel like doing a little hunting today?"

Draco smiled. "Aye, Milord, but whatever will I do if I bag more than we need at the Manor?"

"Perhaps you might show Radolf how to dress some game and, as his reward, send him home with a couple of rabbits."

"Yes, Milord," he replied, reining his horse toward the woods and galloping off.

*   *   *

Regan was startled by a knock on the door as she cleaned up her kitchen that evening. Her heart began to thud painfully against her chest when she saw Calder filling the doorway.

"Good evening, Regan," he said, as he stepped inside and looked around the small, one room cottage. "I hope I am not disturbing you."

"Not at all, Milord. It is an unexpected, but pleasant, surprise," she murmured, as she lowered her eyes, feeling suddenly nervous and shy around him.

"Is Radolf awake?" he asked.

"No, Milord," she said, waving to a corner with a blanket drawn around it. "He fell asleep a short while ago."

"Oh," Calder said, disappointment evident in his voice.

"Why do you wish to see him?" she asked curiously.

"I have to pay him his penny and was looking forward to seeing his reaction. Here are your earnings," he added, laying a small bag on the table. "I apologize for not giving it to you sooner."

Noting the weight of the bag, she said, "I think this is not what we agreed to, Milord. There is too much here." A silver penny was equivalent to one day's work in most trades, and there were many more coins than days that Regan had worked.

"Not nearly enough actually, considering all you have done for me. Your work has been invaluable. Which leads me to my next request," he said with a smile. "Will you compare the information that you have obtained with the books Aric kept? I will pay you a like amount for doing so."

"Certainly, I will do it, Milord. But there is no need for you to be so generous."

"It's the least I can do," he said, reaching over to brush a stray curl from her cheek, his fingers lingering on her face. Looking around, he saw that there was no privacy for the deed his body craved.

Sighing heavily in disappointment, he handed her one more penny. "Will you see that Radolf gets this in the morning?"

"No, I cannot do that, Milord."

He looked at her in surprise, not used to having anyone refuse him.

"May I bring him out to the castle site tomorrow? He is quite excited to see it. Mayhap, you could show him around and give it to him then?"

"I would like that," Calder said with a grateful smile. Leaning down, he took her lips gently with his own, but feeling his pulse quicken and his desire rise, he quickly withdrew his head and moved toward the door.

"Till the morrow then?"

"Till the morrow," she replied softly, her lips still tingling from the feel of his kiss.

*   *   *

"Good morning, Lord Calder," Regan called out the next morning as they approached him at the site where the new castle was being built.

Men were bustling all over, some cutting beams and planks and others carrying them inside the Keep, where loud hammering and occasional cursing could be heard.

"Good morning, Regan. Good morning to you also, Radolf," he said, smiling down at his son.

Radolf hopped from one foot to the other, his excitement almost too overwhelming to contain as he watched all the activity.

"Morning, Lord Cawer," he said absently, turning his head to and fro, trying to take in everything at once.

"Would you like to see the inside of the Keep?"

"Yes, please."

Calder took Radolf's hand and, smiling over his head at Regan, led them up the stone steps on the outside of the building, which led to the second floor.

Regan glanced around as they entered the cavernous Hall. The large stone fireplace took up most of the wall along one side of the room. The Lord's table was set on a dais, higher than the others, away from the doorway and close to the fireplace. Two large chairs were positioned behind it, unlike the benches provided for the other tables.

The floor was not yet covered with rushes and smelled of newly cut wood. Rows of large, wooden pillars were placed strategically throughout the room to support the third floor. The glassless windows were open now and would help the smoke from the fireplace escape when it was in use.

The windows were fitted with wooden shutters, which could be closed and secured with an iron bar, if necessary. Each shutter had loopholes cut into them, which were only large enough for an arrow to be slid through in the event of an attack, the shutters themselves protecting the archer.

Brackets for candles and candelabras were positioned around the room and on the pillars which, along with the oil lamps suspended from rings in the ceiling, would ensure the room could be properly lit even on the darkest night. It was easy to imagine an elegant feast or just a cozy evening being passed in this room.

Calder led them through one of the several screened passageways leading out from the Hall and, within a few short minutes, Regan felt completely lost. She followed along as Calder pointed out the buttery, the pantry and many other rooms, but with each turn down another corridor, she was sure that she would never be able to learn her way around the labyrinthine passageways.

Escorting them along one such passageway, Calder said, "In that direction are the stairs that lead down to the kitchen, which is actually a separate building connected to this one. These are the sleeping quarters for my men. Once all of the work has been completed and things are running smoothly, I will give them the option of taking a cottage and, perhaps, some land of their own, rather than staying here. But, for now, I need them nearby."

Off of the screened passageway, a set of circular stairs led to the third floor. Just above the men's quarters were several small rooms.

"These will be sleeping quarters for guests, or children, should I be fortunate enough to have any," he said, with a pointed look at Regan. She flushed and looked away from him.

He led them down the hallway to the Lord's bedchamber, which was over the Great Hall.

"This is called the Solar," he said, watching Regan carefully, hoping she liked the room as he planned on sharing many nights in it with her.

She wandered around, running her hand over the large wooden chests. Pegs on the wall would hold items of clothing as well, and there was a stool for the Lord to sit on as he removed his boots. Along the same wall as the one below sat another large stone fireplace.

A small anteroom was off to one side, and Regan stared enviously at the great wooden tub that sat within it. Tapestries for privacy were hung alongside and held back with ties.

Most of the room was taken up by an enormous bed which, for now, was just a massive wooden frame with springs made of interlaced strips of leather. In her mind, she could picture the feather mattress that would lay on it, covered with furs and quilts. There would be heavy linen hangings tied back around the posts, which could be left down to ensure privacy, or to keep the cold winter winds at bay.

"It's a lovely room, Milord," she said, looking around and touching the fine pieces of new furniture again. With a heavy heart, she realized that Calder would one day share this elegant, cozy room, and bed, with his wife. Here, they would create their own children.

Being lowly born, and a Saxon as well, she knew there was no hope that he could ever consider her to be his bride. Besides, she was already married. The reality of it left her feeling sick to her stomach and she suddenly needed to get out of the building as quickly as possible.

Calder frowned when he saw the sadness fill her eyes as she glanced once more at the bed, and then walked from the room. He could not understand why the sight of it would upset her so.

"Lord Cawer?" Radolf asked.

"Yes," he answered, looking down at the boy.

"Where is the secret passages?"

Calder knelt down in front of him and whispered, "I'll show you when there is no one else around. It will be a secret for just you and me, right?"

His blue eyes wide, Radolf just nodded.

"But, come over here and I will show you something special." Taking the boy's hand, he led him to a wall with several small peepholes drilled into it. Calder lifted Radolf into his arms, positioning him so that he could look through them and down into the Great Hall.

"These are called squints. I'll cover this wall with a tapestry, so that no one knows about the holes. This way, I can look down and see all that is happening without anyone seeing me."

"Ooh," was all Radolf could say in response.

"Come, let's find your Maman. I think I may have another surprise for you, as well."

"What surprise?" he asked excitedly.

"Come with me and you'll find out," he answered, taking Radolf's hand and helping him down the steep stairs. They caught up with Regan outside of the Keep.

"Lord Cawer has a surprise," Radolf exclaimed excitedly as they walked over to her.

"He does, does he?"

"Yes," the boy said, turning and looking at Calder expectantly.

"Hold out your hands and close your eyes," he commanded.

Radolf did as he was told and his eyes opened to the size of small saucers as he looked down at the two silver coins in his chubby, little hands.

"Momma," he said breathlessly, "look!"

"Two pennies, Radolf. You must have been an excellent assistant," she said, smiling up at Calder. "Did you thank Lord Calder?"

"Thank you, Lord Cawer," he said, unable to tear his eyes from the glittering pieces of silver in his hand.

"You are welcome and thank you, Radolf, for helping out so much." Looking over at Regan, he spoke quietly. "Is all well with you?"

"Yes, Milord. I guess I was just a bit overwhelmed in there. You will have a wonderful home." Lowering her eyes, unwilling to let him see the despair that she felt, she continued, "Radolf and I have work to attend to now. Thank you for showing us around."

He watched in bewilderment as they headed back to the village.

*　　*　　*

Regan's mood did not improve when she arrived at the river to wash their clothes. Maida was already there. She considered going home and coming back another time but, instead, squared her shoulders and headed for the water's edge.

Maida's eyes narrowed as she gave Regan a sly grin. "Well, if it isn't Regan and her little bastard son," she said sweetly. "I'm surprised Lord Calder let you so far away from his bed."

"Momma," Radolf began in confusion, not understanding what Maida was saying, but knowing from her tone that it was not nice.

Regan cut him off by saying, "She's just talking nonsense, Radolf." Kneeling down in front of him, she asked, "Will you do me a favor?"

He nodded, glancing furtively at Maida, who was still watching them. "Remember that patch of daisies that we passed on our way here?" He nodded again.

"Will you go pick a whole bunch for me? We'll put them all over the cottage to make it look pretty, alright?"

"Yes, Momma," he said, turning and running back in the direction they had just come from, only tripping over his own feet once before he was out of sight.

She swung back to Maida. "Listen, you evil-tongued bitch, if you ever speak like that in front of my son again, God help me, I'll cut it from your mouth and tie it around your neck."

Maida was surprised at the venom in Regan's voice but, not one to be easily cowed, strode toward her. Not as tall as Regan, she had to look up to meet her eyes. "You Norman whore, who are you to talk to me like that?"

"I am Radolf's mother, and don't you ever forget it." Furious at the look of superiority on Maida's face, her hand swung out and met the other woman's face with a resounding whack.

The petite blonde stepped away, her hand raised to the red welt on her cheek. Pure hatred poured from her eyes as she looked at Regan. "We know that he even comes to your cottage now, when he feels the need to rut. Obviously, it doesn't offend Radolf's sensibilities overly much when he has to witness you breaking your marriage vows." She quickly took a step backward as Regan moved toward her.

"Whoever your nosy little spy is, they obviously neglected to mention that Lord Calder was only at my cottage for a few minutes, not nearly long enough to do what your filthy mind assumes."

"Just because he can't last as long as Edgar doesn't mean he didn't have the time to do the deed," she answered maliciously, a slight smile on her lips.

"You brag to me about being Edgar's mistress?" Regan asked disgustedly. "It must leave you fairly lonely, what with him running away in such a cowardly fashion. But, of course, you've probably gotten several men to replace him already, haven't you?"

"I have no need of any other men," Maida replied smugly, stooping down to retrieve her wet clothes.

Regan's mind was racing. "Have you seen him, Maida? Do you know where he is?"

"If your husband cared anything at all about you, I imagine that he would tell you that for himself," she stated arrogantly, then turned and walked away.

If her barb was meant to hurt Regan, it missed its mark. Her only concern was that Edgar might be hiding nearby. He might even be watching her and know of her nights with Calder.

Regan viciously washed out their clothing on the rocks while she tried to determine what she should do, if anything, with her newfound knowledge.

CHAPTER 14

That evening, Calder and his men tried to determine how best to stop the rustlers.

"Milord," Draco said, "we send just a couple of men out at a time. There is too much ground to cover to protect all of the livestock with those few men."

"I know, Draco, but we need sleep. With everyone working on the castle all day, how can we remain up all night to catch these bastards?"

"Tonight, we all go, groups of two, surrounding the perimeter. As soon as the thieves are spotted, an arrow with burning straw on it will be sent into the air. We all converge and take them down. One night without sleep, we can handle."

"What say you, men?" Calder asked, looking around at his knights.

"Better one night with no sleep at all, than many with but little," Garrick answered. The others all nodded their agreement. No one noticed Maida, who was now a household servant, listening carefully to their conversation as she set tankards of ale down in front of the men.

A short time later, with their plan set, Calder and his men rode out to their positions. It was not until several hours later, well after the moon had fully risen, that a lit arrow flew into the sky across the field from where Calder and Skeet were keeping watch.

He kicked Alerio's sides and galloped through the herd of cattle with Skeet close behind him. The metallic sounds of swords meeting could be heard over the lowing of the cattle, as he spooked them out of his way.

As Calder approached, he saw Holt and Kenny fighting five men. Draco and Philip had just arrived from the other direction. The thieves looked around and, seeing how many of the fearsome knights they were up against, quickly dropped their swords.

"How many were there?" Calder asked.

"At least a dozen," Holt replied, grabbing one of the thieves and tying his hands together with a long length of rope. He secured the other end to the saddle and would pull his captive along behind the horse.

"Most of them lit out when the arrow went up, but these fools thought we were the only ones here."

"Where did they go?" Calder asked one of the hostages, a man he recognized from the village.

The man looked sullenly at him but would not answer.

Calder backhanded him across the mouth, knocking him to the ground. "In the morning, Holt, when they've had some time to think about their situation, spend some time with these men. See if they might be willing to share some information with us then."

The captives' eyes widened in fear at the implication.

"Gladly, Milord," Holt replied as he cast a bone chilling smile at the men. "Tie them in the stables tonight and set a man to watch over them."

*   *   *

At his morning meal the following day, Calder got the news that Jack, the knight who had been guarding the prisoners, had been killed and the prisoners freed.

"Son of a bitch," Calder roared, furious at himself for underestimating Edgar once again.

"Draco," he commanded, his voice filled with rage, "you and I will see if there are any tracks to follow. The rest of you men, see to the work at the castle."

"Yes, Milord," the other knights responded, anger at the loss of their friend evident in their voices as they stormed out of the Manor.

*   *   *

"Do you see it?" Calder asked, as they peered down over the top of a hill and into the gully below.

"Aye," Draco replied, seeing the wisp of smoke rising from what looked like just another grassy area but was, in actuality, camouflage on the roof of a small cottage.

They had followed the tracks all day, sometimes losing them for awhile and having to make wide circles until they came across them again. But at last they had successfully completed their hunt.

"We will not miss another opportunity at them, Draco. Come, we'll get the men together and return shortly before dark. When they go out tonight, we will take them all."

Draco rode to the castle site and collected all of the knights. Returning to the Manor, Calder advised them. "We have located the thieves' hideout. We will position ourselves outside of it just before dark. When they leave, we hit them. Any that are not killed, we will bring back here to be hung, understood?"

"Yes, Milord," the men answered, eager for the chance to avenge their friend.

No one noticed as Maida slipped out of the Manor and headed off through the woods.

*　　*　　*

It was full dark and still no one had left the cottage in the woods. The knights were growing restless and Calder finally signaled them down to surround it. Sword drawn, he kicked in the door and entered to find it empty. Food still sat on the table and it looked like whoever was there had cleared out quickly. Swearing colorfully, Calder and his men left the building. Two of them remained behind to watch the cottage.

"How the hell could they know?" Calder asked bitterly as they rode away.

*　　*　　*

For the next three days, the knights watched the cottage, but no one entered or left. Feeling particularly frustrated by the third night, Calder was in a foul mood when Filbert arrived for his instructions as to the work for the following day.

"Is there a problem?" Calder asked, finally fed up with Filbert's surly attitude.

Filbert stared hard at him, his thick white brows converging as he tried to work up the courage to speak his mind.

"My daughter and grandson have no food to eat, and it is because of you, Lord Calder."

"I paid Regan for the work she is doing for me. There is no reason that she should not be able to purchase food." His voice was cold as he stared the old man down.

"The villagers know what is going on between the two of you. We are not the idiots that you take us for, Milord. I look the other way because she is my daughter, but the others will not. They no longer speak to her, nor will they sell her any food. I have tried to buy some for her myself, but even that is beginning to get difficult."

"Thank you for telling me. I will see to Regan's needs. And if you continue to have problems yourself, let me know, Leave me now, Filbert," he said, looking over at the man with a thoughtful frown on his face.

Calder sat silently, brooding for a long time, sipping at his tankard of ale and ignoring the talk of the men around him.

*   *   *

The next evening, Regan was summoned once again to join Calder for dinner. She had not seen him in several days and, although she looked forward to being in his company, was nervous about how the evening would end. She wanted it to end with her lying beside him, being held tightly in his arms, but she knew it would be best for all concerned if she left as soon as she finished eating.

"Good evening, Regan," Calder said with a smile, taking her arm and escorting her to his table. "Thank you for coming."

"My pleasure, Milord," she said shyly.

"How goes the bookwork?" he asked, once he was settled in close beside her. "A bit tedious, Milord, but I am making progress."

"Good," he answered, happy to be so close to her once again and to be able to gaze freely upon her lovely face.

The blood drained from Regan's cheeks when the serving girl placed a trencher of food in front of her, and Calder looked carefully at the servant. He had paid no attention to her before this night but realized now that she looked familiar to him.

"Who is she?" he asked Regan, as the girl left to serve the other knights.

"Maida," Regan answered, adding nothing further.

Turning back to Calder, she said softly, "You look tired, Milord. Is all well with you?"

"We've found the thieves' hideout, but now cannot find the thieves. When we plan to be at the fields with the livestock, they do not show. When we watch their hideout, they steal the cattle from the fields. It is as if they know our plans before we do."

He watched Regan lift her head and narrow her eyes as she stared at Maida, who was laughing and jesting with the knights while she made her rounds.

"How long has she worked here at the Manor?" Regan asked quietly.

"I'm not sure. I hadn't really noticed her before," he replied, curious because he knew that it was not jealousy that prompted the question.

She hesitated a moment, then stated, "Maida is Edgar's mistress. I believe she knows where he is."

"How do you know that?"

Regan responded with a shrug. "Just something she said to me in passing."

"Thank you, Regan," he said, taking her hand in his. "That information will be very helpful to me. It must have been difficult for you to share it."

"Not so difficult," she replied, her green eyes holding his. "He may be my husband, but I have no feelings for him other than contempt. I worry only about Radolf."

"That is how it should be," he said, squeezing her hand. Lowering his voice even more, he asked, "Will you stay tonight?"

He felt his heart drop in his chest as he watched her lower her eyes to the table. "I cannot, Milord," she answered unsteadily. "Many people already suspect we have been together. The situation is getting much more difficult for Radolf already."

She would not tell him about the older boys who had called him names while they threw rocks and sticks at him earlier that day. It was not Calder's concern and she would not burden him with her problems.

She raised her eyes back to his. "I wish that I could, but it is too difficult right now." Her heart ached at the thought of not being able to feel his hands on her body, his lips on hers, the weight of him on her as he drove her to heights of passion the likes of which she wanted only to experience over and over again.

"Somehow, Regan, I will resolve this between you and your people. I am not sure how yet, but I will make it right."

"Yes, Milord," she replied softly, loving that he cared, but knowing that there was nothing he could do to mend the situation.

"Please, stay," he whispered, his mouth so close that his breath brushed her hair.

She could feel herself weakening and stood up from her chair, leaving most of her trencher still filled with food. "I cannot, Milord. I must go now. Please excuse me."

Regan quickly walked away before she could change her mind.

Calder's disappointment at her departure quickly changed to renewed anger at Edgar and anticipation at finally finding a way to get to him. "Men," he called loudly, so all in the room could hear him. "I have come up with a plan for tomorrow night. Rather than split our forces again," now that she had been brought to his attention, he could not help but notice Maida's interest in his words "we will all surround the hideout tomorrow night. We will arrive just before dark and wait till dawn, if necessary."

Hearing his men's groans of frustration, he continued. "They have been gone too long from their home. They will have to return, and I believe it will be soon. We will catch them as they try to sneak in with the darkness. Trust me men, I know this will work."

Pulling Draco aside a short time later, he pointed Maida out to him. "Do not lose sight of her when she leaves tonight, Draco. She will go to tell Edgar of our plans. Follow her and find him, then return here. We will set out immediately to apprehend the thieves. They will not get away this time."

"Yes, Milord," the massive knight responded with a smile, the anticipation in his face evident as he went outside the Manor to lay in wait for Maida.

After the serving women left and his men were starting to make themselves comfortable on their pallets, he called them together once more.

"Draco follows the spy," he said. "Tonight, we hit them, so sleep lightly."

He noted their smiles with satisfaction. Rather than sleeping, they chose to use whetstones to sharpen the blades of their swords as they talked quietly amongst themselves. When Draco arrived a short time later, they were awake and ready do battle.

*   *   *

"They are staying in a grove not far from here, in the opposite direction from where we keep the livestock. I saw at least a couple dozen of them huddled around their fire, and I believe there were more standing guard in the woods. All have weapons," Draco stated.

Silently, they left the Manor and saddled their horses. Draco led the way as they entered the forest. He gestured to them when it was time to dismount. They tied their horses far enough away that their noise would not attract any attention, and each man was given instructions on where to position himself once they reached the site.

"Edgar is mine," Calder said, blood in his eye at the thought of finally being able to meet his nemesis one on one, and dispatch him back to the hell he had come from.

They situated themselves around the group of thieves. A few men had been set as lookouts, but they were removed quickly and quietly, before they were able to call out any warning.

Slowly, the knights made their way down the hillside, carefully moving branches out of their way and stepping over any sticks that might break and give them away.

When they were a few yards from the campsite, Calder nodded to Draco. He let out a bloodcurdling war cry, which all the other knights joined in on as they ran at the cluster of men around the fire.

Mayhem reined as the thieves quickly grabbed up their weapons and turned to face this threat. Most were just farmers and no match for Calder's trained soldiers. They were easily dispatched as the knights moved on to the more experienced men.

Calder's eyes met Edgar's across the fire and he smiled. Fear flickered in Edgar's gaze, but he was not easily cowed. Leaping across the fire, he engaged Calder with his own sword.

Wishing Edgar were a better swordsman, so that he would not have to feel bad when he killed him, Calder toyed with him awhile. He allowed Edgar to believe he had the upper hand, only to thrust upward, knocking the sword from his grasp.

Edgar lost his balance and landed on his back, the tip of Calder's sword tickling his throat.

"Now you will die like the dog that you are, Edgar," Calder said coldly, ready to thrust the blade home.

He saw Edgar's eyes flicker over his shoulder and, turning just in time, was able to deflect the blow meant to sever his head from his body. The man was close though, and Calder was unable to prevent the sword from striking his right arm, cutting him deeply. The limb went numb instantly and the sword dropped from his useless fingers, leaving him at the mercy of the thief.

An evil, toothless smile lit his attacker's face as he walked slowly toward the defenseless Calder. Backing slowly away, the injured knight breathed a sigh of relief when Skeet suddenly appeared from the shadows. Thrusting his sword into the thief's back, Skeet efficiently skewered him before the man could dispatch Calder as he had intended.

In the meantime, Edgar rolled away and retrieved his own sword. He faced Calder now with a sinister look on his face.

"Who will die like a dog now, Milord?" he asked, a grin spreading across his face as he relished the thought of killing his foe, feeling much more confident now that Calder had only bare hands with which to fight against him.

Edgar continued to thrust at the defenseless Calder, but was not close enough to do any damage. So far, Calder was able to keep away from the sharp blade, but Edgar was closing in and the knight was losing a lot of blood from the cut on his arm. He could feel himself weakening and knew he must make his move soon.

Skeet stood nearby. He would gladly have taken on Edgar himself, but the warning look Calder sent in his direction reinforced his earlier words. Calder wanted this man for himself.

Edgar's face gleamed with overconfidence as he continued to toy with his enemy, close enough now to nick Calder occasionally on the arms and legs. His grin widening, Edgar paused a moment to savor his anticipated victory.

Unfortunately for Edgar, Calder had maneuvered himself close to where his sword had fallen. He took that moment to dive to the ground, rolling away from the deadly tip of Edgar's sword as he grabbed his own with his still useful left hand.

Edgar roared in rage and ran toward Calder, who was now crouched on the ground. Holding the hilt of the sword in his good hand, Calder thrust upward with all of his strength, watching as the point buried itself deep into Edgar's chest.

Edgar eyes widened in surprise, then they glazed over and he sank to the ground as the life left his body.

Calder stood and looked around at the battle still raging. "Your leader is dead." His voice roared above the sound of steel striking steel. "Give up now or join him in hell."

The men hesitated as they glanced at Edgar's motionless body. Most were already wounded to one degree or another and slowly they lowered their weapons to the ground.

"Bring the bodies and the prisoners," he called to his men, tearing his sleeve and binding his wound to staunch the flow of blood.

When they reached the village, Calder sent Skeet to find the woman called Maida and bring her to the Hall. She entered the room a few minutes later and walked slowly toward Calder, where he stood talking with Draco. Maida eyed him suspiciously.

"You've been injured, Milord," she said, trying to sound concerned rather than curious.

"That I have, lass. I've heard you've a way with mending a man's wound. Would you be able to sew it up for me?"

"Of course, Milord, just let me go get my supplies," she replied, hurrying away.

Maida returned a short while later and began to bathe the deep gash with warm water.

"May I inquire as to how you came by such a wound, Milord?" she asked, as she began stitching it up.

"A minor skirmish," Calder said, gritting his teeth and watching her every move closely. "You can be sure the man on the other end of my sword suffered much worse than this."

She faltered as she tied the knot, but recovered quickly and tried to appear nonchalant. "And who would that be, Milord?"

"He is of no consequence. What is that?" he asked, wrinkling his nose at the vile mixture of herbs she gingerly began to remove from a bowl.

"Just a poultice to help the wound heal," she replied.

Calder's brow furrowed when he noticed that she used a spoon to scrape the substance from the bowl, carefully avoiding any contact with her own skin. He stepped back.

"There is no need for it," he said, unable to miss the look of disappointment on her face. His own features paled somewhat, as he realized how close he had just come to suffering the same fate as his brother.

"Are you sure, Milord?" she asked, her eyes narrowed. "It will take the sting away and help it heal more rapidly."

"Put your hand into the bowl," he ordered.

She looked at him quizzically. "What?"

"Put your hand into the bowl," he repeated.

"But, I have no wound, Milord. There is no need."

"Put your hand into the bowl," he said once again, his voice quiet but commanding.

"No, I will not, Milord," she answered. Her face was ashen and beads of sweat broke out on her brow.

"Why not?"

"There is no need for it," she said, turning to walk away.

"Maida," he said, his voice still deadly quiet, "you would not have thought to poison me, would you?"

The remainder of the blood drained from her face as she turned back to look at him. The bowl trembled in her hands.

His ice-cold eyes stared hard at her. "Do you know what happens to traitors, Maida?"

She refused to answer, her eyes narrowing as she studied him cautiously.

"They are blinded, Maida," he continued softly, inching closer to her. "Is that what you prefer? Abetting Edgar was bad enough, but you also attempted to take the life of your Overlord. It's your choice now. Which will it be, Maida? If not to be blinded, then put your hand in the bowl."

With the screech of a banshee, Maida hurled the bowl and its contents at Calder. He easily ducked out of the way and turned back just in time to see Draco's dirk fly through the air and embed itself in her chest.

Calder shook his head sadly as he watched her sink to the floor and take her last breath. "Put her body out with the others. I must go tell Regan of Edgar's death. And, Draco," Calder said gratefully as he turned back toward him, "thank you."

With a nod of acknowledgement, Draco bent to pick up Maida's now lifeless body and carry it outside.

CHAPTER 15

Regan was startled to find Calder at her door at such a late hour. She looked nervously about to see if anyone was watching them before leading him inside her cottage.

"What is it?"

"Is Radolf asleep?" Calder asked, his voice low.

"Yes, he is."

"Edgar is dead," he said bluntly, not knowing a way to break the news that would make it any easier.

Regan felt her knees grow weak and quickly sat down at the table. A myriad of emotions ran through her right then and, shamefully, she realized that the strongest of them was relief that he was gone.

"I will call the villagers together tomorrow to let them know, but I did not want you to hear it that way."

"Thank you, Calder. I appreciate your thoughtfulness," she said, taking his hand in hers. She knew, somehow, that it was Calder who had taken Edgar's life, but wanted him to realize that she did not harbor any ill feelings toward him because of it.

He watched her face reflect her emotions and wished he could take her in his arms and hold her while she dealt with them.

"I must tell Radolf when he wakes," she said, wondering with concern how the boy would take the news.

"Would you like me to come back in the morning and help explain Edgar's death?" Calder asked. He curled his fingers around hers, wanting her to tell him, and Radolf, the truth, and thereby allow him to be by his son's side to help him through this. He could not understand why she continued to keep her silence.

"No," she said, gratitude filling her eyes, "but thank you, anyway. It would be best if I try to explain. He is so young, I don't know how much he will understand."

She stared into the deep blue depths of Calder's eyes, feeling her own fill with tears at her deception, to Edgar, to Calder and, particularly, to Radolf. He was so young; she must take this slowly. First, he must be given a chance to deal with Edgar's death. Only then could she consider being honest about who his true father was.

"You should go now," she said tearfully, needing to be by herself.

"Yes,", he said, worry showing on his face. "Will you let me know how Radolf handles the news?"

"Of course, Milord," she answered, not finding his concern for the boy at all strange. Calder watched her for a moment longer, and then turned and walked out of the cottage.

* * *

The next morning, all of the villagers were gathered once more in the Courtyard.

"Yesterday, we killed or captured the men behind the thievery of your livestock. Many were members of this village. Those who survived yesterday, will be hung in the square today for their traitorous behavior." He paused as the noise from the crowd grew louder. "I imagine some of you other men may have participated in these raids, as well. Consider yourself fortunate that you were not with Edgar last night. But, know this, should more livestock disappear, we will hunt down those responsible until each is dead, even if that leaves us with a village of nothing but women."

He watched as some of the men stared down at their feet or shifted uncomfortably, refusing to meet his eyes.

"Take your beasts and graze them on your own lands now, and I'll hear no grumbling about which belongs to whom. You must work it out amongst yourselves."

Calder nodded and Draco and the other knights led the prisoners out to the square, where a sufficient number of ropes had been hung for each of them. Calder dreaded the thought of the coming executions. But, harsh as the punishment may be, it was perhaps the only way to ensure no similar problems would occur in the future.

He stood tall and proud, ignoring the looks of hatred cast upon him by the crowd, as he pronounced judgment on the thieves and watched as they were hung. Leaving the villagers to collect and bury their dead, he slowly made his way to the stable and saddled Alerio.

Pushing the horse as hard and as long as he could that day, he was finally able to clear his head. Making his way back toward the village, he watched the sky burn a brilliant red as the sun slowly began its descent.

Calder spotted a flash of yellow in the woods ahead of him and cautiously approached it. Recognizing Regan sitting beneath a tree, he dismounted and walked over to her. His brow furrowed in concern when he saw her face buried in her hands and her shoulders shaking as she wept.

"What is it, Regan," he asked gently.

Raising her tear-filled eyes and seeing who spoke to her, she flung herself into his arms. Calder grasped her tightly, running his hand through her hair and murmuring words of comfort as she sobbed against his chest.

Regan regained control a few moments later and tried to step back, but Calder kept his arms circled tightly around her waist.

She placed her hands on his chest and raised bloodshot eyes to his. "I'm sorry, Milord. You caught me at rather a weak moment, I fear."

He leaned down and gently kissed her lips, then silently took her hand and led her to the fallen trunk of a dead tree. Sitting on the log, he gently pulled her down beside him.

"Is it Edgar?" he asked quietly.

"Yes," she said, still sniffling a little. "I just feel so horrible about everything." She held Calder's hand tightly and stared down at the ground. "I knew, from the time I was five years old, that Edgar was to be my husband. We grew up together, we were friends. I don't think that I ever truly loved him, but he was a good man, Calder. You must believe that."

She looked up and saw the doubt on his face. "When you and your men came here the first time, he lost everything and it changed him. He lost his pride, his family, me."

Taking a deep breath, she continued. "He kept getting worse. He let his anger and his hatred eat him up inside and it turned him into someone I didn't know any longer. He took all of his anger out on Radolf and me, and I grew to despise him for it."

"That is understandable," Calder replied softly.

"Not really. I caused so much of his pain." She hesitated, unable to tell him how crushed Edgar was when he realized that he was not Radolf's father. "He knew I did not love him or want him anymore. I gave you the means to find and kill him. I betrayed him in every way possible, and I feel such shame for it when I remember the man that he was."

Calder put his arm around her, hugging her close. "You never betrayed the man that he was, Regan," Calder said gently. "What happened between you and I when we first met was not your fault. You did not betray him then.

Anything that happened after that was not a betrayal of that man, either. He was a thief, a criminal. We would have caught him eventually, but it's possible that I would have lost even more men in the meantime. You helped prevent that, Regan. You did what was honorable and necessary."

"No," she said, burying her face against his chest, "I cannot relieve myself of my guilt that easily. We both know what I've done."

Running his hand over her hair, he murmured, "We both also know the evil that he did to you, and to your son. He was treating you that way long before I returned. Are you going to accept the responsibility for that, as well? Was it anything that you did that caused him to mistreat Radolf as he did?

"Yes," she answered silently, *"I bore your son and he knew it."*

"Keep your memory of him as he used to be alive in your mind. As Radolf grows older, tell him of the goodness that was inside of Edgar. There is no need for him to remember the bad.

You cannot feel responsible for his death, he chose his own path and knew what the consequences would be if he were caught. Let him go in peace, Regan, don't allow him to continue to torment you."

She did not answer, just wrapped her arms around his waist. She felt the steady thudding of his heart beating against her ear and drew comfort from it.

"How is Radolf?" he asked, breaking the silence a few minutes later.

"I think he will be all right. He cried at the funeral, but he doesn't really understand anything other than that Edgar won't be coming home again. He wasn't around much anyway, so it won't be so different for Radolf."

"Would it be agreeable to you if I stop by to see him occasionally?"

Regan lifted her head to look at him. "Why would you want to do that?"

"A boy needs a man in his life," Calder replied brusquely, feeling a little embarrassed. "Some things a woman just doesn't know how to teach a boy."

"I see," she said with a sad smile. "By all means then, feel free to visit anytime."

"Come along," he said, standing and taking her hand. "We should get back."

"No," she said, shaking her head. "I'd rather stay here for a little longer."

Calder knew she did not want to be seen with him, particularly on the day she had buried her husband. "I will walk with you until we get near the village. No one will see us. It's getting dark and I would not feel comfortable leaving you out here alone. Come with me."

Regan took his hand and he trailed Alerio's reins behind him in the other. They walked in silence toward the village, both lost in their own thoughts.

*   *   *

The next few weeks passed quickly and quietly. Calder left for the castle site at dawn each morning and did not return until well after dark each night. He was filled with an overwhelming sense of foreboding that caused him to push the workers hard, and himself even harder, to get as much of the castle done as possible before winter arrived and halted the work until spring.

During that time, Regan found herself spiraling downward into a deep depression. Her guilt about Edgar ate at her continuously. She spent her mornings doing the tedious figures for taxes, grateful that focusing on them kept her mind so fully occupied that, for a few short hours at least, she had no time to think of Edgar, or of Calder.

For the remainder of the day, she listlessly went about her own chores. Besides tending to the cottage and laundry, she picked vegetables from her small garden and preserved them for the coming winter. She and Radolf frequently took walks through the woods, where they would pick berries, wild herbs and vegetables that she would put up for the barren months ahead.

Food was more plentiful this time of year, and she and Radolf were able to eat much better than they had been. Draco came by once or twice a week. Sometimes he took Radolf hunting or fishing, always leaving half of their booty with the boy at the end of the day. If he did not take Radolf, he would stop in to visit for a few minutes and drop off a hare, or a venison loin, or some of whatever he had been hunting that day.

Regan was grateful to him for his kindness and tried to give him some coin to compensate him. But, after he showed how insulted he was by the gesture, she never offered again.

As if they knew that Regan was responsible for the death of Edgar and his men, the townspeople were now even more openly hostile to her and Radolf. It was seldom that they were able to make their way through the small hamlet without snide, hurtful comments being yelled at them. Sometimes they were even struck with small stones or mud.

Radolf was unable to understand what was happening and suffered even more than Regan. If he wandered outside alone, he was inevitably set upon by the boys of the village and returned home in tears, their words cutting him even more than their fists.

Regan's depression deepened as she saw the effects these incidents were having on Radolf. She struggled to find a way to make his life better, but realized that the only true solution was to take what little coin that they had and leave the village; take Radolf and start over where no one knew them. She accepted that, but was unable to bring herself to do it just yet.

She had not seen Calder since the day of Edgar's funeral. He was working at the castle during the times she was at the Manor doing the figures for the taxes. Although he had summoned her for dinner several times, she always sent Skeet back to Calder with some flimsy excuse as to why she could not join him.

Her emotions were all tangled up inside of her and she needed to work them out by herself. Regan knew that if she allowed Calder near her, she would weaken. Her body would take over and she would willingly give herself to him. It was their relationship that caused Radolf's life to be pure hell and she could not allow it to continue.

Besides, she would be leaving soon and it would do no good, to either her or Calder, to allow their feelings to deepen at this point. It would just cause that much more pain when the time came for them to separate permanently.

*   *   *

"Please, thank Lord Calder for the invitation," Regan said to Skeet one evening, "but I fear I have a touch of the ague and dare not eat at the Manor with him. Besides, Radolf is off fishing with Draco and I must wait for his return."

"Yes, Milady," Skeet said respectfully, backing away from her door.

"Skeet?" she asked hesitantly.

"Yes, Milady?"

"Is all well with Lord Calder? I know he drives himself hard to finish the castle."

"He is well, Milady, just tired most evenings. He will be very disappointed that you are unable to join him."

"Please give him my regards," she said, biting her tongue to keep herself from withdrawing her refusal to join him. She felt so lost and alone. Calder's comfort and strength would do much to help her get through this bad time, but that same strength might also make her lose her resolve to leave and she could not allow that.

A short while later Regan was startled by a loud banging on her door. She jumped, and the dirk that she had been using to chop leeks for soup slipped and cut deeply into her finger.

The relentless pounding continued, so she stuck the bleeding finger in her mouth and crossed the room. She stood motionless when she opened the door to find Calder' broad frame filling the opening.

"Are you injured?" he asked brusquely, the anger on his face swiftly changing to concern as he saw the blood on her lips.

"Just a slight cut," she answered, after removing the digit from her mouth. "Your visit is an unexpected surprise, Milord."

"I'm sure that it is," he said dryly. "I have been very lenient with you these past weeks, Regan, but I cannot allow your insubordination any longer."

Calder strode angrily into the room.

"My insubordination?" she asked nervously, wrapping a cloth around her bleeding finger.

"When your Overlord summons you to his table, it is insubordination when you refuse. You have done so thrice in as many weeks."

"Milord, I do apologize, it is just that..." Her words faltered as she looked into his angry blue eyes.

"Do not attempt to deceive me, Regan. I can see that you are not ill. A little too thin," he said eyeing her from top to toe, "but not ill."

Sighing heavily, she sat down at the small table. "In truth, Milord, I think it is best if we do not see each other and are not seen together."

"Why?" he asked, his eyebrow raised. "Have things gotten worse for you?"

She looked at him silently. Even without words, her anguish and despair were evident. Calder walked over and took her hand, lifting her to her feet. He stared deeply into her eyes. The spark, the light that was Regan, no longer shown through those green orbs and, seeing that, he felt more pain than any wound had ever caused. He watched in dismay as tears began to swim in her eyes.

Regan longed to feel his arms around her, longed to let him hold her and take her burdens from her. She felt her own strength draining as she saw the depth of concern shining through his eyes.

"Regan," he said hoarsely, as he pulled her up against his body. She shuddered and began to sob uncontrollably.

When her tears were finally reduced to an occasional sniffle, Calder led her to the table and sat down beside her. Keeping both of her hands in his, he looked searchingly into her face. "Why didn't you come to me?"

"Calder," she said, resignation heavy in her voice, "there is nothing that you can do. Radolf and I are not wanted here."

"There is always something that I can do," he said firmly. "But first, I must know of the problem."

"And what will you do?" she asked, her voice edging toward hysteria. "Will you put someone in the pillory for speaking harshly to me? Will you use a cane to beat a young boy who teases and torments my son? There is nothing that you can do that will not make them hate us even more."

Calder did not respond, but she saw his eyes narrow as he considered her words. His continuing silence was unnerving and compelled her to tell him of her plans.

"I cannot allow my son to grow up in a village that treats him so cruelly."

"Your son?" Calder asked coldly.

"Yes, my son," she answered, wondering at the meaning of his question. She continued hesitantly. "I plan on leaving this place as soon as I finish the taxes for you."

"With Radolf?"

"Of course."

"And where is it that you think you will go?" he asked, his voice colder and harsher than he had ever spoken to her before.

"I'm not sure yet. When you pay me for these services, I believe I should have enough to get us so far away that we will be able to find some peace in our lives." She was unable to look him in the eye as she spoke.

Once again, Calder just sat silently, studying her. Finally, he spoke. "Regan, I know everything that has befallen you and Radolf is because of me, and I want to make things easier for the both of you. I have not had the time to deal properly with this situation and it is, apparently, much worse than I realized."

Releasing her hand, he ran his own tiredly though his short, cropped hair, and then rubbed his brow, attempting to ease the tension in it.

Regan felt a painful squeeze around her heart as she watched Calder struggle to come up with an answer to her problems. He had so many more important issues to deal with right now and she was just becoming more of a burden to him.

"Regan," he said softly, taking her hands back into both of his own, "can you bear this a short while longer?"

"I don't know," she answered in a whisper, her eyes filling with tears again.

"You must stay awhile longer. I know I have spent too much time preparing the castle, rather than taking care of you and Radolf as I should." His voice was strained, his mind continuing to look for solutions even as he spoke.

"We are not your responsibility, Milord," she replied.

"Yes, you are, Regan, and I have not been there for you." Calder stopped speaking, once again running his hand through his short hair and frowning. "It is just that I have this overwhelming feeling that something evil is coming. I cannot even understand it myself, but I believe, with all my heart, that this whole village and everyone in it, is in jeopardy. Until the castle and fortifications are complete, I will not be able to rest easy."

His words sent a shiver of apprehension down her spine.

"I know that does not ease your mind or solve your problems. It is only my excuse as to why I cannot devote enough time to helping you with the other people in the village. I need you to understand and to give me some time before you make a final decision as to what you will do."

It was Regan's turn to remain silent while she considered what he said. The turmoil of her emotions was overwhelming her so much that she had difficulty trying to make any decision at all. She did not want to leave. It made her physically ill to think of leaving Calder, never to see him again. But, she would only be hurt worse in the future when he married and had no further use for her. And Radolf would only continue to suffer if they remained in the village.

She could not tell him now that Radolf was his son; she feared he may not let them leave if she did so.

With a heavy heart, she finally replied. "I did not come to you and ask that you solve my problems. I can do what is necessary to protect my son. I will stay for awhile, Calder, until I finish the taxes. But, then I believe I must go. For my son. He is my life and I, not you, have caused the pain in his. So, I must be the one to make it better for him."

Calder tried to school his features so that she could not see how hurt and angry he was with her answer. There was no way that he would let her leave, particularly not with his son. They were both too important to him and he could not allow it. "Before you make your decision, I pray that you will come to me first. I think you owe me that much."

"I will not leave without telling you, Calder," she said, trying to hold onto her resolve. "But, in the meantime, I believe it would be best if we do not spend any time alone together."

She lowered her eyes to the table, not wanting him to see how much it hurt her to say those words to him. Calder had no chance to respond before the door banged open and Radolf walked in with Draco.

Radolf proudly held a stringer of fish in his pudgy hands. Draco looked curiously between Regan and Calder, feeling the tension in the room and realizing their arrival had interrupted something important.

"The boy improves each time he fishes," Draco said, hoping to lighten the atmosphere. Radolf was grinning as he took his stringer over to Calder to inspect, then handed it to his mother.

"Did they fight hard, son?" Calder asked, pride fighting with envy as he spoke. He should be the one who was teaching Radolf how to fish and hunt, not Draco, but he was needed at the castle and it could not be helped.

"Yes, Lord Cawer," Radolf responded excitedly, running back over to his side and spending several minutes detailing his struggles in landing the fish.

"You are learning well, Radolf," Calder said, smiling down at him. He was unable to miss the bruise on the boy's face and knew it must be a gift from one of the other village children. It infuriated him that he was unable to protect his own son and he resolved to come up with a solution to the problem this very night.

Ruffling Radolf's curls, he stood and moved toward the doorway. "We must be on our way now. I will be back to visit you soon, alright, Radolf?"

"Yes, Lord Cawer, I miss seeing you," he answered shyly.

"I miss you, as well," Calder said sincerely. Then, looking pointedly at Regan, he added, "Both of you. I'll be back soon to look in on you. Is that alright with you, Regan?"

"Yes, Milord," she answered with a sad smile, appreciating his concern, but knowing it was not enough to keep her from having to leave this place.

CHAPTER 16

Surprisingly enough, life did improve after Calder's visit. Albeit, the fact that one of his knights was always at Regan and Radolf's side whenever they left their cottage, was surely the reason why.

Regan felt guilty taking a pair of strong hands away from the work on the castle. She got such delight from the looks on the other villager's faces, however, that she did not complain about their presence. It never failed, someone would start to make a rude comment, then catch the intimidating glare from the fearsome knight by her side and almost swallow their tongue along with their words, and Regan could barely restrain her giggles.

She also noticed a change in Radolf. He was becoming carefree again, able to leave the cottage without worrying where the bullies would jump him this day.

There was only one unpleasant incident, and in the end, it bolstered Radolf's confidence even more. They were walking toward the river to do wash when a large rock struck Radolf.

He fell to the ground with a sob and grabbed his leg. The knight, Kenny, hesitated just a moment to make sure the injury was not serious, then drew his sword and ran into the bushes from which the rock had come.

The massive knight emerged a few moments later. His sword was back in its sheath and he was dragging two young boys along beside him by their ears.

"Apologize," Kenny said sternly to the ragamuffins, neither much older than nine or ten. Their faces were screwed up in fear as they looked at Radolf, who was still lying on the ground.

"Sorry, Radolf," one boy muttered, tilting his head to the side to ease the pressure on his ear.

"Now you," Kenny said, tweaking the other boy's ear until he was almost kneeling from the pain. Both lads were twice Radolf's size, and Regan's heart skipped a beat when she realized that they were among those who had been tormenting and beating up her young son.

"Sorry," the older boy said sullenly, grunting when Kenny pinched his ear once more before releasing him.

"You will both appear before Lord Calder this evening to explain your actions, or I will come looking for you," the knight added ominously, then both boys ran in the opposite direction as fast as they could.

*   *   *

Regan was filled with indecision as to whether or not she should take Radolf to the Manor when the boys went before Calder. On the one hand, she wanted him to see that they would be punished for their actions. On the other, she worried about the harshness of the punishment and was not sure if he would find it more upsetting than the incident itself.

She was saved from laboring further over her decision when there was a sharp rap on her door.

"Hello, Kenny," she said, giving him a puzzled look when she found him in her doorway.

"Milady," he said with a respectful nod, "Lord Calder wishes the presence of you and your son at the Manor. I am to escort you, if you please."

"Certainly, just give me a moment," she answered. He nodded his assent and stepped back outside of the cottage. Regan quickly bundled Radolf up and led him outside and they walked side by side, with Kenny guiding the way. Radolf was almost skipping in his excitement, exhilarated that the bullies were finally going to be punished for hurting him.

The Hall was packed with villagers. Calder's men had positioned themselves along the outside of the group. The two boys stood before the Lord's table, their parents at their sides. The latter looked almost as scared as the boys themselves.

Calder looked around the room and, when he saw that Regan and Radolf had arrived, began the proceedings, he had tormented the boys long enough by making them wait.

"What is your name?" he asked the older boy, using his sternest tone of voice.

"Aart." He tried to act sullen, but sounded instead as if he might cry.

"And you?" Calder nodded to the other.

"Drew," the second boy answered in a trembling voice.

"What happened today?" Calder asked, making sure that he continued to make eye contact with one or the other at all times.

Neither of them responded.

"Answer me." His voice boomed through the hall and the boys flinched as if they had been struck.

"I did it," the younger boy cried out.

"Did what?" Calder asked in a much softer voice.

"I throwed the rock and hit Radolf," he answered, his voice wavering.

"Why?"

"Cause we always do."

"Why?" Calder repeated insistently.

"Cause we don't like him."

"Why?"

The boy shrugged.

"You don't know why you don't like Radolf?"

"My father says he's a bastard and isn't good enough to live in our village."

Calder's eyes narrowed as he looked balefully at the boy's father. In turn, that man's gaze nervously found the floor. Turning back to the boy, he asked coldly, "Do you know what a bastard is?"

The boy shook his head. "No, just that it's bad to be one."

"Do you know that King William is a bastard? He is the most revered man in this country. He leads the world's greatest army. He owns this land and all who live on it. Would you go to him and tell him that he is not good enough to live in your village?"

"No," Drew answered, his voice shaking nervously.

"But, Radolf is no bastard. He was born to parents who love him very much and for you to call him such a name is cruel and cowardly. Has Radolf ever done you harm?"

The boy shook his head, staring shamefully at the floor.

Calder knew his words were not completely the truth, even though both of Radolf's parents did love him. Calder had never thought of Radolf as his bastard child and it cut him to the bone to think of all the wrong he had caused. He searched his soul for the answers that would help him to right this situation, but realized that they would be long in coming, and for now he must deal with these two boys.

"Do you like people to throw rocks at you?"

"No."

"Why would you do it to a boy only half your size, who cannot defend himself, one who you admit has never caused you harm?"

Again, Drew just shrugged his shoulders and looked at the floor, feeling foolish.

"Were I your parent, either of your parents," Calder said with a pointed look at the older boy, "I would be ashamed to call you my son."

"The measure of a man," he continued, "is how he comports himself on a daily basis. You are so close to manhood now that you need to choose the right paths in your lives. Should you choose to remain bullies, only picking on those younger and smaller than yourselves, you will never earn the respect of another person.

The measure of a man is in the battles that he chooses to fight and the honor with which he fights them."

Calder continued to stare at the two boys and they returned his gaze, unable to tear their eyes away as he spoke. Calder was quiet for a moment, considering their punishment.

"The both of you will shovel dung from the stables for the next two weeks. At the end of that time, you will meet with me again, alone," he added, the last directed at their parents. "We will then discuss what you have learned about yourselves and the kind of men that you want to be. Are we understood?"

Both boys nodded quickly, breathing a sigh of relief at the leniency of their punishment.

Regan was also relieved at how the proceeding had gone and turned to leave with Radolf, but stopped short when she found her way blocked by Kenny.

"M'lord wishes to speak privately with you, after the others have left," he whispered into her ear.

"Of course, Kenny," she said, her heart pounding hard in her chest at the thought of spending time alone with Calder.

She waited patiently for the villagers to file out of the Hall, ignoring the caustic stares they threw in her direction, and then Kenny escorted them to Calder's table.

Calder moved to lift Radolf into the air, then hugged him tightly. Most of the knights were already aware of Radolf's parentage, but still found their leader's carefree, affectionate manner completely out of character for the man they thought they knew.

"Please, sit," Calder said, beckoning Regan to the chair next to his and sitting down with Radolf comfortably situated in his lap.

"So, Radolf," he asked, "are you satisfied with the boys' punishment?"

"Yes, Lord Cawer," the boy answered, his lopsided grin firmly in place. He felt very special tonight. Not only had Lord Calder called the boys to task for what they had done to him, but now he was being asked his opinion as to their punishment. His chest swelled with pride and self-importance.

"Why?" Calder asked curiously.

"They have to clean poop. So now, when they see me and want to throw rocks, maybe they'll think about having to clean more poop and then, maybe they won't throw the rock at me."

"Yes, Radolf, that's what I hope will happen, as well. If it doesn't and people still throw rocks at you, will you tell me?"

"I can," he replied, "or maybe I could just throw rocks back at them."

"Well," Calder replied in all seriousness, "if I find out that you have hit someone with a rock, I will have to make you clean poop from the stable, just like these two boys. Throwing rocks is not a nice thing to do and those who do so, must be punished. Do you want to clean poop?"

"No," he answered with a frown.

"Radolf, you cannot let these boys turn you into a mean-spirited person. You must look deep inside yourself," Calder said, poking a finger gently into Radolf's chest, "and realize that you are a better person than that. Only a coward would throw rocks from behind a tree. You aren't a coward, are you?"

"No," he replied indignantly.

"Then you must show these other boys that you will not let them beat you down and turn you into a person like them. You are Radolf, the red wolf. You must first think about what is right, and that is the only thing that you should allow yourself to do. Do you understand?"

Radolf's face scrunched up as he concentrated on Calder's words before answering. "I shouldn't throw rocks?"

Calder laughed out loud and hugged him. "Yes, Radolf, that's right. Now run and find Draco, see if he has any sweets he will share with you."

Regan fought back tears as she witnessed the exchange between father and son. This was what she had always envisioned for Radolf, a proud, strong father, one who could lovingly teach him how to survive in this brutal world and still remain an honorable man.

"What am I to do?" she wondered, filled with despair. *"Do I tell Calder that he has a son, or do I run from here and never let Radolf know his father? If I stay, what will happen when Calder wishes to marry? How will I survive if I am forced to watch him make a life with another woman? And what of Radolf then? Will he take my son and raise him as his own, with another woman as his mother? Or will he reject Radolf in favor of his legitimate heir?*

"Please, God," she prayed, *"help me to know what to do."*

"Regan," Calder said gently, turning to her just in time to see her eyes squeeze shut and her face fill with such sadness that he could not help but reach over and engulf her hands in his own. He wanted to take her into his arms and comfort her, but knew he could not be more familiar than this with her in the Hall, with his men and the servants watching their every move.

"What is it? Are you upset about this evening's proceedings?"

"Oh, no, Milord," she replied softly, blinking away her tears. "You handled the situation very well. I think Radolf is doing much better now and I owe you my thanks. I was wrong, you can make a difference. And I owe you an apology, as well, for doubting you."

"You owe me nothing, Regan. Just honesty. Please tell me why you are so upset."

She lowered her gaze to the table, unable to tell him how confused and unsettled she was.

"I need to find some answers, Milord, and I don't know where to look for them."

"Can you not look to me?"

A wistful smile appeared on her face, but she shook her head. "No, Milord, this is a problem that I must find the answer to myself."

Calder suspected that the issue of his being Radolf's father was what distressed her, but he could not understand why she felt she could not tell him the truth of it. Edgar was gone now and could no longer harm any of them. It made no sense to him. But, he respected the fact that it was a battle she felt she must fight alone and acquiesced to her wishes.

"Just know, Regan," he said softly, "that I am always here for you. I will help you though anything. And I will never, ever allow anyone to hurt you or Radolf again."

Regan wondered if he realized that it was he, himself, who could hurt them most. Calder was the only one who could cut her so deeply that she might never be able to recover from it.

"Thank you, Milord," she whispered, lifting her hand from his and running it gently along the scar on the side of his face. She searched his eyes and hoped that she would know what to do when she saw what they held. Although tenderness and affection shone from them, she was not sure if that was enough.

"I must take Radolf home now," she said, removing her hand and standing up. He grasped it in his own and held her in place.

"We need to talk further, Regan. I will give you some time to work things out in your own heart, but then, we will talk this through. You will not leave here before we do that. Promise me."

She gazed down at him for a moment, his handsome face so confused and unsure, and knew that she could not refuse him. "I promise, Calder. We will talk again, when I have had a chance to think things through on my own. I will not leave before doing so."

"Thank you, Regan," Calder did not know what to say to make her realize how important she was to him and how much he needed her in his life. He was not sure if this was the time to tell her such things anyway and watched silently as she took his son by the hand and led him away.

CHAPTER 17

With the end of summer and the beginning of fall, harvesting began in earnest. Filbert brought that to Calder's attention each night when he gave his report.

"The people worry, Milord," he said, once again. "If the crops are not brought in by the time the ground begins to freeze, much will be lost and people will go hungry this winter."

"Enough, Filbert," Calder responded brusquely. "I understand the need to get the harvest in. Tell your people that they need not report to work on the castle again, not until the crops are brought in and the beasts butchered and cured for the winter."

"Thank you, Milord," Filbert said with relief.

"And, Filbert," Calder added, "at the end of the harvest season, we will have a festival to celebrate. The people, most of them anyway, have helped a great deal on the castle and I wish to reward them for their services."

"Thank you, Milord, that is very kind of you." Filbert could not hide his surprise. There had not been a fair or festival held in the village since the Normans arrived.

"That's the good news," Calder said with a wry grin. "You might as well also tell them that the tax calculations are almost complete. Once the harvest is in, they will become due immediately and I will expect payment in full. Anyone not paying their taxes will be banished from the village."

Filbert looked at him coldly. "Surely, you would not put out a family just before the winter snows.

"Surely, I would," he answered firmly. "They did not pay their proper taxes to my brother and he almost lost these lands because of it. I will not allow that to happen to me."

"As you wish, Milord," Filbert said, his eyes narrowed as he turned and left the Manor.

*   *   *

One evening the following week, Regan made her way to the Manor to meet with Calder to discuss the taxes. She had left word with Garrick several days before that the figures were ready and had been waiting apprehensively to be summoned.

She had made sure to keep Radolf close by for the last couple of days because she wanted him to attend with her. Regan wanted no opportunity to be alone with Calder, in truth, she could not trust what she might do.

Late that afternoon, however, shortly before her summons, Draco had arrived to take the boy fishing. They would be out late, he had told her, as they were fishing for pike, and those could best be caught at dusk and afterward. Seeing the excited look on her son's face, Regan could not deny him, and so the two left a short time later.

It was not long after that when Garrick arrived with her invitation to dine with Calder. She suddenly became suspicious of the last-minute fishing trip and paced nervously around the small cottage.

Regan still had not decided what to do about the situation with Calder and her indecision was tearing at her as deeply as her guilt over Edgar had. She was afraid to have Calder confront her before she knew for sure what her response would be.

Nevertheless, she carefully plaited her hair and dressed as well as she could, considering the frayed clothing that she had to choose from, and slowly made her way to the Manor.

Calder was near the door when she arrived, speaking with one of his men. His face lit up when he saw her and he took her arm and escorted her to his table.

"It's a pleasure to see you again, Regan," he whispered, his breath tickling her ear.

"Thank you for the invitation, Milord. I only wish Radolf could have joined us," she added casually.

Seeing the corner of his mouth curl up in a slight smile, she realized her suspicions were correct. Calder had instructed Draco to make sure Radolf would be busy that evening, so he could not interrupt the conversation that Calder intended to have with her. Regan's heart pounded furiously against her chest as her nervousness increased.

"Where is he this evening?" Calder asked, his voice serious, but a mischievous sparkle lit his deep blue eyes.

"Draco came by earlier to take him fishing. Had I known you would be summoning me here this evening, I would have denied the request, as I'm sure Milord must know."

"A miscommunication on my part, I fear," he said, his eyes smiling into hers as he pursed his lips and shook his head in mock regret.

"Now it will have to be just you and me," he added, his face turning more serious, passion flaring in his eyes as he took her hand in his. "I hope you do not find that too disagreeable."

"I imagine that will depend, Milord," she answered softly, unable to tear her gaze from his, "on how you choose to comport yourself."

With a devilish smile on his face, he replied. "I will do my best to be nothing other than honorable, Milady."

They were interrupted then by servants bringing in the food. Regan was impressed at the richness of the fare and genuinely did regret that Radolf could not be there to sample the delicacies.

Usually when she dined at the Manor, there was a simple meat dish served with bread and, occasionally, a small dessert. This evening's meal seemed more like a feast. The servants brought trenchers, hollowed out loaves of stale bread, piled high with food and cut in half, to be shared by two people.

She savored the taste of the venison, which had been basted with a verjuice marinade and cooked over a spit in the great fireplace in the Hall, its aroma lingering still. The meat was accompanied by a frumenty, the wheat milk pudding which was a common dish in her own home. But this frumenty was different, much richer and spicier than what she as used to, and Calder seemed pleased when she mentioned the fact.

Regan particularly enjoyed the white bread that was being served, helping herself to several pieces. It was a very rare occurrence when she was able to enjoy it, being used to dark bread or, occasionally, some made of wheat or rye.

Although the knights had no trouble keeping up a loud boisterous conversation while they ate, Calder and Regan remained quiet, with just occasional comments about the food. Both felt the need to ease into this evening slowly, neither knowing which direction it would take, each of them having their own idea of how it should end.

Picking at the boiled apples and cheese curds that completed their meal, Calder leaned back in his chair, unable to keep from watching Regan. It had been a long time since they were together and his body craved hers. Having her so close pushed thoughts of anything, other than holding her in his arms, from his head.

Feeling the weight of his stare, she nervously picked up her pewter cup to take a sip of the spiced wine which had accompanied their meal. He saw her frown down into the empty cup and snapped his fingers. A servant instantly appeared and filled it to the brim.

Regan knew she shouldn't be imbibing, she needed all of her wits about her when dealing with Calder. The wine though, was sweet and flavorful and did not taste strong at all, so she allowed herself a little more.

With dinner over and most of the items removed from the table, Calder had Regan's books brought to them. For the next couple of hours, they poured over them, detail by monotonous detail.

During that time, Calder made sure her cup was never more than half empty before quietly signaling the servant to fill it again. He wanted to have a serious discussion with her when this was done and, if the wine loosened her tongue a little, so be it.

Regan was so engrossed in explaining her calculations that she never noticed how much she was drinking, nor how many times the servant inconspicuously refilled her cup.

"You have done an excellent job, Regan. I am very pleased," Calder said sincerely, smiling down into her brilliant green eyes.

"Thank you, Milord," she replied, flushing at his praise. "I fear the villagers will not feel the same, once they've seen the amounts that are back due."

"I'm sure that you are right about that," he agreed. "But, they only have themselves to blame. Had they paid my brother what was due him, they would not now owe so much to me."

"Yes, Milord," she answered softly, unable to keep from watching his wide, full lips as he spoke.

"It has been too long since I held you in my arms," Calder said quietly, his body responding to the longing that he saw on her face. Leaning forward, so that only she could hear him, he whispered, "I need you, Regan."

She patted her hair nervously, feeling herself blush crimson at his words. She suddenly found herself wanting him so badly that she was afraid she might do something embarrassing if she did not leave his presence soon.

"I believe it would be best if I go now, Milord," she answered, not able to look him in the eye and see his disappointment. Regan did not want to leave, but was afraid that she would not be able to stop what might happen if she stayed.

"Will you take a walk with me first?" he asked, not willing to give up just yet.

"I shouldn't, Calder," she replied, making the mistake of looking into his eyes and losing herself in their depths. Every nerve in her body tingled in anticipation of his touch.

"But you will," he said softly, his lips brushing her hair as he spoke.

He stood and took her hand, helping her to her feet and leading her to the entranceway. Making their way around the boisterous knights, who had consumed as much ale as they had food, Regan and Calder grabbed their mantles and stepped out into the cool, crisp fall night.

Still hand in hand, they walked along a trail behind the Manor. They continued deeper and deeper into the woods, where even the strong beams from the full moon had difficulty making their way through the thick evergreens.

When he felt they had gone far enough from the Manor, Calder led her to a mossy area under a large tree and sat down. He pulled Regan down firmly on his lap.

She began to protest but, even in the dim light, his lips found their way to hers. Instantly, all fight left her body and her arm encircled his neck. Her breasts flattened against his hard chest and all thoughts of protest fled from her mind.

Calder released her hair from its confinement, allowing it to envelop them as their lips met. His hands roamed freely over her body, his excitement building.

Their kisses were frenzied, their bodies trying to make up for all the time they had spent apart. Urgently they tried to touch and taste every inch of the other as, without even realizing it, layer after layer of clothing fell away. They rolled in the soft moss, their naked bodies entwined, Regan's soft, satiny skin caressing Calder's hard, muscular body.

Pulling his lips from hers, Calder rested on his elbow, looking down at her in admiration as the faint glow from the moon illuminated her body. The light reflected itself in her wide passionate eyes and shimmered off of her porcelain skin as he ran his fingers over the satiny expanse ever so slowly.

Her body moved in response to his touch. She turned toward him, needing to feel his body against her own, needing to feel him inside of her, bringing her the fulfillment that only he could.

He wrapped his arms around her and rolled onto his back. Carrying Regan with him, he waited breathlessly as she pushed herself up to straddle his hips, and then took him within her and rode him to heights neither could have imagined.

A short time later, regretfully, Calder rolled away from her to retrieve their mantles, which lay nearby. The night was growing cold and he had felt the goosebumps rising on her skin.

He wrapped the cloaks around them and held her tightly in their little cocoon, continuing to trail his fingers along her satiny skin. Their passion spent, he was still unable to keep his lips from lingering tenderly against hers.

Taking his finger and moving the long curls from her face, he slowly kissed her cheek, then trailed soft kisses down her jawline to her chin. "I can't get enough of you," he whispered against her mouth.

Regan captured his lips with her own, caressing them, teasing him with her tongue as she savored the feelings that came in the aftermath of loving him. "I shouldn't be here," she said softly a few moments later.

"I cannot imagine a more right place for you to be." Calder's voice was low, more relaxed than she had heard it in sometime, as his hand continued to explore the silky skin hiding under her mantle. "You make me complete, Regan. I don't know how I ever made it through my days before you were in them."

"And you confuse me so," she replied, kissing the pulse at the base of his throat.

Calder raised himself on his elbow in order to talk with her more easily and not be so tempted by the smoothness of her skin or by her lips, slightly parted and waiting to be kissed once again.

"How do I confuse you?"

Regan remained silent, trying to find the right words. She wanted to bare her soul to him, as she had bared her body just a short time before. Maybe it was the wine, but she believed it was more than that. She believed that what they had just shared went beyond the physical, but how far beyond?

"Please, Regan, talk to me. I would do anything, anything at all for you."

"I know you would, Calder. I know that you feel as if you need to protect Radolf and me, and I love you for it."

"You love me?" Calder asked, his voice soft and filled with a bewildered awe. He had never considered love being a part of what they shared, had never thought to define it.

"Of course," she answered with a warm laugh. "You did not know that?"

Caressing her face, he spoke thoughtfully. "I don't think that I know what love truly is, so it had not occurred to me that you might love me, or that I might love you."

"You are an odd man, Calder. But know this, whether you understand the meaning of the word or not, you do know how to express the depth of your feelings. And for that, I can say that I do love you."

"So, if you love me, why would you consider leaving me?"

"There are so many things that you do not know, Calder," she said, lying on her back and staring at the stars twinkling between the branches of the trees above them. Maybe there, in the heavens, she would find the answers she sought.

"Then you must tell me, Regan. For otherwise, we can never find the answers that we both need to learn." He watched as tears escaped her eyes and slid down onto the moss beneath her head. "Is it the way that you are treated by the villagers?"

"Not really. Having your men with us has made a great difference in the way we are treated." Her voice was soft, her brow furrowed as she struggled to come to a decision.

"Then what is it, Regan? Please trust me."

Gracing him with an angelic smile, she suddenly realized what she must do. Finally, she was able to acknowledge that Calder was the only man who had stood up for her; the only man who protected both her and Radolf and tried to make them safe; the only man who cared when she was unhappy and tried to make things better for her. The only man that she had ever loved.

And with that knowledge, she felt an overwhelming need to believe in him and trust him to do what was right, for all three of them.

Regan sat up, pulling the mantle closer around her to ward off the chill, and touched his face. She traced her finger over his strong features, wanting her son to learn to be a man from such an honorable, noble person such as he.

"It's about when we were together," she began hesitantly, knowing now what she would say, but not how he would react, "before, when you first came here."

"Yes," he urged, his heart thundering in his chest, eager to hear her tell him the truth about his son.

"You and I," she said, tears forming in her eyes, "we created Radolf. He is not Edgar's son."

Having already known the fact did not matter to him, hearing her say the words brought back the same exhilaration he felt when he first learned the truth.

Feeling the heat of his own tears burning along his cheeks, he lifted her face toward his and kissed her with all of the depth of the emotions coursing through him. "Thank you," he said in a low, choked voice. "No one has ever given me a greater gift."

"You are not angry?

"How could I be angry with the one woman who is able to fill my whole being with such contentment. And now she tells me that, by some miracle, one of the most extraordinary boys I have ever known is my son. God has truly smiled on me this day."

With a cry of relief, Regan kissed him repeatedly between sobs, then stilled when he pulled her tightly against him. Calder rolled her over, until his body lay on top of hers.

"Thank you," he whispered softly once again. He gently nudged her legs apart and, finding her ready, thrust deep inside of her.

As she arched her body against his, welcoming him, Regan realized that there was much more for them to resolve. Tonight though, just having his love, for both her and their son, was enough.

CHAPTER 18

Calder's heart was much lighter after his pleasant romantic evening with Regan and her subsequent honesty about their son. Still though, he did not have much time to sit back and savor the feelings that night had created. With the majority of the villagers working hard at the harvesting of their crops or the preparation of meat for the winter, he and his men were left to do what they could themselves on the castle.

After a long week of hard labor, and a particularly brutal day lifting large blocks of stone for the wall around the bailey, Calder dragged his exhausted body back to the stables. He wanted only some food and a soak in a tub of hot water to ease his aching muscles before bed and, hopefully, a peaceful night of rest.

Brushing down Alerio before releasing him into his stall, he realized that, even more that those basic things, he wished he could share his bed with Regan. Not for the sex, although that would also have been welcome, he mused with a wry grin, but just to have her close by his side. He longed to rest his weary head against her chest and hold her throughout the night, her warm body molded against his, comforting him when those inevitable dark dreams sought to overwhelm him. *Yes,* he thought with a sigh, *she would be my greatest comfort this night*.

Calder slapped Alerio on the rump and closed his stall door, leaving the animal to munch eagerly on the oats and hay, as he wearily made his way towards the Manor.

His mood darkened when he entered the building and found a variety of villagers inside the Hall, all apparently waiting to discuss their troubles with him. Pinching his brow and trying to rub some of the fatigue away, he took a deep breath and made his way to the Lord's table.

He refused to speak to anyone until a large tankard of ale had been placed before him. After taking a healthy draught of it, Calder looked up and saw Filbert sitting at the front of the crowd, an ominous look on his face and his hands twitching nervously in his lap.

"What is it, Filbert?" Calder asked impatiently.

"Milord," the old man said quickly, coming to stand before him, "your knight, Draco, has been visiting my people's homes and giving them the amounts that they supposedly owe for taxes."

"Yes, I know. I asked him to do so. And those are the amounts your people owe. The figures have been carefully calculated and the taxes in arrears included."

"Well, that is the problem, Milord. No one anticipated that the amounts would be so high. Our crops were not so good this year, what with all the time we had to spend on the castle." He added the last in an attempt to gain a little sympathy. "Many of us will not be able to pay so much. I ask that you grant us a reprieve, Milord. Let us pay a little to you now and more next year, when we can better afford it."

Calder leaned back in his chair, narrowing his eyes at Filbert and drinking the remains in his tankard before answering. "We have been through this before, Filbert. Why do you continue to make me repeat myself?"

"Milord, you cannot expect so much from these people. Why, you take more than half of what they have. It is not right."

"Enough already." Calder's voice boomed across the room, quieting the disgruntled murmurs of the villagers who had come to hear his response to Filbert's pleas. "I will not continue to have this conversation with you time and again. Listen well, because this is the last time I will say it. Most of what I collect will be given to the King as his heregeld. These lands rightfully belong to him and those taxes are his due."

"I will be damned," he continued, his voice cold and angry, "if I will dig into my own pockets, as my brother did, for monies that have been due from your people for the past several years. They were well aware of their responsibilities and, in their stubbornness and disrespect, refused to pay.

Your people must learn to accept that they are now *my* people. I am here by order of their King. They are able to live on and farm these lands only because I allow them to. They will not do so freely. Their taxes will be paid in full or they will leave immediately."

The insolent look on Filbert's face infuriated him further and he could hear the murmurs of the crowd increasing again.

Filbert's voice was hard and his anger almost matched Calder's when he replied. "These people will starve or freeze to death if you put them out."

"Then they should pay their taxes."

"That is easy for you to say, Milord. It is not your child whose belly will be empty this winter. Not your wife who has not enough to eat and cannot fight the cold and sickness that will come."

Calder was silent a moment, the scar on his face a livid red as he sought to control his anger. "I have suffered much from you, Filbert, for your daughter's sake. But do not think that my patience is infinite or that, because of your daughter, I will not have you punished for your insolence. Think carefully the next time you open your mouth in my presence, for it may be your last time. You are relieved of your duties for me. Now leave the Manor immediately."

Filbert's face was as pale as his flowing white beard when he walked, with as much dignity as he could muster, from the room. Many of the villagers in the Hall began to raise their voices and move toward Calder. For a moment, he feared there might be trouble, until his men, led by Draco, quietly pulled their swords from the scabbards and, holding them with the points to the ground, formed a line in front of his table.

The villagers slowly backed away, only muttering once again, as none wanted to be singled out. Many of them followed Filbert from the building.

Calder sighed with relief, hoping that the rest would leave as well and let him get some sleep. But then Kenny appeared at his side and whispered in his ear.

"Bring them to me," he said resignedly, realizing sleep would have to wait a while longer.

The two boys that had thrown rocks at Radolf appeared in front of him. They had witnessed his conversation with Filbert and could not keep their knees from knocking together in fear.

"Has it been two weeks already?" he asked them.

They nodded, keeping their heads down, afraid to look him in the face.

"Kenny, have they fulfilled their requirements?"

"Aye, Milord, the avener says they shovel shit as well as a grown man," Kenny responded with a laugh.

Calder looked them both over carefully and decided to speak to the older boy first. He was probably only about eleven or twelve years old, but was burly already, with thick arms and torso, and dark brown eyes sunk in his chubby face.

"You, boy," he said, nodding to the older one when they both finally looked up at him, "what have you learned?"

"That I don't want to work in the stables, M'lord."

Using his hand to smother the grin that threatened, Calder nodded. "Didn't enjoy the shoveling?"

The boy shook his head emphatically in the negative.

"But, did you learn anything about the man that you do want to be?" he asked more seriously.

"I watched the smithy shoe the horses. He let me help and said I did real good and can apprentice with him next year." The boy's eyes were shining and his voice rose in excitement.

"I'm, glad for you," Calder said sincerely. "But what of throwing rocks at small children and hiding your deed. Did you learn nothing about that?"

The boy lowered his gaze to the floor and said quietly, "It was wrong and I'm sorry. I won't do it again."

"Do you swear it?"

"Yes, M'lord."

Calder stood and walked over to him, clapping his hand on the boy's shoulder. "You have done well, son. I look forward to seeing how you do as the smithy's apprentice. You go now, but remember, I will hold you to your word. If I find you have lied to me, your punishment will go much worse for you the next time."

"Yes, M'lord," the boy said, bobbing his head and backing swiftly toward the door.

Calder turned his attention then on the younger boy, smaller than the other, wiry and thin. His sandy brown hair was thin and straggly, his clothes torn and dirty. Obviously, his family did not have much money. Calder had more respect for this boy, as he had the courage to admit to the deed he had done.

"And you," he said, his voice lower, his weariness causing it to be raspy as he spoke, "what have you learned?"

"I'm sorry I threw the rocks, but I don't want to work in the stables or with the smithy." His voice trembled as he spoke but, even in his fear, he forced himself to look at Calder.

"Why are you sorry about the rocks?"

The boy looked at him quizzically for a moment. "Radolf din't never do nothing to me. I shouldn't of hurt him like that."

"I see," Calder replied, not sure if the boy was sincere or just saying what his parents had told him to.

"Will you give me your word that you will do nothing like that again?"

"Yes, M'lord. I give you my word."

"Will you be apprenticing for anyone next spring?"

"No," he answered sadly and Calder knew the reason why. Most masters required a fee be paid before taking on an apprentice, and the boy's family did not have the money.

"When the Keep is ready, I will have need of a page. Do you know what that is?"

"No, M'lord," the boy answered cautiously.

"You would do work around the Keep itself, replacing rushes and doing other menial tasks. I will sometimes need you to run errands or do special services for me. After you are old enough, if you prove yourself worthy, you might become a squire, such as Skeet," Calder said, indicating the lad standing nearby.

"Then your duties would become more involved and my men and I would begin to train you with arms, so that one day you might become a knight in his majesty's service. Does that sound like something you would like to do?"

"Aye, M'lord," the boy responded, his eyes shining in anticipation.

"Talk to your parents, and then come see me in the spring," Calder told him, hoping he was not getting the boy's hopes up for nothing. He was not sure how these Saxons would react to one of their own becoming a knight for a Norman king.

"Aye, M'lord," the boy said, a grin stretching across the width of his face as he sprinted from the room.

After the boy left, Calder sat back in his chair and lifted the large tankard to his mouth again. He was thoroughly drained now and did not even care if he ate before seeking his bed.

"Is that it, Draco?" he asked hopefully, noting that there were still several people sitting in the Hall.

"One more, Milord," Draco replied in his gravelly voice. His pale blue eyes studied his leader with concern. He knew how hard Calder had been pushing himself and could see that the physical work, as well as the pressure of ensuring that all was going well within the village, was starting to wear on him.

Calder's fatigue was evident in the dark circles under his eyes and the way he held his body. It angered Draco to see these ungrateful peasants give Calder nothing but further aggravation, when he was killing himself seeing to their safety.

"You've asked the Saxon carpenter, Wallis, to speak with you this evening," he said. Coming to a decision about something that he knew he had no business in, he added, "I must run a quick errand now, Milord. Good evening to you."

"I completely forgot about Wallis. Call him forward before you leave, if you please." Calder said absently, too tired to even be curious about where Draco could be going at this time of night.

Wallis came forward, a fairly young man with intelligence shining through the dark brown eyes of his handsome face. He was slight of frame, but Calder had witnessed his surprising strength while working with him on the castle.

"Wallis," Calder said with a nod, "thank you for coming."

"My honor, Milord, thank you," he said, his nervous hands grasping the large tankard of ale placed in front of him. He had never been called before the Overlord before and worried about what it might mean, particularly with what he had witnessed earlier between Lord Calder and Filbert.

"I have been very pleased with your work at the castle, Wallis. You are a fine craftsman and you put in many more hours than are required of you. I was wondering if you would be interested in working for me fulltime. Over the winter, no work can be done on the outside. We have most of the Keep done and the exteriors to several outbuildings. I thought, mayhap you, and whatever men you select, could work on the interiors of those buildings until spring. I am anxious to have it all done as soon as possible."

Wallis stared at him in stunned silence.

"I will pay you handsomely for the work that you do," Calder said, misreading his expression. "Although, you will be required to work closely with me."

"Yes, Milord," Wallis replied, smiling in gratitude. "I would be honored to work for you. I will do everything that I can to get it ready."

Calder was pleased to see the excitement and anticipation on the carpenter's face. This was one Saxon that he felt he could work well with, and respected Wallis for his ability to solve any problems that arose. He always made sure to check with Calder before making any changes, but Calder had agreed with all that he proposed and felt he could rely on this man's judgment.

"Good," Calder said, raising his tankard of ale to Wallis. "Let us drink to our new arrangement. Will you join me for dinner?"

Feeling overwhelmed, Wallis mumbled an answer and, before long, full trenchers were placed before the two of them. While enjoying the food and ale, they discussed at length the work that would, hopefully, be accomplished before the snow melted in the spring.

The other villagers had all left while they were eating and when Wallis took his leave, Calder wearily made his way up the stairs to his chambers. A fire burned brightly and he crossed to it, mesmerized by the flames as he soaked up the heat emitted by the great fireplace.

Suddenly, he felt soft feminine arms wrap themselves around his waist and, with a wave of relief flooding through him, turned and pulled Regan into his arms.

"How did you know I needed you so this evening?" he whispered against her hair.

"A rather large birdie told me," she answered softly, brushing her hand across his brow, and then trailing her fingers along his cheek. "One who now sits with our son, so that I can try and ease Milord's troubles for a short while."

She removed the belt from his waist, letting it fall to the floor, then pushed his tunic up and let her hands slide across his chest as she pulled it over his head. His breath caught in his throat as she knelt in front of him, slowly, tortuously slowly, loosening his breeches and lowering them, again letting her fingers brush against his skin as she did so.

His hands wrapped themselves in her hair, drawing her even closer as she took him in her mouth. His heart almost thundered out of his chest and he thought his knees might actually buckle as he relished the incredible sensations coursing through his body. All fatigue was miraculously washed away as he closed his eyes and enjoyed the moment.

Feeling his body fast approaching the point of no return, he pulled her to her feet and carried her to his bed. He teasingly ran his lips and tongue over every inch of her naked body until she writhed uncontrollably. With both hands holding her face as his lips tenderly caressed hers, he lowered his body and entered her.

They moved against each other in a slow, seductive dance until their bodies took over and the thrusts became deeper and faster, carrying each of them to a fulfillment so intense that they cried out their release, and their bodies quivered and shook in the aftermath of the passion they had shared.

Holding her tightly while stroking her smooth skin, feeling completely satiated and relaxed, he lay there quietly, savoring the feel of her in his arms. "I am so happy that you are here," he whispered, nibbling at her ear.

"Draco is worried about you, as am I," she said, turning in his arms so she could look into his incredible blue eyes and run her hands over his hard, furred chest.

"Although, I don't necessarily think Draco expected this to happen," she said with a giggle, waving her hand at their entwined bodies. "I think he expected that you just needed some comforting."

"Oh, I am surely comforted," Calder replied with a lazy grin. "I think I should worry the two of you more often."

"Your stamina is noteworthy, Milord," she said with a mischievous smile. "I was told that you worked so hard this week that you were exhausted. I must have been misinformed."

"I think not, Milady," he answered quietly, and she saw that his eyelids were getting heavy, although he tried his best not to let them close. "Will you stay awhile longer?"

"Yes, Calder, if you wish," she answered, running her fingers over the deep lines in his forehead until they relaxed and then through his hair until his eyes finally closed and his breathing became deep and regular.

She laid with him until just before dawn, watching him sleep in the flickering firelight. When he moaned or murmured in his sleep, she would caress him until he quieted again.

"Good-bye, Milord," she said, kissing him lightly on the lips before leaving his bed. He startled her by grabbing her hand and turning her back around to face him.

"Thank you, Milady, for coming to me. You help me keep my sanity amidst all this madness," he said softly, with a vague wave of his hand.

"I am glad, Milord," she replied with a warm smile, but then her expression sobered as she looked down at him. "I must go now, it is getting light. Take care of yourself, Calder."

She leaned down and kissed him thoroughly before retrieving her clothes and putting them on. He watched silently as she dressed and left the room. He lay there for a long while afterward, not even hearing the sounds of the village and Manor waking up to greet the new day, as he considered Regan. It was time to make a decision as to what he would do so that she could be with him every night, and not have to sneak out of the Manor in the dark so that no one would see her.

Soon, he promised himself, *she will be mine in every way.*

CHAPTER 19

The cold and frost came early that fall. Everyone was in a fever to finish what needed to be done so that they could survive the long winter ahead. The entire hamlet was a frenzy of activity.

Calder was forced to put a complete halt to the work at the castle while he and his men oversaw the supplying of the Manor. Calder's duties mainly involved being available for the villagers when they came to discuss the amount of grain or slaughtered meat that they would barter to the lord, in lieu of paying coin for their taxes.

Once an agreement was reached, after much labored debating, Calder then had to see to it that the barley and apples were taken to the Brewster for ale and cider, the hay and oats to the Avener so the horses could be fed over the winter, the meat to the Butler for smoking and storage, and so on and so on.

The area beneath the Manor was brimming with foodstuffs of all kinds, and the haze never cleared from the air over the village as mutton, pork and beef were smoked continuously. The meat and fish not smoked were put into barrels with salt to preserve it over the winter. Onions, potatoes, turnips and other vegetables were stored in bins throughout the great room and barrels of spices lined the walls to dry.

Many were disheartened when the snows arrived early, the sight of its pristine whiteness beautiful to behold, but its arrival deadly due to the amount of crops it killed before they could be harvested. It would be a lean winter for them all.

Calder announced the time of the Harvest Festival and, before long, merchants and peddlers began to arrive with their carts and wagons full of items to barter or buy. Word had spread throughout the countryside and people from all over arrived to join in the fun.

There were games of chance and a wagon full of gypsies, ready to foretell anyone's future, for the right coin, of course. The villagers were more lighthearted than they had been since the Normans first reached their shores and enjoyed themselves to the fullest. There would be time enough to worry over their current state of affairs once the festival was over.

The festival continued for several days. Each night, Calder saw that his own cattle or pigs were slaughtered and cooked over a large outside spit for everyone to share. He made sure that there were plenty of kegs of ale opened to accompany the meat, and his men found them empty each morning.

There was music and dancing, and people were able to forget for a short while about the difficult months that lie ahead of them. Some of the villagers were so carefree that they even spoke to Calder as he strode through the festival periodically. He tried to be pleasant to them in return, but could not forget that these were the same people who had mumbled and sworn about his every move since his arrival, the same people who tormented Regan and his son. He would be as nice as possible, but he would not trust that their congeniality would last any longer than the length of the festival.

Neither he nor his men spent much time at the festival. The villagers seemed less subdued if they were not around, and he did not want to give them a chance to let the ale work them up into a frenzy and have them start trouble with his men. Calder did spend some time around the merchants' wagons until he found what he was looking for and then made several purchases. With Draco's assistance, he carried them toward Regan's cottage.

*　　　*　　　*

Regan took Radolf to the festival on the day that it began and, although the townspeople had not been so blatantly offensive to them since the rock throwing incident, the cold stares and muttered names as they walked by made her uncomfortable. They returned home again after just a short time and, although Radolf was disappointed, he did not fuss too badly.

She was surprised by a knock on her door one evening and even more taken aback when Calder and Draco strode through it with their arms full. "Milord, what is this?"

Calder smiled triumphantly, as he carefully set some items on the table. "Is Radolf here?"

"He's sleeping."

"Wake him, please. I have a present for him."

Smiling to herself and feeling warm and happy just because Calder was nearby, she hurried over behind the blanket to wake Radolf. Gently shaking his shoulder, she said quietly, "Lord Calder is here with a surprise for you."

Yawning and stretching, the boy made his way over to Calder, his eyes widening and all sleepy thoughts disappearing as he looked at what Calder held in his hands.

"What is it?" he asked.

"A marionette. Watch." Calder played with the strings on the colorfully clothed puppet, making it appear as if it was moving its arms and legs on its own.

Radolf laughed with delight and clapped his hands together. "Zounds," he said excitedly, "can I try it?"

"Of course, it's my gift to you."

Radolf ran toward him and started to grab the puppet, but was stopped cold by a stern matronly voice.

"What do you say first, Radolf?"

"Thank you, Lord Cawer."

"You're welcome, Radolf. Give me a hug and then run and play."

He hugged Calder tightly, then turned and ran back to his pallet, lost to them now, as he became completely engrossed with his new toy.

Realizing that this was his cue, Draco cleared his throat and said, "I will go now and make sure all is well at the festival. Good evening, Milady." With a nod in her direction, he walked toward the door.

"Good evening to you, Draco," Regan replied, just before he shut it behind him.

"And what is this, Milord? More gifts?" she asked, indicating the large wooden crate sitting on the floor between them.

"I thought some eggs might be welcome by you both, so I brought you chickens." He flushed, feeling silly suddenly for doing such a thing.

She smiled warmly at him. "You are a very thoughtful man, Milord. Thank you for both gifts."

"Twas nothing," he said, looking abashed.

"Twas much, Calder, and I do appreciate it." He was sitting in one of the small kitchen chairs and she moved closer to him, pulling his head against her chest and running her hands through his hair. He wrapped his arms around her waist.

Leaning down, she kissed the top of his head, then whispered, "Thank you."

Unable to resist her nearness, he raised his face and drew her head down toward his own, kissing her deeply and savoring the taste of her, the feel of her in his arms.

"I've missed you, Regan. I fear I've been so busy lately, that I've not had any time to spend with you or Radolf."

"We have all been busy, Milord. It is that time of the year....oh!" she exclaimed breathlessly, as he deftly turned her around and sat her on his lap.

Checking quickly to make sure Radolf was still playing with his puppet, he turned his attention back to Regan. Burying his fingers in her long, rich hair, he drew her forward until their lips were barely touching, flicking his tongue playfully over hers before taking full possession.

He finally released her mouth, but the passion in his eyes belied his desire to do so. Running his finger around her full lips, then caressing her cheek and staring deeply into those luminous green orbs, he said, "The King has ordered my presence. I must leave for London in a few days."

He watched those same beautiful eyes cloud over as his words registered and she sat watching him quietly. "Will he let you come back to us?"

"Of course, he will," Calder replied, curious at her response. "Why would you ask that?"

"It is the King's land that we live on, is it not?"

"Yes."

"He can make anyone that he chooses our Overlord, can he not?"

"Yes."

"Why else would he call for you to return to London? Your brother was never required to go." Tears began to form in her eyes and a strong fist squeezed her heart, as she realized how close she might be to losing Calder forever.

"Don't cry, Regan," he said softly, using his finger to wipe away the single tear traveling down her cheek. "King William is my friend. He asked me to come here, gave me these lands against my wishes. He wouldn't take them back now. He wants me to let him know how the castle is coming and to bring his heregeld, of course. That is all."

"Are you sure?"

Calder smiled. "Yes, I am sure. You can't be rid of me that easily, cheri."

Feeling embarrassed at her insecurity, Regan buried her head against his chest and held him tight. "How long will you be gone?"

"I am not sure. It will depend on how long it takes me to get an audience once I reach London. The King is very busy and everyone wants his time. With any luck, it'll just be a few weeks."

"I will miss you," Regan said, her tears burning his skin through his tunic. She had come to rely on him so, for protection, for love, for his kindness and gentle words, and she did not want to be left there alone. Even though she was not able to see him often, just knowing that he was somewhere nearby if she did need him was enough.

"And I, you," he answered sincerely, wishing he could throw her onto her small pallet right that moment and show her how much she meant to him. Instead, he just held her tightly and tried to make her feel safe.

"Will you join me for dinner tomorrow night, Regan? I would like to see you alone before I must leave."

"A little something to remember on your long, cold trip?" she asked with a tremulous smile.

"Something like that," he answered warmly.

*   *   *

The winter storms started in earnest the day Calder and his men rode off to London. As much as he hated the thought of it, he was forced to take a dozen knights along with him, including Draco. The wagons contained a great quantity of silver for King William, and he had to ensure that no thieves or brigands had an opportunity to steal it.

He worried at leaving the village unprotected but knew Garrick would do well acting in his stead. And the bad weather conditions would lessen the chance of any mischief occurring.

*   *   *

Over the next few weeks, the weather continued to worsen. On many days, the strong winds carried chips of ice along with the snow, pelting the flimsy cottages, within which the villagers found small protection.

The cottages were made of a framework of timber, supporting oak or willow wands, which were then covered with a mixture of clay, chopped straw or cow hair and dung. The wind tore through them unmercifully at times.

The thatched roofs suffered the greatest from the blustery winds and the weight of the icy snow, and repairs were being done continuously throughout the village. Many could feel the icy flakes hitting them inside their homes, as the wind and snow whipped down the vent in the roof, which was used to release the smoke from the open hearth inside.

Old men sat around their fires, telling tales of winters past and vicious snowstorms endured, but none could recall one that came so early and blew with such constant ferocity as this one.

It was Regan's first winter alone, without Edgar, and she was worried. Although food was still plentiful, there was not enough wood to keep the fire going, and its meager heat was all she and Radolf had to keep them from freezing to death.

Edgar always made sure that they had a good supply of wood in the past, but Regan was so occupied with her own responsibilities in preparation for the winter, it had not occurred to her to stock up before the snow hit.

Each day, she wrapped a woolen blanket around her head and donned her thin, worn mantle as she struggled through the drifts into the forest. The men had axes and were able to chop down small trees and carry them back. Regan did not have the strength to do so and was forced to break off small branches or dig through the snow for limbs that had broken off due to the weight of the ice and snow.

Wrapping her treasures in another threadbare blanket, she would drag it along behind her as she trudged back to the cottage.

On the days that the blizzard let up, she would try and make at least two trips, so there would be extra wood in the cottage and it had time to dry a little before they used it. The wet wood smoked horribly, burning their eyes and throats as they sat close to the fire to absorb its meager warmth.

Each time that she went out, she as forced to go further and further into the forest. Others were also out collecting wood and it became scarcer and more difficult to find. The long, cold journey through the deep drifts sapped Regan's energy quickly and she had little left by the time she returned to her cottage.

By the end of the first week, she had developed a cough deep in her chest that refused to lessen its hold.

*   *   *

"Good morning," Regan said, opening the door and allowing her mother in, out of the frigid, biting wind.

"Hello, my dear, how are you feeling?" Gayle asked in concern. Regan' face was alarmingly pale and there were deep shadows under her eyes.

"I'm better, I think. The syrup you brought helps with the cough," Regan answered, sitting down at the table and hoping her mother would not realize that she did not have the strength to stand any longer.

"It's the strongest that I know how to make," her mother stated absently, still watching Regan. "I mixed finely ground licorice in with the vinegar and honey to help with the bitter taste. You look very tired, my dear."

"The cough returns in the night and keeps me from sleeping. Radolf, as well, I fear," she said, looking down at where the boy slept on a pallet near the fire.

"Perhaps, Mother," Regan continued hesitantly, "Radolf could stay with you and Father for a few days? I feel terrible keeping him awake all night with my coughing and he worries so about me."

"Certainly, Regan. That would be fine. Why don't you stay with us, as well?"

"Thank you, but I need to stay here to care for the cottage and the chickens. It will just be for a few days, till the cough is gone."

"As you wish," Gayle replied, brushing a curl back from Regan's ashen cheek. "But you've had the cough for over two weeks already, haven't you?"

"Yes, but I feel it's getting better now."

"Will you at least come over and join us for our evening meal?"

"Not tonight, mother. But I'll join you tomorrow, if you don't mind."

"Every night would be wonderful, Regan. We do not get to see you enough anymore."

"Is Father still angry at Lord Calder for discharging him?"

"Some days, he is. Others, he realizes that it was his own sharp tongue that caused the problem. Mayhap, he will apologize to lord Calder and get back into his favor. He enjoyed the position that he was in and would like to be there again."

"Should I talk to Lord Calder about it when he returns?"

"No, dear. Even though he is old, your father still carries the pride of a young man. He would want to do this himself."

"Thank you for taking Radolf," she said, kissing her mother on the cheek before waking Radolf and bundling him up as warmly as possible before he left with his grandmother.

After closing the door tightly behind them, Regan made herself a cup of barley water, vainly hoping that it would relieve some of the stuffiness in her head and the tightness in her chest.

Sighing heavily, and wishing Calder were there to take her into his strong, warm embrace, she set her empty cup on the table. Wrapping a thin blanket around her shoulders, she curled herself up into a ball on the pallet by the fire.

As the days wore on, Regan found herself growing weaker and weaker. Her trips for wood, more often than not, ended with little to nothing to show for it. She no longer had the energy to dig through the deep snow or travel far into the forest.

She would eat a little when she joined her parents and Radolf for their evening meal, but did not have much of an appetite. When she returned to the cold, dark cottage, she would curl up next to the meager fire and sleep.

The cough continued to worsen and, some nights she just lay shivering near the fire, her clothing drenched in sweat produced by her raging fever.

Some days, she would not wake until the sun was high in the sky. Even then, her body ached so that she found it difficult to make herself go back out into the fierce, howling wind to find more wood.

And one day, she did not wake at all.

CHAPTER 20

Calder pushed his men as hard as he dared in the deep snow. The heavily loaded wagons they were bringing back with them made the journey twice as long as it would have been. The conveyances continuously got stuck in the huge drifts that blew across the road, and his men were forced to push them until the wheels were free enough for the oxen to continue on.

He had been away much longer than planned. The King was too busy to see him for the first couple of weeks that he was in London. Even when he had finally been granted an audience, the King had but a few minutes to spare and Calder was not able to broach the subject that he most wanted to discuss.

Calder was not sure how King William would react to the news that he wanted to take a Saxon as his wife. He did not know whether the King would find it acceptable and, therefore, could not mention it to Regan until he was sure that he had the King's permission.

If Calder married her without His Majesty's sanction, he risked having the union annulled. He could possibly even be banished, and he would not take the chance of losing Regan and Radolf.

He was dismayed and frustrated that he had been unable to clarify the situation with King William now, but resolved that when he returned to London in the spring for the tournament, he would convince the King to give his blessing. In the meantime, he must keep his plans from Regan, so that he did not get her hopes up, only to have them crushed later on.

Never had Calder considered marrying before and he was surprised at how strongly he felt about it now, and how anxious he was to have the deed done. He had thought through their situation and realized that the best way to protect Regan, and Radolf, was to marry her. As the Lady of the Manor and the son of the Overlord, no one would dare insult or hurt them any longer for fear of serious reprisal.

Calder was honest enough to admit that this was not something that he was doing solely for their benefit. He wanted his son near him. He wanted to spend time with Radolf; to teach him to hunt, to fish, to sit a horse properly, to watch him grow and help him along on his journey into manhood.

And he wanted Regan always near his side. He wanted to hold her in the dark of the night, wanted to see her bright smile and let it lighten his heart as he went through the rigors of daily life at the castle. He wanted to be able to take her into his arms whenever the mood struck him and not have to worry about who might see them and what repercussions she would suffer because of it.

Calder smiled as he thought of how their life together would be and spurred his horse on, barely able to contain his desire to be back at the Manor with the two of them.

*   *   *

As soon as they arrived at the village, he impatiently instructed his men as to what should be done with the items on the wagon and left Alerio for Skeet to tend as hurried toward Regan's cottage. The smile disappeared from his face when the door was opened by an attractive older woman, not Regan.

"Who are you?" he asked gruffly.

"I am Gayle, Regan's mother, Milord," she replied, with a slight curtsy.

Looking over her shoulder, Calder saw Regan lying on a pallet by the fire. He brushed past the older woman and went to her. Kneeling down next to her unconscious form, he placed his hand on her burning face and looked up at Gayle.

"What has happened to her?"

"Regan is very ill, Milord," Gayle replied, her eyes filling with tears. "She has not been well for several weeks. She did not come to our home last night to join us for our evening meal. When I came to look in on her, I found her like this. I cannot get her to wake, Milord."

"Have you no healer in the village?"

"Yes, but she will not come."

He looked at her sharply. "She refuses to help Regan?"

"Yes, Milord."

"Where is Radolf?" Calder asked, looking around the spartan cottage.

"He has been staying with Filbert and me. Regan refused to."

"Tell me the name of the woman who would not help Regan," he demanded.

"Esme," Gayle answered reluctantly, seeing the anger in his eyes and fearing what he would do.

Calder realized that there was not enough time to send to London for Gideon. By the time he got the message and returned to the village, Regan could be dead.

"Is there anyone else in the village who knows of healing?"

"Bernia," she answered hesitantly, "but she is young and just an apprentice."

A tendril of fear crawled up his back and panic threatened to overwhelm him as the reality of the situation registered. He could not, and would not, allow Regan to die.

"I am taking Regan to the Manor so she can be properly cared for. Go to your home and get Radolf. Bring him to the Manor, he will stay there, as well."

Gayle frowned, not feeling at all comfortable with her grandson staying amidst the Normans. All she knew of Calder was that he was her grandson's father, and that he was a strict, and sometimes heartless, Overlord whom most of the villagers hated and feared. She also knew that it was because of this man's violation of her daughter, that Regan had come to be so mistreated by others in the village.

"I do not believe that would be proper, Milord." She said it quietly, but her voice was filled with determination.

"You worry about Regan's reputation?" Calder asked incredulously.

"Of course."

"What good will her reputation do her if she is left here to die?" he asked angrily. "Get Radolf and bring him to the Manor immediately."

There was no misinterpreting the tone of his voice and Gayle quickly donned her mantle and headed for the door. Before opening it, she turned back to Calder. Tears filled her eyes and worry lined her face, as she asked softly, "May I come to the Manor and help with the care of my daughter?"

Calder softened a little and, with an apologetic smile, said, "Of course. You may spend as much time with her and Radolf as you wish."

He turned back to Regan then, and covered her with the threadbare blanket. Listening the wind howling fiercely outside, he realized the meager covering would not be enough. Removing his own heavy cloak, Calder wrapped that around her also. He quickly made his way back to the Manor with Regan held tightly in his arms, trying to use his own body to block her from the wind.

Draco frowned as he saw the limp, lifeless body that Calder held in his arms. Their eyes met in mutual concern as the Overlord carried her rapidly upstairs to his chamber. Draco began bellowing orders and had servants scurrying around in their haste to obey. Then he made his own way to the bedchamber.

"Seems we've been here before," Draco said in his deep, gravelly voice, recalling the first time they had come across Regan.

"Let's hope we have not come full circle, my friend. She is very ill and I am not sure that this time she will be able to walk out of here."

Calder removed her clothing and placed her under the heavy quilts. Her face was flushed and her skin clammy with the sweat from her fever. Calder tenderly wiped her face with a cool cloth as she tossed and turned restlessly.

Several servants arrived then, some with ewers of water, others with armloads of wood. After the fire had been stoked and they left the room once again, Calder turned to Draco.

"I need you to fetch two women from the village. One is called Esme and the other Bernia. Esme is to wait in the Hall until I come down. Send the other to me as soon as possible. Regan's mother will be bringing Radolf. See that he is taken care of and allow Gayle up here if that is her wish."

"Yes, Milord," Draco replied, and quickly left to do his bidding.

Calder continued to use cool water on Regan's face and body. She moaned and writhed on the bed as her fever raged. He preferred that actually, over the way she had been in the cottage, completely still, as if she were already dead. He could not bear to see her like that.

He sighed in relief when he saw Gayle enter the room, followed by a young woman.

"This is Bernia," Gayle said, glancing worriedly at her daughter, who looked so small and fragile lying beneath the covers of the huge bed.

The girl with her watched Calder in fear and confusion, unaware of why she had been called to the Manor. She was thin and not unattractive, with light brown hair and pale blue eyes. Calder looked at her pointedly.

"You are a healer?" he asked, trying to keep his emotions, which were running rampant, from his voice as he spoke.

"An apprentice, Milord," she said is a shy, quiet voice, lowering her gaze to the floor.

"This is Regan," he said, waving toward the bed, "and she is very ill. Will you help her?"

The girl glanced at the bed and then back in Calder's direction. "As I said, Milord, I am just an apprentice. If she is very ill, you should have Esme look to her."

"I have asked if you will help her. Will you or not?"

"Of course, Milord," she responded nervously.

"You harbor no ill feelings that would keep you from doing your best for her?" He was hesitant to ask anyone in the village for their assistance in this matter, but realized he had no other choice.

"No, Milord. I will do all I can for her, I swear." She spoke sincerely, looking him straight in the eye.

"I will hold you to that," he answered, in a soft but threatening tone of voice. "Gayle will be here to assist you. If there is anything that you need, just ask and you shall have it."

"Thank you, Milord. Now, if you will excuse me, I must see to Regan." Bernia hurried over to the bed and started examining her patient with shaking hands. She could not concentrate with Calder watching her every move and turned back towards him.

"Mayhap, you could go down to the Hall for a short while, Milord. We will call you when we have finished examining her."

Calder stood by the door, feeling inadequate and useless. Anger and fear boiled up inside of him as he realized that he could do nothing for Regan. "Of course," he answered hesitantly, afraid to leave her side. "But call me if there is any change."

"Yes, Milord."

He reluctantly left the bedchamber and made his way downstairs. He had no sooner sat down and taken a healthy draught of ale than Radolf jumped on his lap and wrapped his arms around his neck.

"Lord Cawer," he said excitedly, "you're back."

Calder returned his hug, having to restrain himself so he did not hurt Radolf, as he engulfed the boy in his arms and held him close.

"I missed you. Have you been well?" His voice was tight, strained with worry.

"Yes, Lord Cawer, but my momma is sick." Radolf blinked back tears as he spoke.

"I know, son. That is why I brought her here, so that we can help her get well. I would like you to stay here also. Would you mind that overly much?"

"No," Radolf answered, a smile lighting his face, his worries over his mother suddenly forgotten at the thought of the new adventures to be had inside the Manor.

"You'll have to sleep on a pallet here in the Hall with my knights."

"I can do that," Radolf answered happily.

"And I will take you to see your mother as soon as she feels better."

Radolf's smile faded a little as he thought of his mother, but brightened again at Calder's next comment.

"I have a gift for you that I brought from London. Would you like it now?"

"Yes, I would," he answered, unable to continue sitting still in Calder's lap in his excitement and jumping down to stand beside him.

"Garrick," Calder yelled, "where is Radolf's gift?"

"Taken to the kitchen, Milord. Shall I go get it for you?"

"Yes, and quickly, Garrick. Poor Radolf is getting quite impatient."

A few moments later, Garrick arrived holding a fluffy, wiggling bundle in his arms. He released it onto the floor and the puppy ran in circles around the room, barking shrilly and wagging its tail in happiness.

"He's for me?" Radolf asked in wonder and, at Calder's nod, scampered over to the puppy.

"He is not just to play with, Radolf. You must also feed and care for him." Calder had to raise his voice so that the boy heard him, so engrossed was the child with his new friend.

"Yes, Lord Cawer," he answered absently, rolling the puppy onto its back and tickling its belly. The puppy squirmed out of his grip and leaped onto him, retaliating by knocking Radolf onto the ground and licking his face unmercifully, while the boy giggled and tried to escape.

Calder could not help but feel some of the tension leave his body as he watched Radolf and the puppy disrupt the entire room. His knights were kept busy trying to prevent any serious injuries. Radolf managed to trip over his own feet often enough, but now made several extra trips to the floor as the puppy ran between his legs or grabbed his tunic with its sharp little teeth and caused him to lose his balance.

Calder's mighty knights stood at the ready, making sure there was no contact with any of the large heavy pieces of furniture.

The smile Calder was wearing as he watched their antics dropped from his face when he saw Draco approaching with an old woman. Her white hair and bent frame were covered by a heavy mantle. Her wizened face was set as she approached, and he could see the hate and mistrust in her eyes when she glared at him.

"Garrick, take the boy and his puppy to the kitchen for a bit," he ordered, not wanting Radolf to hear what was about to be said.

"You are Esme?" he asked, after he was sure Radolf was gone from the room.

"Yes," she answered sullenly.

"You are the healer of the village?"

"Yes," she answered again, knowing why she was there, but feeling no compulsion to make excuses to this man for her actions.

"You were asked to help Regan, but you refused?"

"Yes," she answered, this time somewhat arrogantly.

"Why?" Calder could feel the anger growing inside of him and tried to subdue it.

Esme studied him for a moment, then shrugged, deciding that she was the one with the power at this moment and that she had nothing to fear from the Overlord. He needed her and she knew that he would not harm an old woman, not when she was the only one who might, possibly be able to save Regan.

"She is a whore and a traitor to her people. She deserves to die."

Calder's face froze and his knuckles turned white with tension as he gripped the tankard of ale. He had to wait a moment before speaking, until the red haze of fury cleared from his head a little and he was able to voice words in a reasonably calm manner. "You will leave my lands this day, old woman, and never return."

His voice was cold and his eyes were chips of blue ice. The scar along his cheek was a vivid red against his skin. He felt no remorse for banishing the hag, in his eyes, he was being as merciful as his anger would allow. The old woman was lucky that he did not run her through with his sword at that very moment.

The wrinkled skin on her face sagged as she stared at him, her mouth open in astonishment.

"You cannot do that, M'lord," her voice came out no louder than a whisper.

"Yes, I can and I have. Now leave my sight before I do you harm."

Everyone in the room watched silently.

"Graeham," Calder yelled, when the woman made no move to leave, "escort her home. Do not leave her side until she has left my lands."

"But," the old woman whined, "I will freeze to death. I have nowhere to go. Please, Milord, have pity."

Calder stared at her coldly. "I show you the same pity that you showed Regan."

"She deserves no one's pity," the woman cried shrilly.

"Graeham," Calder said, with a nod at the woman. Graeham took her arm and dragged her toward the door.

Yanking her thin arm from his grip, she turned back toward Calder with narrowed eyes. "Your whore dies as we speak, as it should be. Whether I live or die once I leave this place, I will not rest until I see you and your bastard son join her in hell."

Graeham roughly grabbed her arm again and dragged her through the door before she could say anything further.

"Post more guards this evening, Draco. I fear there may be some trouble."

"I believe you may be right, Milord." Draco replied dryly as walked over to advise the men.

CHAPTER 21

Gayle returned to Regan's room at daylight. She had gone home to sleep for a few hours, but it was difficult in coming. Between her worry for Regan, and the comings and goings of the villagers all night, she had gotten little rest.

She found it ironic that the people came to Filbert for help in dealing with the Overlord, when it was Esme's treatment of their own daughter that had started the wheels in motion for this particular situation.

Esme and her husband had been escorted off the lands, but some members of the village were making plans to sneak them back and hide them without Calder's knowledge.

Filbert had warned them not to do so, at least not until he had a chance to try and reason with Calder. They had agreed to wait one day before taking matters into their own hands, but the anger and tension against the Normans was palpable. Nothing good would come of this, Gayle feared.

She would not speak to the others or involve herself in their mischief. She was consumed with fear that her daughter might die. And it was because of Esme and the others that it might happen. Gayle had tried to maintain a healthy relationship with the other villagers, even though she was well aware of how they treated Regan and her grandson.

It broke her heart, but what could she do? There were so many of them and she was afraid that they would ostracize her as well. But now they had gone too far. Her daughter's life was in danger and she would no longer forgive and forget. She was filled with shame that it had taken something so extreme for her to be able to place her daughter's well-being above her own.

Gayle hesitated when she opened the door to Regan's room and found Calder asleep in a chair next to the bed. His face was relaxed while he slumbered, but then his brows creased and he began to mumble incoherently. The only word she was able to make out was her daughter's name.

"Mayhap, I have been wrong about this man," she thought. He was an enigma to her. She held him responsible for violating her daughter and causing all that had befallen Regan since, and blamed him for the death and destruction that had come to their village with the Normans arrival. Yet, there he sat all through the night, unable to leave her daughter's side in his worry.

"Mayhap, Regan was the only one of us that was able to see what his heart truly holds," she thought, a slight smile gracing her lips.

She roused herself from her thoughts when she saw that he was awake and studying her as closely as she had been him.

"Good morn to you, Lord Calder," she said nervously. "Has there been any change?"

"No," he replied sadly, gently pushing a curl back from Regan's flushed cheek. "I fear the fever may be worse now. She tossed and turned restlessly all night. Nothing seems to help. Will Bernia return?"

"I hope so, Milord. But," she hesitated, unsure of how much she could trust him, "feelings are running very strong right now amongst the villagers. If she returns to the Manor, they will make her suffer for it."

"I created those feelings and may have killed Regan in the process." He felt so disheartened and guilty that he buried his head in his hands. "I was so angry at the old woman that I did not consider the repercussions of my actions."

He felt a hand on his shoulder and looked up into Gayle's eyes, which were brimming with unshed tears.

"I can see how much you care for my daughter, Milord, and I know that you would never do anything to deliberately cause her harm. Her father and I failed her. Edgar failed her. This whole village failed her. But you have not. We will see her through this. She is a very strong woman. She would not let her own people beat her, and she surely will not let a silly illness beat her. Have faith, Milord."

Calder took her hand and kissed it gently. "Thank you, Gayle. I think it must be you that she gets her strength from, and I know that she will not give up the fight. You are right. We must have as much courage as she, to help her through this."

He was interrupted when Bernia opened the door and approached the bed. "Thank you for coming," he said, looking at her with a mixture of profound relief and gratitude.

"I have a patient to care for, Milord," she answered simply. Her brow furrowed as she felt Regan's forehead and realized the fever still raged as strong as ever.

"Milord," she said, suddenly realizing the limits of her knowledge and becoming unsure of herself. "I am only an apprentice and do not know all the ways of healing. We must break her fever or she will die. I am not sure how to do so. I have tried all the herbs and tisanes that I know of."

She looked at him, pleading silently for his understanding and trust.

He gave her a wan smile in return. "So, there is nothing more that can be done?"

"I have heard tell of dunking a person in the river. The cold water makes the body cool down and rids them of the fever."

Calder looked hopeful for a moment, then crestfallen. "It is too dangerous. There is too much snow and ice along the banks of the river now. We could easily lose her in it and cannot chance it."

He paced the room in frustration, feeling so inadequate and angry at what was happening that he wanted to scream his rage and bury his sword into something, anything, but realizing the futility of it. Fate had caused Regan to become ill, and fate was a fickle master that could not be challenged.

Turning to Bernia, he grasped both her hands in his own. "She is all that is good and right with my life. I cannot, and will not, live without her. Please help me."

Bernia was taken aback by the pain and devotion with which he spoke those words and touched by the depth of his emotions. She had never spoken with Regan herself, several years separated their ages and by the time she was old enough to understand, all she heard was that Regan was possessed by the devil and had turned against her own people and into the arms of the Normans.

Looking at this handsome Norman warrior in front of her, his love so evident on his face, she wondered if she might also sell her soul to the devil and turn her back on her own people, if it was she that he felt so strongly about. Inspiration suddenly struck Bernia like a brick hitting her between the eyes and she knew what they had to do.

"Milord," she said sharply, "have you a bathing tub?"

"Yes."

"Have it brought here right away. Have your men bring in as many buckets of snow as they can carry. We will pack Regan in the snow to see if that will break the fever."

She spoke excitedly, confident that her idea would work. Calder was encouraged by her attitude and quickly bolted down the stairs to do as she asked.

For the next several hours, a battalion of servants and knights continuously brought up buckets of snow to replace that which melted. At long last, Regan's body responded and Bernia declared with a tired smile that the fever had broken.

Calder gently lifted Regan from the tub and dried her off carefully with a towel before placing her back under the heavy blankets on the bed.

"Bernia," he said softly, unable to remove his eyes from Regan's now pale face, "I always remember a good turn done me. You will be richly rewarded for this."

"I do not expect payment, Milord. I did what I have been training to do most of my life. And she is not out of the woods yet. We still do not know for sure if she will recover." She did not want Calder to get his hopes up, only to lose Regan later this day.

She touched his arm. "You should go rest now. I will call you if she wakes."

He shook his head wearily, smiling at her. "No, I will be here by her side when she wakes. But, thank you. You have worked hard, go downstairs and eat something. As you said, it is not over yet and she will still need you."

"As you wish, Milord," the girl replied, turning and walking toward the door.

Gayle had been working with them in the room the whole morning. As the hours passed, she had become more and more convinced of Calder's love for Regan. After witnessing his conversation with Bernia, she realized that he was not the demon that the other villagers had made him out to be after all.

She approached him slowly, as he tucked the blankets tighter around Regan's sleeping body. "Thank you, Milord, for interceding and saving my daughter's life."

"She is not well yet, Gayle. And there is no need to thank me. I do what I do for purely selfish reasons. I do not want my son to grow up without the love of his mother. And I cannot imagine how I would get through my days if Regan were not in them."

He spoke softly and tenderly, and tears rose in Gayle's eyes as she listened. She looked down at her sleeping daughter and ran a hand over her hair. Her voice was almost a whisper as she said, "Talk to her, Lord Calder. I'm sure that wherever she is right now, she will hear you. Tell her how much you love her and how much we all need her. Help her the rest of the way through this, Milord."

*　　*　　*

"You came back to me," Calder said softly, almost in disbelief, as Regan opened her eyes and looked at him in confusion later that day.

"Came back?" she croaked, her voice cracking, her throat parched.

"Here, love," Calder said tenderly, lifting her head and bringing a cup of water to her lips.

"Where am I?"

"You've been ill, Regan," he said, running his hand over the porcelain skin of her face. "You had us very worried."

His voice broke as relief flooded through him. Unable to help himself, he pulled her into his arms and held her tightly. She groaned softly and he forced himself to release her. "I'm sorry, are you alright? Can I get you something?"

She smiled weakly at him. "I feel like I've been run over by a team of oxen and so hungry that I could eat those very same oxen."

"Of course, I will see to it right away." He ran to the door and bellowed for Bernia and Gayle, and for food to be brought up posthaste. The women arrived moments later, smiling in relief as they ran to Regan's bedside.

Bernia respectfully had the trencher, which was piled high with food, sent back to the kitchen and asked for broth to be sent up instead.

"But she is hungry," Calder stated angrily.

"Milord, she has not eaten in days. She must start with something light or she will not be able to keep it down."

"Oh." Watching the women take over with Regan's care, Calder felt out of place and in the way. He slowly backed toward the door. Regan caught his eye before he left and, to his surprise, winked at him. He blew her a kiss in return and slipped quietly from the room.

*   *   *

"You've drunk enough for three men, Milord. Perhaps you would like some food to go with the ale?"

Draco's raspy voice barely registered, but Calder turned toward him and smiled. "She will live," he said softly, raising his tankard in a toast.

Draco laughed and raised his own against it. "She is one hell of a woman, Milord."

"Aye, that she is. And she will be mine, Draco. Make no mistake about that." His words were slurred, relief and lack of food and sleep contributing to his inebriation as much as the ale itself.

"You should sleep now, Milord, she will need you on the morrow. You'd best be ready for her."

"Yes, my friend," Calder replied, clasping Draco's shoulder. "You are right, as always. Thank you for tending to things while I sat with her. Did all go well?"

"Tomorrow is soon enough to discuss those matters, Milord. Get some sleep now."

As if he had been waiting for permission, Calder's head slowly sank to the table. He was snoring lightly just moments later.

*   *   *

Even his pounding head could not keep the jubilance off Calder's face as he raced up the stairs and into Regan's bedchamber. "Hello, love," he said tenderly, as he leaned down and kissed her dry, cracked lips. "How do you fare this morn?"

"I feel very sore and tired but, other than that, I am wonderful," she said with a weak smile. "And you, Milord?"

"I feel as if I have been reborn, Regan. Had you died, the most important part of me would have died with you. I love you, Regan, and cannot live without you by my side."

"Oh, Calder," she said softly, tears slipping quietly down her cheeks as he took her in his arms.

Relinquishing his grip on her, he laid her back against the pillows. "Don't ever scare me like that again."

"Yes, Milord," she replied with a smile. Her face was still very pale, with deep, dark shadows under her eyes, and she ached in every joint of her body. He could see that she was still very tired and, with a peck on her cheek and a squeeze of her hand, he admonished her to get some sleep.

"Will you stay with me awhile longer?"

"Of course, love," he responded, getting into the bed and pulling her head against his broad chest as she fell back into an exhausted sleep.

Gayle and Bernia entered the room a short time later and found the two of them sound asleep, cuddled in each other's arms. Smiling at one another, the two women quietly stepped out of the room and closed the door behind them.

*　　*　　*

"So, Draco, what has been happening?" Calder asked later that day, feeling completely refreshed and at ease now that Regan was improving.

"I hate to ruin you high spirits, Milord."

Calder looked at Draco and, with a heavy sigh, said, "Let me hear, Draco. From the look of you it has not been going well."

"Someone started a fire in the stable and several of our men were attacked with stones thrown at them in the dark as they hurried to put it out. I do not know the identity of the culprits as yet, and feel the mischief has only just begun."

"How much damage to the stable?"

"Little, we were able to put it out quickly. None of the horses were injured."

Calder nodded. "Well, that is something good, at least."

"And Filbert wishes to speak with you as soon as possible. I'm sure it's to plead for the hag."

"And if I do not allow her to return, things will get worse."

"So, it would seem."

"We shall see about that," Calder said thoughtfully. "Bring him to me."

"Yes, Milord," Draco said, as he stood and made his way from the Hall.

* * *

"Good e'en to you, Milord," Filbert said as he leaned forward on the table, hoping Calder would offer him some ale so that he could settle his nerves. His last conversation with the Overlord had not gone well and he anticipated that this one may not either.

"The people are very upset that you would banish two elderly people with little money and nowhere to go. You have sentenced them to death."

"I banished only Esme, no one else. Are you aware of why I did so?" Calder was leaning back in his chair, staring at Filbert with cold eyes.

Pausing momentarily, Filbert replied, "Yes, I am, Milord."

"And still you come to me asking for leniency?"

"You must understand, Milord, these are my people. They look to me to ask you for fairness, for justice."

"Your daughter almost died. You did not even come here to see how she fared. You did not come to see if she still lived. You spent that time plotting with the same people who contributed to her circumstances, the ones who would not help her when she needed it most."

Calder paused to stare at Filbert. He wanted to understand why a father would do such a thing, but was only able to find pity for an old man who was too weak to stand up for himself, a man who valued the opinion of others more than he did the welfare of his own daughter.

Filbert refused to look away from Calder, but could feel his face flushing in embarrassment.

"How can you come to me and ask leniency for a woman who called your child a whore and said she deserved to die, for an evil woman who wished for the death of your own grandson?"

"There is much you will never understand, Milord."

"Enlighten me," Calder replied coldly.

"You Normans came here and took everything from us. We have spent years rebuilding our homes, mourning the deaths of our kin and friends that were murdered on behalf of your King William. We finally got our crops growing again, and then you arrive. You take us away from our own fields to build your grand castle. We give you our blood, our sweat and our time, all at the risk of our crops, and then you take more than half of what we have for taxes. A man can only tolerate so much before he must forget about his fear and take a stand against his oppressors."

Calder sat quietly, watching in amazement as Filbert continued his speech.

"Forgive me, Milord," Filbert's voice was rising as his emotions surfaced, "but we have given all we have to give. We cannot just accept it when you arbitrarily banish valued members of community, people we have known and loved for many years and who will die if they are sent from here. You have no right to do such a thing."

Filbert jumped as Calder slammed his tankard of ale onto the table, spilling it onto both of them.

"You, hypocritical bastard," the knight stated softly, shaking his head in disgust. "When my brother came here, he taught you all better ways of farming. He increased the yields of every member of this village and, in return, they refused to pay him his due in taxes. I build a castle to protect you and your people and my lands. That has been my primary purpose since I arrived here, but you refuse to see it."

"I understand the anger you must have felt when we arrived, but enough time has passed and I have been very patient and very fair with all of you. I now expect my due. I expect the loyalty and the fealty of these people. They are no longer *your* people, Filbert. They will be *my* people and will do my bidding with no argument."

"That will not happen, Milord," Filbert replied bravely.

"Yes, it will. If not, they will not live on these lands. It is as simple as that. King William rules this country. I act in his stead, with all of the powers that he has granted me. There are homeless people throughout the country. They would be happy to come here and be part of my community, should you, and others like you, decide you cannot swear fealty to me."

"I do respect you, Milord," Filbert said icily. "You are intelligent, and when your anger does not cloud your judgment, you do try to be fair. But you will always be a Norman."

"And what is your grandson?"

There was a momentary silence, and then Filbert replied, "A bastard, Milord, never to be accepted by either people. And that is your doing."

The silence was so heavy in the room at that moment, that only the jangle of chainmail could be heard, as the knights shifted uncomfortably. Filbert misjudged the extent of their loyalty to Calder, and many were hard put to keep their swords sheathed when the old man spoke to him so disrespectfully.

Calder's voice was cold and steady when he replied. "Yes, Filbert, it was my doing and it fills me with the greatest pride to know that I could create such a child. As Radolf's father, I will let no one, Norman or Saxon, harm him. I will make sure that he feels so loved that it matters not if he is one or the other. He is my child and that is enough for me. Can you say the same?"

Filbert stared at him defiantly. "I love my daughter and my grandson, even if they have been disgraced because of you. You have no right to imply that I do not."

"Even as you ask me not to punish the woman who would let your daughter die? Who said Regan was a whore and deserved such a fate."

The silence was forbidding as Filbert answered. "That is what you made her in their eyes."

A strong, feminine voice came from the bottom of the stairs. "And what of *your* eyes, Filbert? Do you also think of your daughter as such?"

All heads turned as Gayle walked toward the two men. Her face was set, her eyes snapping in anger.

"Of course not."

"Then leave here. You will not defend the woman who was willing to let our daughter die. Do not embarrass me like this, Filbert."

Their eyes met in a heated stare, each angrier than they had ever been with one another before.

"Regan is our daughter," Gayle continued. "She is much more important than anything we have, including our so-called friends and neighbors. It's about time that we started showing her that."

Filbert glared at his wife for a moment longer, then stated quietly, "I will not be the one responsible for what happens now."

He stood then and strode angrily from the Manor.

CHAPTER 22

Calder's knights were busy that evening. Many of the villagers braved the cold night air to start fires and throw rocks and chunks of ice at the knights as they attempted to douse them. The knights' frustration and anger increased and, inevitably, violence broke out.

"Milord," Garrick said brusquely, as he strode into the Hall, "we are unable to control the mob. Per your instructions, we have not drawn our weapons. Now our men are getting injured."

His tone was angry, almost accusatory.

Sighing deeply, angry himself that the situation was still so unstable, even after all of this time, Calder turned toward Garrick.

"From this day on, there will be a curfew at dark. Take all the men and roam the village. Be sure everyone knows that they must be inside their homes by the time the sun goes down, which will be shortly now. Anyone found outside once darkness comes will be tied in the cellar until it is my pleasure to release them. We will talk more this evening, Garrick, and decide what else needs to be done. But make sure we keep enough men outside on patrol during the night."

"Yes, Milord," Garrick said with a nod, turning to leave.

"And Garrick," Calder said, halting him mid-stride.

"Yes, Milord?"

"I will allow no further violence against my knights. Use whatever force is necessary, but try not to let our men get out of hand."

"As you wish, Milord," Garrick said with a slight, satisfied smile.

Calder turned back toward the flames and watched, mesmerized, as they danced in the great fireplace. Staring intently, he tried to determine what his next course of action would be. He had tried to be fair with these people, but they only continued to thwart his every move. The time for leniency was over. Now he would show them who owned these lands, once and for all.

His thoughts were interrupted as Gayle quietly approached.

"Milord," she said nervously, finding it difficult to meet his angry gaze.

"Yes?"

"I wish only to try and explain my husband's actions, if you have the time."

Calder stared askance at her. "Why would you feel the need? Is that not his responsibility?"

"I think, mayhap, he does not even understand his own actions all of the time."

"What would you have me believe of them, then?"

"Filbert is an old man. He has lived in this village, with these people, his whole life. During that lifetime, he has lived under seven different sovereigns and even more Ealdormen." She spoke rapidly, trying to keep her courage up. "Each time the power has changed hands our lives have been changed. We have lived at the whim of many different men. Sometimes, it has not been easy."

Calder watched her closely, admiring her for speaking to him so and, helping him gain an inkling of what ran through these Saxons' hearts and minds.

"During all these times, we have had only each other to count on. It is difficult to choose a new Warlord over one's own people; friends who have stood beside us and helped us, as we have helped them when needed. Filbert has been the spokesman for the village for many years. In his mind, he is responsible to them and for them, to ensure the treatment that they get is as good as can be obtained. It is difficult for him to change his loyalty after all this time."

"Thank you for explaining," Calder replied, without much warmth. "But, even so, I will never be able to understand how he could choose anyone over his own daughter. She has been mistreated for years and he has not made any attempt to correct the situation. With his strong position in the village, he should have taken a stand. Because he would not do so, I will not take pity on him now."

"It was because of his position that he did nothing," Gayle answered nervously, her voice shaking as she realized how angry Lord Calder was at her husband. Her own anger at Filbert began to fade as fear for his safety took its place.

"I do not understand."

"His loyalty is with the people of this village. Regan let you, a Norman, bed her and get her with child. She embarrassed him in the eyes of his own people. He loves her dearly but, I believe that, deep down, he feels she deserved the treatment that she got."

"And you?" His voice was even colder and harder now and Gayle worried that she was making the situation worse.

"I could do little, Milord. But I always did whatever I could for my daughter and my grandson. And I will continue to do so. I have never been ashamed of Regan, nor of anything that she has done. Having met you, I can understand her attraction to you. I can only hope that you care enough about her in return to put right the situation you created for her, and not hurt her any further by hurting her father. She will see that it is due to her own plight and will blame herself. Please do not cause any more harm to my family."

Calder graced her with a slight smile. "I can see where Regan gets her courage, and her skill for persuasion."

His smile faded and his eyes shone with sincerity as he continued. "You may trust me on this, Gayle. I will not harm your husband, unless he does something further that leaves me no choice. And I will make right the situation with Regan and Radolf. You have my word on that."

"Thank you, Milord," Gayle said, breathing out a great sigh of relief and, after curtsying to him, quickly left the room.

Calder leaned back in his chair, taking a long swallow of ale and thinking over what she had said to him. He wondered if Filbert had the slightest idea how graced his life was with those two women in it. He thought not.

*   *   *

Regan moaned softly as he brushed the hair from her forehead. Turning to Bernia, he said, "She does not seem to be doing any better."

"But she is, Milord. She sleeps peacefully most of the time. The fever is gone. It will take some time of rest for her body to fully recover, but she is doing as well as can be expected."

"I have imposed a curfew on the town and everyone must be in their homes by dark. You should go now. I will have one of my men escort you, so that you will not run into any trouble."

Bernia heard the sounds outside and knew there had been fighting between the knights and the villagers. She was afraid, not for herself, but for what was still to come. "Thank you, Milord. Gayle will stay the night with Regan. I will return at first light."

"I appreciate all that you have done for Regan. I will not forget it." With a blush and a curtsy, Bernia headed for the door.

"Draco is in the Hall. Tell him that I would like him to escort you home. And then send Gayle up and ask her to bring Radolf with her.

"Yes, Milord."

*   *   *

"But, M'lord," Holt interrupted, holding a cloth to his bleeding forehead. The cut was due to a piece of ice, thrown from the shadows as he was making his rounds. "The curfew is a start, but these addle-headed simpletons need a show of force. We have been too soft on them and now they think they can dictate to us. It is unthinkable and must be dealt with."

"I agree, Holt," Calder replied, much to everyone's surprise. He had done his best to be lenient and fair with these people, hoping that, over time, a relationship of mutual trust might develop between them. Obviously, that had not worked and now these people's misconceptions as to their own power must be corrected. "How many are in the cellar?"

"Seven, M'lord," Graeham replied. "I worry about the servants, though. They are friends to these men and may loosen their ties so that they can escape or cause trouble here in the Manor."

"Post a guard at the entrance to the room. One will have to be on duty at all times as long as there are prisoners. See that they receive no food or water until tomorrow morning, Graeham."

"Yes, M'lord," he said, leaving quickly to do as he was ordered.

Calder had just opened his mouth to continue when the door to the Manor banged open and Davis came in, carrying a limp, lifeless body in his arms. Calder and the others ran to his side.

"Damn these people," Calder said angrily, when he saw that it was Bernia that Davis carried. "What happened to her?"

"I found her on the ground outside one of the cottages. It looks like they beat her, and then threw her out in the snow."

"Take her to one of the empty bedchambers, quickly," he added, as Davis continued to stare at the young girl in his arms. "Draco, get Gayle from Regan's room and bring her to me."

Bernia had bruises from one end of her body to the other, but she regained consciousness quickly and it seemed she would suffer no permanent injury.

"Who did this to you, Bernia?" Calder asked softly, after Gayle had tended to her.

The tears slid down her bruised cheeks as she looked at Calder, "I cannot say, Milord."

"You cannot or you will not?"

"I will not," she replied bravely.

"Why? Those cowards beat a woman. Where is the honor in that? What is the good in hiding their identities? Tell me who they are and I will show them justice." His tone was hard and cold as his dark blue eyes bore into hers.

She just shook her head and sobbed into the pillow

Calder forced himself to soften his tone and turned her face back to his. "You did nothing wrong. You gave aid to another human being who needed you. Why do you protect these people after what they have done?"

"Because they are my people," she answered tearfully. "I will not see them hurt because of me."

Calder shook his head in disgust. "You will stay in the Manor for now. You will not return to your home without my permission and the escort of my guards. Do you understand?"

She nodded her head hesitantly, frightened at the thought of having to be around these Normans day after day, but even more frightened now of her own friends and family. She understood suddenly how Regan must have felt all these years and a rush of empathy engulfed her. *How had the world turned so crazy in such a short time,* she wondered dismally.

Once back in the Hall, Calder addressed his men.

"This madness stops now. I will have all of the villagers called to the square first thing in the morning. There will probably be trouble and we will be prepared to crush it as soon as it begins. I will tolerate this sanctimonious treason no longer."

His men actually look excited at the prospect of an altercation. After spending so many years defending their lives while fighting Saxons, it had been difficult to sit back and watch these peasants treat their Overlord, and themselves, with such disrespect. They were ready to put these people in their place and show them who their conquerors were, hopefully, for the last time.

*   *   *

The following morning, the sun was bright but the frigid temperatures kept the villagers subdued. Calder made them wait in the Square a suitable period of time before going out to stand at the top of the stairs. His men wore full battle dress. Some were astride their great destriers, circling behind the crowd. The rest of his men formed a semi-circle in front of him, facing the villagers with their hands resting on the hilts of their sheathed swords and a look of deadly intent on their faces.

Draco stood next to him. As always, he wore only a sleeveless jack over his leggings, his mantle thrown over one shoulder as if he had no need of it, even in this bitter cold.

Calder himself wore only chainmail over his tunic and leggings. His heavy fur mantle was wrapped snuggly around him, but could be thrown off instantly should he need more freedom in the event fighting ensured.

"Almost five years ago now, we came to this village and took it back in the name of William, the true King of these lands." Calder began to pace back and forth along the top of the steps, turning to stare out at the crowd periodically as he did so. There were disgruntled murmurs but, so far, the crowd remained calm.

"King William is a just and fair man. When he took over the throne, he admonished all of his castellans that they were to treat you people as they would villagers from our home country."

"For cripe's sake," one man bellowed, "ye killed half of us afore you even won the lands. And we've heard about the murdering you Normans did elsewhere. Killing women and children and leaving most to die of starvation after you burnt their homes and fields. How fair and just is that?"

The man fell to his knees with a woof as he was struck in the kidneys by the flat side of Davis' sword.

"Do not interrupt me," Calder said in a quiet tone, but one nevertheless filled with a dangerous promise should he be disobeyed. "King William also instructed his men that any revolt would be quashed quickly and with definite finality. There was to be no question as to who these lands belonged to. That was done, sometimes a little more zealously than may have been necessary," he added, with a pointed look at the man still on his knees. "But, then, the lesson was learned and, had some ruthlessness not been engaged in, mayhap there would have been more deaths, on both sides."

"Both my brother and I tried to be reasonable with you. Aric helped you learn better ways to farm and increase your crops. In return, you poisoned him and caused his death. By doing so, you brought me here."

He stopped pacing and stared down into the crowd. The mumbling was getting louder, but he had not lost control of them yet. "I am trying to build a castle, which will be used for your protection, should there be trouble.

I asked for your help in doing so, you refused, and so I had to force you. I asked that you pay your taxes as decreed by King William and you refused, so I had to force you. In an attempt to hurt me, you stole from yourselves and caused the death of one of my men and many of your own in the process. You have rallied against me at every turn, and still I sat quietly and attempted to be lenient so that we could learn to work and live together."

The villagers' grumbling became louder as they scoffed at the thought of Calder being lenient. In their eyes, he ruled with a heavy hand, one that allowed him to take even more from their already meager lives.

"When the castle is completed in the spring, there will be many jobs to fill. The people that fill them will have to consort with me and my men on a daily basis. How will the rest of you treat them, should they choose to take a position with me that will give them more income and, perhaps, more power in the community?"

"I have watched you all terrorize and humiliate one of your own time after time, simply because of her association with me. Last night, a bloodied and beaten young girl was brought to me. She was brutalized by you, her friends and family, simply because she did as I asked and helped save the life of another. It is time for you to look to yourselves and see the poison that festers within you. We are the not the barbarians here. You are."

The disgust was evident on his face, as well as in his voice now. "I have tried to treat you like fellow human beings. But, again and again, you show me only how shallow and backward you are in your thoughts and in your feelings. Well, I have finally learned all that I needed to from you. You cannot be treated as civilized people. You respond only to brutality and punishment. So be it then."

The disgruntled murmuring of the crowd grew stronger, but none would call out, not wanting to be singled out by one of the armed knights patrolling so closely to them.

"It ends today!" Calder shouted suddenly at the group. "Any further violence against my men, or anyone who is doing service for me or has an association with me for one reason or another, will be dealt with swiftly and severely. I will no longer tolerate your intolerance. Learn this well, people, for it will not be told to you again."

He could not miss the hatred in the faces that looked up at him. "Now, go to your homes and cause no more trouble. Should the old hag be sneaked back into town, neither she, nor anyone that helps her, will be shown any mercy. Should you refuse to help me in the spring, when work on the castle resumes, I will immediately banish you from my lands. There are many people who would gladly trade some of their time for the privilege of farming this soil. Remember that, if you think to play me false when next I ask for your assistance."

The mumbling and grumbling raised a notch or two in volume as people began to disband. Calder was just turning toward Draco when a sharp stone suddenly struck him in the cheek. Turning back immediately, Calder saw one of the village men look at them in terror and turn to flee. Draco bounded down the steps before Calder even had a chance to move.

Draco thrust his large body through the crowd and launched himself at the man. Rolling with him on the ground for a moment, knocking the wind out of the smaller, thinner man, he grabbed him by the scruff of the neck and stood up.

"Hang him," Calder announced as coldly as any executioner ever had.

All hell broke out after his decree. The villagers allowed their pent-up anger and frustration to get the better of them and began to attack Calder's men. They used their hands, homemade weapons they had secretly made and hidden in their tunics, rocks, ice, anything they could lay their hands on. But they were no more successful than they had been the first time Calder and his men arrived on their soil and were easily subdued by the well-trained knights.

Dead and injured villagers littered the ground within minutes, no match for the mighty broadswords swung effortlessly by the knights. Women screamed and cried as they threw themselves on the bodies of their men where they lay in the bloody snow.

Calder, seeing that his men had the situation under control, had not joined in the melee. He was so angry at these people that he was afraid of what he might do to them. He was furious that they had brought the situation to this point, consumed with a deadly rage because they refused to be conquered and submit to his rule.

"What did you hope to accomplish?" he bellowed, his voice filled with loathing and contempt. "Did you really think that you were men enough to defeat my knights? And had you been able to do so, did you not realize that King William would have come down upon you with all of his vengeance, and no one in this village would have survived? Get to your homes now. Leave the dead. They will be buried another time. I will not have any of you in my sight at this moment."

The injured were helped to their homes and the dead lay where they had fallen.

Seeing that Draco still held the man who had started the whole incident, he called out, "Hang him now. Then take your men and search each home for weapons. Confiscate what you find and bring the owners to the cellar. If you have any trouble, deal with it as you see fit."

"Yes, Milord," Draco replied, as he dragged the struggling man along behind him.

*　　*　　*

"You're awake," Calder whispered softly, brushing back the limp curls that framed Regan's face. Even her hair seemed to have lost its luster and buoyancy due to her illness.

"Yes," she responded weakly.

"Are you feeling any better?"

"Yes, much," she answered. "I am just so tired all the time. I feel as if I have aged twenty years."

"Sleep will help you, love. Rest as much as you can. Radolf is being well taken care of by Gayle and my men." With a wry smile, he added, "They are teaching him some interesting new games, and the colorful language that goes into playing them properly."

Regan smiled at him, groaning in mock despair, then her smile faded as she studied his lined face more closely. "You seem upset, Calder. Is all well?"

He wished that he could share with her what he carried inside; wished he could unburden himself by explaining how frustrated and angry he was at the rest of the people in the village. But it would serve no purpose other than to upset her and delay her recovery.

Being a leader of men, he had learned long ago never to show when he was unsure of himself. It would only cause his men to worry needlessly and lose their respect for his actions and decisions. It was so ingrained in him that he would not now change who he was and unburden himself, particularly on the shoulders of a woman.

"Everything will be fine, Regan. You must not concern yourself with anything other than getting well. I miss your company and pray you will be back by my side soon."

Looking at him thoughtfully, realizing there was much more happening than he was letting on, she reached her hand up to his face and traced the thin scar on his cheek. Worriedly, she said, "That is my wish, as well, Milord. After all, I must fear for my son and fret over the influence of your bawdy knights on his very soul." Then she smiled up into his stunned face. "'And I miss your smile and your touch and your conversation, most heartily, Milord."

Calder's face softened as he stared down into her luminous green eyes, which were fixed so pointedly on his own. "God only knows what I would do if I could not have you near me, Regan. You are all that is good and true in my life and I would give my own for you, need be."

She was surprised and touched by his words, which were spoken so fervently, and tears filled her eyes as she demanded softly, "Come, lay with me for a short while."

He gently lowered his muscular frame onto the bed and wrapped his arms around her. Regan fell asleep a short time later, with her head resting comfortably on his chest, listening to the persistent thumping of his heart. Calder stroked her hair and studied her face as she slept. He felt so relaxed and comfortable with her in his arms that he too drifted off to sleep, able to forget for a short time the troubles and pressures still to be dealt with.

CHAPTER 23

Over the next few weeks, Regan slowly recovered her strength. Tension remained high between the villagers and the Normans, but there were no further altercations. No one had been restrained in the cellar since that first week. The cold, damp room, along with only bread and water to eat, made a lasting impression on those that had been there, and none of the others cared to enjoy the same discomfort.

Calder had his men on the training field daily, regardless of the weather. He realized how soft he and his men had become and was determined to remedy the situation. The uneasy feeling that had pushed him to get the castle built had lessened during the winter season, but there was still a small niggling of uneasiness that he could not rid himself of.

Besides, he and his men would be attending the tourney in London come spring and, although it was, purportedly, just fun and games, the participants knew better. Depending on the terms agreed to, a man could lose much should he be defeated, including his gear, his horse, his lands or even his life. Calder had rarely lost any contest, but he would be up against Roderick's men, and they were as underhanded and deceitful as their leader. It would not be easy to beat them, but Calder had no question in his mind that it would be done.

*   *   *

Regan slowly made her way down the stairs with Gayle's assistance. She had insisted on getting up and dressed, although that act itself had sapped most of her strength.

She paused, with a slight smile of triumph on her lips, to catch her breath at the bottom of the stairs. Calder was sitting at the Lord's table, pouring over some papers in front of him. Wallis peered over his shoulder, pointing his finger at certain areas. She was too far away to hear their words, but could see that Wallis was very enthusiastic about the points he was trying to make.

Sighing contentedly at the sight of Calder's handsome face, she pulled her gaze from him and glanced around the rest of the Hall. Most of the knights appeared to be relaxing near the fire while the wind whipped and howled outside the Manor. She smiled as they laughed and swore quite heartily as they threw their dice, or moved their men on one of the many board games that some of them chose to play.

The smile abruptly faded from her face and her brow creased in concern when she saw Radolf. The boy was kneeling on the floor. A cloth was wrapped around his head, covering his eyes, and his hands were extended out behind him. Several of the knights took turns slapping his hands, and a large, gangly puppy barked shrilly as it ran in circles around the laughing group.

"Let the boy be," Regan called out, anger ringing in her voice.

Everyone in the room stopped what they were doing and watched as Regan strode determinedly over to her son.

Radolf stared up at her in surprise as she snatched the cloth away from his eyes. "What is it, Momma?" he asked, seeing the worry on her face.

"Were these men hurting you?" she asked with a scathing look at the knights who had been striking him. They, in turn, stared shamefully at the floor, shuffling their feet and refusing to meet her eyes, which were snapping in fury.

Radolf just giggled. "No, Momma. We're playing a game."

"A game?" was her incredulous reply.

"Yes, Milady," one of the knights answered in relief. "Hot cockles."

"Hot cockles? The game is to strike my child for the fun of it?" Her brittle tone left no doubt as to her opinion of such a game.

"Yes, Regan," Calder replied, from very close behind her. "It is very popular among the men and Radolf asked to join them. It was his turn to guess which of them slapped his hand. If he guesses correctly, he wins a ha'penny."

Feeling her face begin to flush, she looked up into Calder's eyes, which were sparkling with amusement. "Radolf, stop the pup from yapping so," Calder instructed, giving Regan a chance to recover from her embarrassment.

"I apologize," she said quietly to the knights, who were still standing uncomfortably in front of her. "I did not realize it was a game."

She twisted her hands together, suddenly feeling foolish and unsure of herself amidst the large, fearsome men.

"No harm done, Milady," Garrick said warmly, hoping to ease her discomfiture.

The knights were aware of her situation with Calder but, unlike the villagers, were delighted about it. Their leader had never had a woman around long enough to give him any comfort and, even though she was a Saxon, they were able to see how much this wench meant to him. For that reason alone, they would treat her with the utmost respect and protect her with their life, if need be.

"Come, sit with me," Calder said gently, taking her arm and leading her to his table.

Wallis hastily collected the plans for the castle that he had been going over with Calder. "Good day, Mistress Regan," he said politely.

"Come back with the drawings this evening and we will finish our discussion," Calder ordered, dismissing him.

"Please, Calder, don't let me interrupt your business," Regan said worriedly.

"It is no problem. Both Wallis and I need a break from it anyway. We've been pouring over the damn plans all morning." He rubbed his eyes wearily, and then offered her some wine.

"No thank you, Milord. Are the plans for the castle coming along well then?"

"Wallis has a fine mind and has come up with some very interesting ideas. Now we are trying to figure out best how to implement them. The weather will be improving soon, so we need to get a better idea of what our first steps will be. It is a slow, tedious process, but we are making some headway on it. But, what of you? You must be feeling a great deal better."

"Oh, yes, Milord. I tire easily still, but I couldn't bear to lie abed one more minute."

"You mustn't try to do too much too soon, you know." Pulling his chair up close beside hers, he added, "I've never had such a scare as you gave me. I couldn't bear it if you fell ill again."

Smiling tenderly, she said, "Please accept my apologies, Milord. I will certainly be more cautious in the future."

"I would appreciate that," he answered, with a slight nod of his head and a sardonic grin on his face.

She reluctantly pulled her eyes away from his magnetic blue ones and turned to watch Radolf play. He was wrestling now with one of the massive knights, laughing and giggling as they tossed and turned around the floor of the Hall, the puppy nipping at both of them all the while.

"It seems that Radolf has made himself some friends," she said, her heart swelling at the sound of his gaiety while he played.

"Yes," Calder replied dryly. "I'm just not sure if the men felt he needed to be taken under their wings, or if they use him as an excuse to act as children themselves."

He shook his head in mock dismay as Garrett wailed in pain. Having been knocked away from the boy by Holt, his momentum caused him to crash into a nearby table, shaking everything and spilling the contents of cups and pitchers along the length of it.

The puppy gave up chewing various body parts on the players and hastily ran over to lick up the spilt ale. Having cleaned up as much as he could before being booted out of the way, he then proceeded to spend the next several minutes endlessly chasing his tail. He finally gave up and plopped down in an exhausted heap in front of the fire.

Smothering a laugh, Regan turned back to Calder. "Will it be alright if he returns here occasionally to spend some time with his new friends?"

Calder's brow furrowed in confusion. "What do you mean, return here?"

"I am almost well, Milord. Radolf and I will have to return to our cottage soon."

"No."

"No, what?" she asked, her voice quavering slightly, a sliver of fear creeping into her heart at the thought that he might try to keep her son, their son, from her.

"Neither of you will be returning to that cold, drafty cottage. You will both stay here in the Manor."

"Oh no, Milord," she cried. "What will people say?"

"I haven't a care what they say," he replied firmly. "The winter is not over. There is still snow on the ground and it is too difficult to get the supplies needed to repair your cottage enough to make it livable. I will not have the two of you struggling through the winter, trying to keep from starving and freezing, not when there are beds and food and warmth available here."

He had not been entirely honest with her. He and his men could have fixed up her cottage in no time, and they could also ensure that she had enough firewood and food. But he enjoyed having the two of them close by and, selfishly, would say or do whatever he had to in order to keep them there.

Regan stared into the deep grains of wood in the heavy table. On the one hand, she was relieved that they would be staying. She certainly did not want to have to struggle into the forest every day for wood anymore. But her mother had told her about the rebelliousness of the villagers. She knew that it was because of her and did not want to make the situation any worse than it already was. She had already placed Bernia and her mother in danger, just for the part they played in helping during her illness.

"There is naught to worry about, Regan," Calder said.

"What of the villagers?"

He scowled as he replied. "There is much that needs to be done as far as my relationship with them. Come spring, I hope to improve the situation, but I will not have them dictate to me who shall live in my house."

Seeing her worried face, he continued. "Already more and more people pour in from the countryside, looking for land to farm, or jobs within the castle. When it is completed, your villagers, the ones here before we Normans came, will have choices to make. They will be able to see how much richer this area will be, as will the people that dwell in it. Hopefully, they will strive to cooperate and better their own lot in life."

She smiled as she squeezed his hand, hope glistening in her eyes. "You truly believe that?" she asked.

"I have to believe it," he replied matter-of-factly. "If the troublemakers do not desist, I will be forced to banish them. I do not want to have to do that, but I will if it becomes necessary. If we cannot make a community that works together, we will have nothing."

"Does not my remaining here encourage more trouble?"

Leaning close and whispering against her ear, Calder said, "Whatever trouble you cause is well worth it. I need you like the air I breathe. I cannot bear to have you far from me for any length of time."

Regan blushed and stared down at their entwined fingers.

"Momma," Radolf yelled as he ran toward her, the puppy, refreshed from its short nap, now nipping at his heels once again.

"Hello, my handsome man," Regan greeted him, removing her hand from Calder's and reaching toward Radolf. "Are you behaving yourself for Lord Calder?"

"Of course, Mamma," Radolf replied, crawling into her lap and hugging her waist. "Are you all better now?"

"Almost. I am well enough that you can sleep upstairs with me on the big bed now."

She was hurt and bewildered by the crushed look that appeared on his face. "I thought you missed me," she said forlornly.

"I do, Momma," he answered, his brow creased and his lips twisted as he fought his disappointment.

"I believe the boy enjoys the camaraderie of the knights, who also sleep in the Hall," Calder interjected.

Radolf nodded his head vigorously.

"His pallet always lies closest to the fire, and the mutt," Calder inclined his head toward the puppy, which sat patiently staring up at Radolf, his tongue lolling comically out the side of his mouth "sleeps on his feet to keep them warm."

"It's fun, Momma. I'm not alone anymore."

Regan blinked back her tears and brushed a curl back from his forehead. "My little boy is growing up," she said quietly.

It saddened her to realize that he no longer needed or depended on her as he always had. But at the same time, it filled her with a profound joy that he was finally happy, that he had people to play with and to look out for him. Hopefully, he might even have friends his own age to play with before too long, rather than these large, brutish knights, who only behaved as if they were children.

"I can sleep down here, Momma?" he asked, his beautiful blue eyes, so like his father's, gazed at her, wide and trusting.

"If it pleases you, Radolf, you may."

"Thank you," he said with a loud, wet smack on her cheek. Then he leapt off of her lap and ran squealing across the room.

"Don't look so sad," Calder said to her softly, his voice filled with tenderness. "I will see to it that you do not get lonely in that big bedchamber all by yourself."

"That is most reassuring, Milord," she replied with a measured look. "You would not have had anything to do with Radolf insisting on sleeping down here, would you? I'm sure you could not be so deceitful as to take advantage of a young boy for the sole purpose of leaving his mother unprotected in the Lord's bedchamber, could you?"

With a mischievous grin, he replied, "Fortunately, I did not have to try my powers of persuasion on the boy this time. He came up with the idea all on his own. But, know this," he lowered his voice even more, his breath tickling her ear as he spoke, "nothing will stop me from sleeping by your side any longer. And as soon as you are strong enough, there will be a little less sleeping than you have become accustomed to."

"I grow stronger by the minute, Milord."

*   *   *

The Christmas season was fast approaching and the tension in the village seemed to dissipate as anticipation of the Winter Solstice infected everyone. Entertainers of all sorts had been arriving for the fortnight of celebrations, and spirits were high in both the Manor and the village.

Christmas Day dawned bright and sunny, with no hint of snow in the air. There had been an Angels Mass at midnight and Regan, feeling much healthier now, sat proudly between Calder and Radolf in the front pew, ignoring the hard stares of the other attendees.

The new priest, Father Simon, gave a beautiful sermon. He expounded on the notion that the light of salvation appeared at the darkest moment of the darkest day in the very depth of winter, The Winter Solstice, when the sun stands still, making it the shortest day of the year.

Regan took the time as she listened to him to hope and pray that this was, indeed, the darkest time for them all. That from here on in, life would continue to improve so that they could work together as a community once again, giving Calder his due as a fair and just leader, as their leader.

CHAPTER 24

The feasting and partying began that afternoon. Calder had Gayle extend invitations to several families in the village, asking them to join him at the Manor. He left it to her discretion as to whom to invite, but hoped this would be another way to get to know these people and, perhaps, allay their suspicions and fears about him and his men.

At first the villagers seemed uncomfortable and out of place, but Gayle had been shrewd enough to bring young couples with children. They had none of the reservations of their parents and gleefully joined in the fun, forgetting even that it was Radolf they were allowing to play with them.

There were tumblers and minstrels, music and dancing, as well as mummers in curious costumes who acted in verse. Wine and ale were plentiful and the Christmas feast was magnificent.

Calder brought back a chief cook from London, Julian, who had apprenticed in the castle of the King himself. He outdid himself as he prepared roasted salmon with wine sauce, poached fowl and bacon with pudding, fried fig pastries with warm honey spooned over them, Grete Pye—chicken, duck and hare mixed with eggs, fruits and spices, then put into a pastry pie. And, of course, the succulent slices of the Yule Boar, which had been basted in wine with garlic, coriander and other spices as it roasted over a spit, filling the room with its delectable aroma.

Once the dishes from all of the various courses had been cleared, Julian's wife, Carina, who was now the Manor's patisser, brought out the subletie, a sculpture made of a jelly and sugar paste several tiers high. She made it in the shape of the castle which would soon be completed, and Calder was very pleased.

Radolf ate little of the feast, having gorged himself, along with the other children, on pine nut candy, Leche Lumbard and other sweetmeats for most of the day.

The banquet lasted long into the night, with much gaiety and laughter. Calder was relieved to see that his men and the villagers in attendance were able to get along and enjoy themselves. He had no doubt that the presence of Bernia, Gayle and Wallis helped in that matter. They had spent enough time in the Manor to become acquainted with his knights and were able to help the others relax and join in the festivities.

Regan had never participated in such an event and enjoyed herself immensely. Calder's men insisted on taking their turns leading her across the dance floor, and she felt like a young girl again. She did not mind that the villagers tended to ignore her; she was having too much fun anyway, and her heart threatened to burst with joy as she watched Radolf playing with the other children.

The only sad part of the entire day was Filberts refusal to join them. Regan could see her own heartache reflected in her mother's eyes. It seemed as if he had chosen his side in this breach between the villagers and the Normans, and it was not the same side as theirs.

Calder's lascivious glances at her throughout the evening warmed her cheeks, and she felt her desire for him rising as she watched his muscular frame glide effortlessly across the dance floor.

The guests from the village returned to their homes in the early hours of the morning. The Hall was already ringing with the drunken snores of Calder's men, some of whom actually made it to their pallets. Others slept where they fell, or with their heads on the table, unfinished tankards of ale still gripped in their hands.

After tucking a blanket around Radolf, Regan turned to find Calder at her side. He smiled down at her tenderly as he took her hand and escorted her upstairs to their bedchamber, where they completed the celebration in their own way.

The feasting continued every day for a fortnight, although not on quite such a grand scale. Different village families were invited to attend each day. Some refused, as Filbert continued to do. Some came out of curiosity, but found themselves having a good time, even though they had not intended to.

Calder was able to take advantage of having them there and tried to spend time with each of them, listening to their concerns and explaining his vision of the future and what it could hold for them. He made sure that he had a lengthy discussion with Drew's father and convinced him to allow the boy to move to the Keep when it was completed and become his page. Overall, the festivities were a success as far as assuaging the bitter feelings of some of the villagers. Although it was just a handful of them, Calder was optimistic that it could be a good beginning for them all.

On New Year's Day, gifts were exchanged. Radolf received presents from all of Calder's knights, who had developed quite an attachment to him. The clothes that Regan made for him paled in comparison to the dice they fashioned from deer antlers and the board games they made for him. Draco gave him a battledore and shuttlecock. The battledore was a piece of wood whittled into a bat, which was used to hit the shuttlecocks—corks with feathers stuck in them—back and forth.

The greatest gifts by far though, were the bow and arrows that Calder made for the boy. Poor Radolf was not sure which of his presents to play with first and ended up spending most of his time chasing the puppy around the Hall, trying to retrieve one or another of his treasures from its mouth.

Regan felt like a young girl, being spoiled rotten by a loving family, which is how she had come to feel about Calder and his men. Calder gave her a magnificent woolen mantle, which was lined with ermine and etched in gold along the edges.

"But, Calder," she said in dismay, "my gift was the bolts of cloth that you brought back from London. This is too generous of you."

He smiled in pleasure, fondling the bone-handled dirk that she bought for him with her few silver pennies. "They were only a part of your gift, love. I just gave them to you early. Do you like it?"

"It's lovely," she murmured, rubbing the ermine lining against her cheek. "And Draco, the brooch will go with it beautifully."

The knight had carved her a brooch out of ivory, in the likeness of a swan. Looking uncomfortable at her praise, he stared at the table and grunted. "Lord Calder had not the foresight to give you a way to secure the mantle once you put it on. Seems I must always finish his tasks for him."

Calder raised an eyebrow and looked at him, replying dryly, "'Tis good to always have you at my back, Draco. I need never worry about loose ends or things left undone."

Noting the sarcasm in Calder's voice, Draco grunted again and gave him a low bow. "Milord," he said, backing away and going in search of a tankard of ale, feeling out of place and uncomfortable in situations such as these.

"Calder," Regan said softly, her luminous green eyes glittering as she looked up at him, "I have another gift for you, one I would like to share in private. May we go somewhere and be alone?"

"I would have thought that what we shared this morning would satiate you for a short while, you minx, but I am always at your service," he answered with a lewd grin.

"Not for that," she said, her face turning a deep shade of red.

He gave her a perplexed look and took her hand, leading her up to the bedchamber. When they arrived, she walked around the room, nervously twisting her hands together, not sure if she should do this or not, but unable to keep from sharing her happiness with him.

Suddenly she turned and he could not miss the radiance of her smile. "We are going to have another child, Calder."

He sat in stunned silence for a moment, then rushed over and took her in his arms, hugging her tightly. "Regan," he murmured softly, running his hands through her hair, so happy that it felt as if his heart had actually swelled in size. "Oh, Regan, you just continue to make my life better and better. We must have a girl child this time, one who will be as beautiful as her mother and bring nothing but joy to all who behold her."

"You are not upset then?" she asked nervously.

"Of course not," he replied, as giddily as a child. "It is known to happen when two people enjoy each other as we do."

"I wonder though, Calder," she said hesitantly, "what will everyone think?"

He knew that she worried about the fact that they were not married and wanted to ease her mind, but was not sure how much he should tell her yet. The trip to London was nearing and he wanted to be sure of the King's support before taking the next step.

If the King would not give his permission, Calder would still marry her, but it would entail deceit and, ultimately, treachery against the King that he had served and respected for such a long time. They would have to leave this country, and he would have to be sure his plans were properly laid and his men taken care of first. He did not want to burden Regan with these possibilities, unless they became a reality.

"Do you trust me?"

"Of course, I do," she answered, tilting her head back to look up into the depths of his dark blue eyes.

"Then you must believe that I will make this situation right. The time is fast approaching for a resolution to everything. You must be patient just a bit longer, and then all will be as it should be."

Regan felt her pulse quicken as she considered his words. She even allowed herself to hope that he would marry her, although he had given her no indication that was his intent. Her pregnancy would make things even more difficult for them in the village now. There would be no doubt as to the true relationship between her and Calder any longer. But she did love him, and she did trust him, and she would do whatever he asked of her.

"I know that you will do what is right for all of us. I love you, Calder, with all my being."

"And I you, never doubt that," he said tenderly, as he lowered his head and took possession of her lips.

The weather began to improve shortly after the celebrations ended and work began again in earnest, on the castle and in the fields. Calder had to reinstitute his decree that the villagers work every third day on the castle, but all showed for their duties. Even they could see that the end was in sight and were as anxious to end their time working on it as Calder was to have the job done.

Wallis had accomplished a great deal over the winter months and the majority of work left to be done was on the outer stone wall and the drawbridge.

The villagers were too busy preparing their fields to stir up any trouble and Calder took advantage of the opportunity they afforded him to work his knights. They practiced hard every day in preparation for the tournament.

Although he still felt tense about the tourney and about completing the castle, life seemed to go much smoother these days. He realized that lying with Regan each night could not help but improve his outlook on life. And with Radolf near him each day, and another child soon to join them, he felt a contentment that was alien to him, but which he, nevertheless, embraced with open arms.

He did resent being kicked out of his own bedchamber each morning before dawn. Even though everyone soon would know about the child she carried, Regan still insisted that no one see him leave her. Because it eased her mind, and because he knew it would not be for much longer, he did as she requested.

The villagers no longer taunted or tormented Regan. They chose simply to ignore her rather than incur Calder's wrath. Radolf still played with a couple of the children that he had come to know during the festivities. He became especially close with Drew, and no one tried to hurt him any longer.

His puppy had grown by leaps and bounds and now stood almost as tall as Radolf. The bullmastiff was his constant companion and, even in a friendly game of wrestling, he could get overprotective of the boy and drag his opponent off of him, whether it be another child or one of Calder's knights. No one wanted to take the chance on how he would react in a serious altercation. With Draco's help, Radolf had named him Orvyn. It meant brave friend, and they both felt it was suitable for the beast.

Regan spent her time finishing her new clothes from the materials that Calder had given her and tidying up the Manor. She made a daily trip to the fields to collect fresh rushes for the floors and early spring flowers to dry and spread on them, hoping to sweeten the air in the Hall. With the dog and the knight's sweaty bodies, it did become somewhat overpowering on occasion.

She also began to spend quite a bit of time in the kitchen with Carina and Julian. They were very pleasant and Regan was enthralled by their tales of London and the King's court.

One morning, she sat at the table helping Carina prepare vegetables while water heated for her morning bath. Carina was a short, stout woman, her dark hair was always pulled tightly back way from her round face, emphasizing her large brown eyes and red lips that always appeared to be pouting.

"Mistress," Carina asked, looking somewhat bewildered, "why do you heat your own water? Should not the servants be doing it for you?"

"Carina," Julian said sharply. "Do not be impertinent. It is not your business."

This was Julian's first kitchen as chief cook and he feared losing it. He was a tall, thin man, his nose turned up slightly and his eyebrows arched in such a way that he appeared to be perpetually surprised. And, although more serious and less gregarious than his wife, they seemed to balance each other out nicely.

"She's not being impertinent," Regan responded, her face flushing slightly. "I was ill and Lord Calder was kind enough to let me stay here at the Manor so that I could be properly cared for. I fear I may have overstayed my welcome, though. I am not the Lady of the house. The servants have no duty toward me."

Carina was a compassionate woman and not unintelligent. She had seen Regan with Lord Calder and knew that there was much more to their relationship than Regan was admitting to. "But, as his guest, you should be entitled to the proper treatment from his servants," she said kindly. She liked Regan and could not help noticing how shabbily she was sometimes treated.

Regan shook her head sadly. "No, I take of myself. I have no need of their services." She was embarrassed to tell Carina of her true circumstances, with Calder and with the other villagers.

Noting her discomfort, Carina quickly changed the subject. "I heard several more wagons full of people arrived today. Word must have spread throughout the countryside about the castle being built. So many come every day now. Julian is hoping that Lord Calder will hire some on to help him in the kitchen."

"Carina," Julian said in warning, knowing that her tongue had the tendency to get carried away.

"What?" she answered tartly. "I am just saying that we need more help in here."

She turned to Regan and whispered conspiratorially, "Don't take this wrong, but your fellow villagers know nothing about the proper preparation of food." She shook her head dismally and Regan could not help but smile at her.

"I believe that Lord Calder has hired on just about everyone that he needs for inside the Keep. They are all over at the castle already, getting it prepared so that he can move in when he returns from London. Mayhap, I could put a bug in his ear about more kitchen help?"

"That would be so dear of you, Regan," Carina exclaimed, clapping her hands in delight and looking smugly over at her husband.

"When does he leave for London?" Julian asked.

"Within the week," Regan answered despondently, staring down at the table. Both of them noted her sadness and looked at each other curiously. Then Carina briskly removed the buckets from the fire before they became too hot and insisted that Julian help her carry them upstairs.

*   *   *

"So, love," Calder said quietly that evening, holding her closely and reveling in the aftermath of their lovemaking, "are you ready to go to London?"

"What?" she screamed, pulling out of his arms and staring down at him. He could not help but smile at her discomposure.

"You didn't really think that I would go away and leave you again, did you, especially after the way I found you when I returned last time?"

"But...but...I can't go to court. I don't know what to wear, I won't know what to do or say. I don't belong there."

"You belong by my side, wherever that happens to be. Don't worry, I will help you with whatever you feel insecure about. But, always remember this, you are my lady, Regan, and you are as noble and gentile as anyone else who will be there. You have nothing to fear."

CHAPTER 25

The trip was long and not very comfortable in the big, heavy wagons, but Regan hardly noticed. She had never been away from her own little hamlet and the thought of seeing London filled her with a sense of great excitement. She was disappointed that Radolf could not come with them, but he would be well taken care of by her mother and the handful of Calder's men who had been left behind to mind matters in the village, so she was not overly concerned about leaving him.

And to her delight, Bernia was accompanying them. She now had another female for companionship on the trip, one who also had never been to the great city and could share her excitement and nervousness about it.

Calder was going to try to make arrangements for Bernia to apprentice under Gideon for a few months, so that she could finish her training.

"Our village has need of a good healer, Bernia," he told her. "Gideon is the best and can teach you much. If I pay the fee, are you willing to apprentice for him and return here as our healer?"

Bernia could hardly get the words out of her mouth, as she replied, "Oh, yes, Milord. I would be very grateful for such an opportunity."

Both of the women were somewhat disappointed at their first view of the city. They entered in one of the poorer sections and the stench and squalor was overwhelming. Chamberpots were emptied into the streets as they passed by, pigs rooted in the garbage lying all around, and beggars ran up to their wagons, displaying their stumps or running sores as they begged for coins.

But, soon conditions began to improve and they sat in awe of the endless procession of humans and animals. Women hurried from the open markets, carrying baskets of fruit and other necessities, whole herds of sheep were driven through the streets around them. And they watched in delight as jugglers and minstrels entertained passersby and accepted coins in return from their appreciative audience.

All too soon, they arrived at the palace, and Regan could feel her heart racing when she realized that she was actually going to stay at the home of the King of England. Her hands were sweating, her knees felt weak, and she was afraid that she might actually faint.

"You will do fine, Love," Calder whispered in her ear as he passed by her on the way to direct the unloading of their wagons.

They were all escorted to rooms in one of the wings of the labyrinthine building and Regan, without even realizing that she was doing so, reached out to take Calder's hand for support as they followed the servants deeper into the recesses of the castle. Her mouth was agape as she stared at the rich decor of the building, so ornate and beautiful that she was overwhelmed by the sight of it.

"You will share a room with Bernia, for now," Calder said, as he stopped outside one of the portals. The thought of sleeping without her vexed him, but until he could speak with the King, this was the best way to handle the situation.

"You won't be with me?" she asked nervously.

"I'll be staying right next door. For now, there are some things that I must attend to. If you leave the room, take Bernia with you. Ring for the servants if you need anything at all. They can show you to the gardens if you would like to take a walk. They are quite beautiful and you would enjoy them. I'll be back later to escort you to dinner. Will you be alright?" he asked, concern evident in his voice as he saw how distressed she looked.

"I'll be fine," she replied, taking a deep breath and smiling up at him. "Go, tend to the matters that need your attention. Bernia and I will keep each other company."

Decorum be damned, he thought, as bent down and softly kissed her full on the lips. Bernia, who stood nearby, blushed and looked away.

After stabling their horses and tending to their gear, Calder and his men walked down to the tourney grounds. One always had the upper hand when they knew the layout of the battlefield.

"You know that Roderick will request a melee, don't you?" Draco asked.

"Yes," Calder replied thoughtfully. They were all aware that a melee was a contest between two groups of knights which had no rules and, unlike some of the other contests, the sharpest and deadliest weapons were used. Knights died during this particular type of game, more so than any of the others.

"And they will use every dirty trick that Roderick has been able to learn. We must be at our best men, or some of us will not be returning home."

They all nodded silently as they stared solemnly out over the grounds.

"Calder will need the most protection," Draco said sternly to them. "Roderick wants him dead, as we all know. He is not man enough to do it himself, so he will team up his knights against Calder. Even in the heat of battle, do not lose sight of your leader."

"Yes, Draco," they answered in unison.

*   *   *

Calder spent the rest of the afternoon unsuccessfully attempting to get an audience with the King. The closest that he came was meeting William Fitz Osbern in one of the hallways.

"There are too many people here for the tourney," he replied in answer to Calder's question. "The King cannot take the time to meet with everyone individually, so he will listen to petitions after dinner this evening. You will have to bring your matter up to him then. I'm sorry, Calder. I wish I could help."

"Thank you, anyway, William. I appreciate it," he said, unable to disguise his disappointment.

*   *   *

"Tell me about your day," Calder said to Regan, as he escorted her to one of the long banquet tables for dinner. Garrick was close behind them with Bernia on his arm, surprising them all of them with his gallantry and attentiveness toward the young woman.

"It took us the entire afternoon to make our way through the gardens. They were magnificent," she said, her voice filled with awe at the splendor of everything that she had seen since arriving.

"I ran into Devona, your sister-in-law, in the gardens. She was quite surprised to see me and I didn't really know how to explain why I was here," Regan said, gazing into his deep blue eyes, gaining strength and confidence just from having him back at her side.

"It is none of her concern why you are here and you need offer no explanations to anyone. I didn't realize that she was still in London though," he replied, his voice thoughtful as he considered what repercussions Devona's presence might have, especially if she was still petitioning to get his lands back for her son.

Regan ate little of the opulent meal that was presented. Her stomach was a tight knot of nervousness as she tried not to show how unrefined she was. Watching all of the people in the room carefully, she tried to mimic their actions, so that she would not look too out of place.

The array of glorious colors and rich fabrics of the tight, form fitting kirtles worn by the other women amazed Regan, and she was left feeling self-conscious about her own clothing. She was wearing a dark green, silk kirtle which, fortunately, still fit since her pregnancy was not yet showing. Her long hair was plaited and hung down her back, covered by a linen wimple.

Regan had other tunics made of rich fabrics, thanks to Calder, but she owned none of the jewels or fur trimmings that adorned the nobles' attire. She felt like a peasant.

But, she could not help but feel proud to be at Calder's side. He was resplendent in his dark blue tunic, which was decorated with gold etching and hung to just above his knees, drawn tightly around his waist by a belt with a wide gold buckle. His muscular legs were shown off in all their glory in his tight-fitting hose, and she could not miss the lascivious glances of the other women at their table, as they tried to catch his eye.

As if sensing her mood, Calder reached for her hand under the table and squeezed it lightly. "Is there something wrong with the pheasant, love?" he asked tenderly. "You do not seem to be enjoying it much."

"It's delicious, Calder. I just haven't much of an appetite this evening."

"Is it the baby?" he asked, his voice so low that only she could hear. He found her to be the most brilliant jewel in the room and had no idea of the insecurity she was feeling amidst these people. He had also noted looks in their direction from the romantic young swains waiting to pounce on a beautiful, single woman, and he determined that he would not let her out of his sight to be at the mercy of these randy knaves.

There were other looks cast in their direction, as well, more malevolent and directed solely at him. Most were from Roderick and his men, but there were others that harbored naught but ill-feelings toward him and his men. Being one of the King's favorites did have its accompanying problems.

After dinner, the tables and benches were cleared from the room and King William took his position on a dais overlooking the crowd.

"Who here has a petition for the King?" cried out his steward.

Several people rushed to the front, all wanting their few moments of the King's ear. William was not an especially attractive man, but his bearing was proud and regal, and power emanated from him, making him more attractive than he might have been.

As they rushed through their petitions, Calder was in a quandary as to what to do about Regan. Should he allow her to stay and hear his own petition, and the arguments that would flow forth because of it, or send her back to her room? To do so would embarrass her, as she would feel that he did not believe her good enough to stay and participate in the festivities later that evening.

He was absolved from laboring any further over a decision when he heard his name mentioned a few moments later. Curiously, he looked over toward the dais and saw that Devona was fervently making an appeal to the King.

"Stay here," he said brusquely to Regan, as he shouldered his way through the crowd to reach Devona.

"My husband was one of your most devoted servants, Sire." Her high, mousy voice was almost shrieking in her enthusiasm, and Calder could see the King wince as he listened. "You gave him lands after his great support for you in your conquest of this barbaric country. In return, he gave his life for you, living amongst these savages and being poisoned by them after trying to acquiesce to your wishes. Then, rather than let his son, Harlan, inherit, as was the right and just thing to do, you gave those lands over to his brother. To Calder, who is a simple soldier, not a nobleman, and who has no right to them."

The King's displeasure, at her tone and her turn of phrase, was evident on his face, but she was so carried away by finally having a chance to speak her mind to him that she failed to notice.

"Enough, Devona," he said sharply. "You have made your thoughts on this matter perfectly clear and you need add no more insults. Calder became a nobleman when I made him such. What is it that you are asking of me?"

"Sire," she said a little more contritely, "I know Calder has been invaluable to you, but these lands should go to Aric's son. If you do not see fit to return them to him, please allow me to marry Calder, then Harlan will inherit them after his death. It is the only fair and just thing to do."

The King tried to smother his grin as he glanced askance at Calder, whose face had suddenly paled. He looked almost panic stricken at the thought of having this woman as his bride.

"What say you, Calder?"

"I cannot marry, Devona, Your Highness. In fact, I intended to bring a petition myself, to get your permission to wed one called Regan."

The King looked at him in surprise, caught off guard at such a request from his most respected knight.

"But she is a Saxon," Devona screeched. "Will you now let the conquered once more take over these lands that your men fought so valiantly for, Sire?"

"Is this true?" the King asked Calder.

"Yes, Your Highness, it is. That is why I came to you."

"Why do you believe that I would allow one of my nobles to take a Saxon as a wife?"

"I believe, Your Highness, that ultimately the decision of whom a man will marry is made less because of whether they are Norman or Saxon and more because of what lies in each of their hearts."

"That is foolishness, Milord," Roderick called out loudly as he stepped forward, eager to add his own opinion. His hawkish features were even more pronounced as he strode toward the small group. He moved with the imperiousness that came from having power and knowing how to use it. Not as tall as Calder, he was almost as broad and muscular, his physique leaving no doubt as to the number of hours he spent on the practice field with his men.

Roderick's dark brown eyes swept arrogantly over Calder before he turned back to the King. "Calder obviously has not learned what it means to rule these people. He chooses instead to bed them and let them run the lands themselves."

"Sire," Calder replied forcefully, "when we first conquered this land, you admonished all of us to do several things. The most important, you said, was to try to work with these people, to develop an agreeable relationship with them, so that the country could prosper and flourish."

"Sire," Devona interrupted shrilly.

"Be quiet, Devona. I will give you further leave to speak. For now, Calder is entitled to explain."

"I have done as you asked, Your Highness. Our castle is almost completed, more lands have been cleared and fields harvested, merchants and tradesmen are clamoring to join our community, which will enrich not just the people of the area, but you, as well. How can we continue to maintain any relationship with these people if we treat them as lesser men, or women, than we are? How can we live amongst them every day and not allow friendships, or more, to develop? How can we ever become one as a country until all are treated as one?"

King William stared pointedly at him, nodding his head at the wisdom of Calder's words. "You make a strong argument, Calder."

"Your Highness," Roderick interjected, "you cannot allow these lands to return to the peasants. The blood of your knights allowed Calder to have them, and you cannot shame their memory by now giving it back to the ones who killed them."

The scar on Calder's cheek was a livid red as he turned toward Roderick. His hands were clenched in fists at his side as he fought to control his anger.

"This woman did not kill any of our men. I lost many myself and would never dishonor their memory. The war is long since done and it is time now to strengthen this country. My marriage to Regan will help bind two peoples together into one, to make us all stronger when the next enemy arrives at our shore."

"Poppycock," Roderick stated disdainfully. "You lust after a young village woman. Take her, Calder, but do not embarrass the rest of us by marrying her."

"Enough," the King said sternly, seeing that Calder was ready to do physical harm to Roderick. "Is the woman here?"

"Yes."

"Come forward, Regan. Let me meet the young woman who has my knights in such an uproar."

Regan had been trying to hide herself in the back of the room as she listened to the arguments. Her face was pale and her hands trembling. She had never expected this and, although pleased that Calder wanted her as his wife, she was dismayed that he must now suffer the wrath of his peers because of his feelings for her.

She walked slowly toward the dais, feeling the curious stares of all as she did so. "Your Highness," she said quietly, with a low curtsey as she arrived in front of the King.

"Is it your wish to marry Calder?"

"Yes, Your Highness," she said solemnly, moving closer to Calder and reaching for his hand. He clasped hers firmly and she sighed in relief. With him next to her, she could handle anything, even an interrogation by the King of England.

"Why? Will it not make you an outcast from your community if you do so?"

"Lord Calder has been trying his best to create a community for us, Sire. There is still dissent from some of my people. We can be a stubborn lot and sometimes we do not, at first, always see the good that can come from a situation. But I love him and would suffer anything to be at his side. If they cannot accept that yet, I am hopeful that someday they will."

The King watched the two of them closely. They made a strikingly handsome pair and he could see how this woman would catch Calder's eye. But still he was troubled. For Calder to petition for marriage went completely against the nature of the man he had come to know over the years.

And, although William was not worried about Devona, Roderick had much support from the other nobles and could create some serious problems should he allow this marriage to go forward.

Calder could see that the king was deliberating, but did not feel confident about what his decision would be. Taking a deep breath, regretting the embarrassment that he knew he would cause Regan, he played his last card.

"She carries my child, Sire, and with or without your blessing, it is a child that I intend to help raise, with Regan at my side."

The King's eyebrows narrowed as he looked angrily at Calder. "Do not get impertinent with me, Calder. You have my utmost respect and I value your friendship and your service. But do not think that you can make my decisions for me. You have done a grave disservice to this young woman, and I must think for a time on what I will do. I will give you my answer after the tournament." He stared pointedly at Calder, daring him to question what he would say next. "Since you obviously cannot be trusted with her welfare, she will be moved to different quarters and watched over by my guards until my decision is made."

In actuality, the King's concern was more for Regan's safety from Roderick and some of the other nobles, rather than Calder, but he did not want to voice his thoughts aloud. Strange things tended to happen in the palace when this many powerful people were gathered, and he would take no chance of any ill happenstance occurring to the young woman.

CHAPTER 26

"But, Calder," Regan said frantically, "where will they take me?"

They were in her room, re-packing her bags, having been escorted there by the King's guards, who waited for them in the hallway.

"If you trust me, Regan, then you must trust King William. He is a good and just man and, once he has a chance to think things through, he will see how right it is to allow this marriage. For now, he has only your safety in mind. He will see that you are properly protected."

"From what?" she asked, her green eyes glittering.

He sighed heavily and sat down on the bed next to her. "There are many dishonorable people here at Court. In trying to thwart me, they may attempt you harm. The King will not allow that, and neither will I," he added, seeing the fear in her eyes and hoping to ease her mind.

"But, what will happen after the tournament if the King refuses your petition?"

"King William has been my friend and my leader for many years. I have faith in him, and so must you."

He would not tell her of the dangers that could await them if the King refused the petition and they chose to defy him. Should it come to pass, he would tell her only what she needed to know.

"Regan," he said softly, running his hand along her cheek, "no matter what happens, I will have you as my wife, please believe that. It is what you want also, isn't it?"

She smiled warmly at him, her heart beating excitedly at the thought of it. "Oh, yes, Calder, it has been my wish since the first night that we were together. I would wither away and die should I not be able to spend the rest of my days with you."

He pulled her into his arms and kissed her thoroughly, wishing he could stay and show her the depth of his commitment to her, but he must return to the party and try to prevent the King's ear from being bent by the wrong people. "Have faith in me then, and have a care for your safety. Trust no one but me and my men," he whispered against her lips. "And I will make your wish come true."

Leaving her a few minutes later, he went in search of Draco and explained the situation. "Even the King's men can be bought, Draco. Have one of our men watching over Regan also, but be sure they know not to be too obvious about it."

"Yes, Milord," Draco answered, his face set as he went to locate their men, leaving Calder alone to return to the vipers' pit.

The following day, the tournament began. First would come the Bohort, where the squires fought each other with blunted weapons and padded armor. Then the individual contests, the jousts and commencailles, where a few chosen knights showed off their skills to the guests with various weapons. Calder and his men had all refused to participate in those contests, knowing they needed to preserve every ounce of their strength and energy for the melee against Roderick and his men.

Regan had just finished dressing and was waiting for Bernia to arrive so that they could be escorted to the Ber Frois—the stands where lady spectators and important guests watched the tourney. At the knock on her door, she rushed over to open it, her surprise evident as she looked up into King William's implacable face,

"Your Grace," she said, with a deep curtsey.

"Forgive me, Lady Regan, for barging in on you like this. I was hoping to have a few words with you before the tourney begins."

"I am at your service, Sire," she answered, nervously wringing her hands together.

"This is a very important decision that I have to make regarding your marriage to Calder. Do you realize the repercussions that could occur if I allow you to do so?"

"Sire, I have little knowledge of your court or the people in it. I truly do not know why the marriage of two people who love each other should have any repercussions at all."

"I believe you are an intelligent woman, Regan, and I think you understand more than you admit."

Regan flushed and looked down at the floor. "Sire, perhaps it is just wishful thinking on my part that Calder's and my life together should have no effect on others, but I do know, from my own people, that it will."

"So, your own people have already made you suffer and you are not yet wed. Are you willing now to suffer at the hands of the Normans, as well as the Saxons? And to possibly have Calder suffer, as well?"

"That is a difficult question, Sire. I would never wish harm on Calder and would do anything in my power to prevent it. He has already left himself open to a much more difficult time because of his feelings for me, and so he tries even harder to make amends with my people because of it. He is a kind and generous man and I love him with all my heart. But, which is the greater harm to him, Your Highness, taking away what he believes is necessary in his life for happiness, or allowing him to have that happiness, a happiness which he can then use to help him deal with the difficulties that will follow because of it?"

King William smiled down at her, admiring her logic. "Can you help him to make his lands more prosperous and the people more complaisant to his ideas and plans?"

"In truth, Sire, I am not sure that I can. Already many of my people are coming to know and admire him for his foresight, intelligence and compassion. It will take some time before there will be complete harmony in our village, but I sincerely believe that it will be our children that will make the difference. They will no longer be just Normans, or just Saxons, they will be Englishmen, Your Grace. And they will be able to see both sides of any problem and meet somewhere in the middle for the answer. My hopes rest with them."

"Well said, Milady. You have given me much to think about, but I must go now. I hope we have a chance to speak again. Enjoy the games."

"I will, Your Highness, thank you," Regan said with another deep curtsey as he left, her heart pounding in her chest as she worried that she may have overstepped her bounds and said too much.

*   *   *

"Men, you must put everything from your mind this day and focus on the battle at hand. And it is a battle, make no mistake about that. You can show no mercy, for Roderick's men will not yield and they will not hesitate to kill any one of us."

Calder and his men were being suited up in full armor for the melee, the squires helping them on with the heavy pieces and tying them into place. The destriers were already prepared, covered from head to tail in heavy armor.

"Be prepared for dirty tricks and questionable tactics, and watch out for your fellow knight. Our backs will be their main target and we will only survive if we protect one another," Calder admonished, as he checked the cinch on Alerio's saddle one last time, and then lowered his helmet into place.

When the trumpets blared, announcing their event, Draco rode beside Calder onto the field, with the others following four abreast behind them.

They made quite an impressive sight as they rode slowly toward the King's box, their horses stepping high, obviously anxious to enter the foray themselves. The knights raised the lids of their helmets and nodded respectfully to the King.

Roderick's men entered from the opposite end of the field and positioned themselves similarly, but to the right of Calder and his men.

When the cheers and applause from the crowd died down, King William stood and stared pointedly, first at Calder, then at Roderick, before he began to speak.

"A melee has been requested and, against my better judgment, I have agreed to it. You and your men are some of my finest knights. Remember that this is a game and do not cause me to lose my knights solely because of the vanity or animosity of their leaders."

"This is a game," he repeated sternly, "for the entertainment of my guests. Its purpose is to unseat your opponents from their horses. You are all experienced enough to show off your skill with weapons without causing any undue injuries, or deaths. See to it that is how you play it."

The King's tone was firm. He knew with whom he was dealing, and he also knew that not all the men sitting in front of him would leave this field alive.

Each of the knights raised their shields to him and bowed their heads before backing up their horses and heading to their end own of the field.

Each man carried a dagger, a broadsword and a lance. Some bore extra weapons, as well, which they preferred over the others. Draco carried a mace, a heavy clublike weapon with metal tipped ends. Only someone with much experience handling one could use it with the ease that he did. A couple of Calder's men preferred poleaxes and, again, only men with experience could wield the long-handled axes successfully.

Their shields were made of wood and boiled leather, with Calder's coat of arms, a golden griffon painted on a red background, on the face of them. The shields were tied across their shoulders on a leather thong for protection, while at the same time allowing them use of both hands.

Regan, watching from the stands, found it difficult to breathe. She heard the King's warning and desperately hoped that the knights would heed it. There was no mistaking the look on their faces as they sat in front of the king. No quarter would be given. Her palms began to sweat and her heart raced in fear for them.

As much as she cared about Draco and the other men, she could not tear her eyes from Calder's tall, proud body as he melded with his horse and began the charge across the field.

Much of her view was blurred as the battle began. The horses' great hooves kicked up so much dust as to render the men almost invisible at times, but never did it dull the sharp sound of metal striking metal.

She gasped as she saw Garrick struck in the shoulder by a lance. He dropped his own, but was able to keep to his horse. Calder and Davis took up either side of him, battling off Roderick's men so that Garrick had time to get control of his horse and draw his sword.

In a blur of armor, the enormous horses were turned in small, tight circles, as the knights sought to fight off new threats. Most of them had thrown down their lances after the first charge. The weapons were fourteen feet long and of no use in close combat. Nervously, Regan watched as three of Roderick's men removed themselves from the heat of the battle, and then positioned their lances as if to for another charge.

Her breath caught in her throat when she saw that they were lined up with Calder, whose back was to them as he battled two others with his broadsword. Regan screamed when she saw them spur their horses forward in his direction. There was too much noise and confusion for any of the knights to have heard her, but Draco saw them coming. With a herculean swing of his mace, he struck his opponent. The blow was so hard that the man's helmet dented and he fell to the ground with a thud.

Turning his horse, Draco arrived behind Calder just as Graeham did and, together, they were able to repel the attack on him. Regan almost fainted in relief as she watched.

Calder grunted in pain as one of the broadswords slipped through the laces that held his armor together, piercing his chainmail and slicing into his side. It was not a deep cut though, and did not keep him from continuing to fight.

Kenny and Holt had dispatched several more of Roderick's men and moved to his aide, as well. The flat of Holt's sword struck one of his opponents square in the back, knocking him ass over teakettle onto the ground. The other, Calder faced down alone as Kenny kept watch for the next attack.

"We have the advantage, Roderick. Will you cede?" Calder yelled. Their numbers were much greater now than his. There was no need for more injuries or deaths.

"To you?" Roderick laughed. "Never."

"Then cause no more harm to your own men. Let this end between just you and me."

Roderick narrowed his eyes through his helmet, his hatred almost palpable. He would look the coward if he refused the challenge, but he could not risk Calder walking off the field alive. "We have fought worse odds and will not run from you now."

"So be it then." Calder raised his sword into the air and his men joined him in a bloodcurdling war cry as the two groups charged each other.

Even with the difference in numbers, always two men attacked Calder. An admirable fighter, even Calder could not continue to ward off two knights at a time. The armor was heavy and stiff, making movement difficult, and there was too much of a disadvantage when attacked from both sides. Draco took up a position at his side, to ensure no harm came to his leader.

Wildly swinging his mace, hitting one man so perfectly that his helmet swung backwards around his head and later had to be removed by a blacksmith, Draco continued to protect Calder's weak side.

Soon Roderick had few men still astride, although many littered the ground around them.

"Stand back, men," Calder commanded as he slowly walked his sweating horse in Roderick's' direction, sword at the ready.

"You and me, Roderick, we finish now what you started so long ago."

Their horses rushed toward each other, their swords clanged unmercifully, the impact sending dull shards of pain up each of their arms, but neither would relent as they continued their deadly battle.

It soon became evident that Roderick was tiring. His thrusts were not as hard, his parries not as quick. Calder was forced to turn away from him though, when he heard Draco roar out a warning.

One of Roderick's fallen men, who was just slightly injured, stood and swung his own sword at Calder from the ground. Calder yanked back hard on the reins and Alerio reared into the air. Sensing danger, the animal's hooves landed directly on the man as he came back down, making an ugly thudding sound as he crushed his chest.

Roderick took advantage of those few moments, having seen the hole already made between the armor in Calder's side. He rushed in and thrust his sword through it, sinking his blade deep.

Calder, ignoring the burning pain, turned his attention back to Roderick. Seeing an opening in the crinet—the chainmail covering over the horse's neck—he, in turn, plunged his sword into it, killing the horse. The great destrier rolled to the ground, pinning Roderick underneath it.

In an instant, Calder was beside him. His anger at Roderick's dirty tricks, his memory of their prior altercations and the adrenaline from the battle, all combined to make him forget everything and everyone, other than his desire for vengeance. He ripped off Roderick's helmet and was gratified to see the fear in the fallen man's eyes.

"Calder," Draco called out sharply, seeing the deadly intent on his friend's face, "now is not the time."

Calder hesitated, sanity returning as he realized where he was. To dispatch Roderick now would be murder, and to commit murder in the King's presence was a grievous offence. He would die himself for doing so, never having seen the babe that Regan carried, never able to watch Radolf grow to manhood. As much as Roderick deserved to die, he would not allow him to take those things away from him.

Instead, he unsheathed his dagger and held it before Roderick's terror filled eyes, then he slowly carved a shallow mark from the bottom edge of his right eye downward to his chin. He stood back then and watched in satisfaction as a thin trickle of blood began to flow from the wound.

"And now we are even, Roderick. That which you give, you should receive, although my cut was much more merciful than yours. Remember this day, for when next we meet, you will not have such an easy time of it."

Mounting Alerio, he rode with quiet dignity off the battlefield, his knights falling in behind him.

CHAPTER 27

Regan paced her room and fretted for hours after the tournament. No one would tell her where Calder was or how he fared. She had seen the blade sink into his side and was sick with worry for him.

She ran quickly to the door when someone knocked and opened it to find Bernia standing in the hallway.

"Come with me, Regan. Gideon has been tending Lord Calder and he asked for you."

They hurried through the well-lit corridors, stopping only when they found Draco standing guard outside one of the doors.

"Milady," he said solemnly.

"Oh, Draco, I'm so happy that you are all right. What of the other men?"

"Some have been badly injured, but Gideon is tending them. None have died."

"I'm so glad," she said, raising herself on her toes and kissing his cheek, sure that she saw a blush appear on his face as she did so.

He opened the door and she rushed over to the bed where Calder lay, pale and asleep. She ran her fingers over his strong jaw line and watched as his chest shallowly rose and fell.

"Gideon?" There was no need to ask anything further. The questions in her eyes were enough for him to know what was going through her mind.

"He will live. He lost a lot of blood and will need some time to get his strength back. I must go now, to tend the others. Bernia, will you assist me?"

"Of course," she replied, as they quietly closed the door behind them. Regan sat with Calder until he regained consciousness a short time later.

"Hello, love," he said hoarsely.

She smiled tenderly at him and raised a glass of water to his lips. "You had me worried, Milord. I thought mayhap I would not get the chance to be your bride, after all."

"Ah, Regan, you should know me better than that by now. When I say something shall be done, it shall be done."

She hugged him tightly and covered his face with kisses. "I love you so much, Calder, and I was so frightened for you. You don't have to do this every year, do you? I don't think I could bear it."

He started to laugh, but it made him cough painfully. She gave him more water and, when he could speak again, he said, "No, love. I think I've had my fill of tourneys for awhile. I'm thinking more of teaching my son how to hunt and fish properly, and of watching my wife become more beautiful every day as she nears the time to bear my next child."

"I can live with that," she replied with a dazzling smile, climbing onto the bed and wrapping her arms around him.

They were interrupted by a loud banging on the door and Regan swiftly jumped off the bed to answer it. Seeing her low curtsy, Calder knew who it must be and struggled to sit up.

"Your Majesty," he said with a nod, as the King approached his bed.

"Once again, Calder, you have proven yourself to be a man of courage and honor. I am proud of you."

"Thank you, Sire."

"I wish that I could say the same about Roderick, but I cannot."

Wisely, Calder chose to remain silent.

"I have given a lot of thought to your petition and what you said. Do not take this wrong, Calder. You made some fine points on your own behalf, but after much deliberation, it was ultimately what Regan said that proved to give me the most hope for our future here."

"If she is right," the King said, in response to Calder's questioning gaze, "we will have a strong and prosperous country, and I am going to let you be the one to take the first step in that direction. If you are up to it, I will marry the two of you myself, tomorrow morning."

Calder's face split into a grin of unequivocal delight.

"But," the King continued sternly, "I leave it to you to make this right with your own kinsmen and the people you rule. See to it that it is handled properly."

"It will be my reason for being, Your Grace. Thank you." There was nothing more that he could say to express the depth of his gratitude to his friend and sovereign.

*   *   *

Calder rode close to the wagon for the entire trip home, unable and unwilling to lose sight of his new bride for more than a few moments at a time. It was as if his heart had increased in size and the joy that he felt, at times, threatened to overwhelm him.

For her part, Regan wore a perpetual smile on her face. Her whole life had changed in those few minutes when King William conducted the ceremony that pronounced them husband and wife. Regardless of how the others accepted this news, for her it was a wonderful new beginning, one that she cherished and intended to make the most of.

They went directly to the Keep, which had been prepared for their arrival and would now be their home. Just moments after they got there, Radolf, followed by his canine companion, came running into the Hall and threw himself into Regan's arms.

"You're home, Momma," he said excitedly. "I missed you so much."

"And I, you," she responded, hugging him and kissing him on both cheeks. Calder strode into the room just then and, seeing the two of them together in his home filled him with more pride than any other accomplishment in his life.

"Radolf," he called, "have you grown too much into a man while I was away to give me hug, as well?"

Grinning in delight, Radolf ran over and leapt up into the large man's arms. Holding him tight, Calder twirled the boy a couple of times, causing him to squeal in delight and the pup to run circles around them.

"I believe that we have some news for you," he said, lowering the boy to the floor and looking askance at Regan. She nodded her head and Calder squatted down beside Radolf. "Your mother and I were wed in London, and from this day forward, you will both live here with me and I will be your father. Is that agreeable to you?"

Radolf stood silently, his brow creased as he tried to grasp what Calder had said. "Forever and ever?" he asked finally.

"Forever and ever."

"Really, Momma?" he asked, as he turned toward Regan. When she nodded her head, his face split into an endless smile. Turning back to Calder and looking at him shyly, he asked, "Can I call you Daddy?"

"I insist," Calder replied. "And, as soon as the work on the castle ends, we must spend lots of time doing things that fathers and sons do."

"Like what?" Radolf asked excitedly.

"Well, to start with, I will have to show you how to use your new bow and arrows, and then there will be many new things to learn and to do."

Radolf hopped around excitedly as Calder went over and hugged his mother, taking her into his arms and kissing her tenderly on the lips, no longer caring who might be around to see them.

Draco arrived in the room just then, and after his share of hugs and news from Radolf, sat down at the table with Calder.

"Let the villagers know that I will be speaking to them tomorrow morning. After I am done, I will expect them all to swear their fealty to me. I have not asked that of them in the past, but now it is time. Make sure they realize that should they refuse, they will be turned out immediately."

"Yes, Milord," Draco answered solemnly, and left to see to his instructions.

*   *   *

The following morning, the square outside the new Keep was filled with people, the villagers who had been there when the Normans arrived and all of the new people who came looking for jobs and new lands to farm.

Calder stood on the top step with Regan and Radolf at his side. "Today, I expect each and every one of you to swear your fealty to me as your Overlord. The time has come to prove that you will serve me without question. In return, you will have all the protection that I can provide. I will also have work to keep you busy and lands to keep you fed. If you feel you cannot swear your support to me, you will be asked to leave these lands. But first, hear me out.

I have brought builders from London and will not require any more service from you to complete the castle. We will be clearing more of the forest and developing more farm land. Each of you who were here before we came will get an additional piece to work. The grants given to those newly arrived will be equally as large. You will have an opportunity to increase your yields and your wealth."

He stood quietly for a moment as they turned and talked amongst themselves. "But, more importantly, know this. Regan is now my wife and Radolf, my son and heir. If you continue to live in this community, you will show them the proper respect that is their due. To insult your Overlord, or any member of his family is a grave offense, one that will not go unpunished. If you do not feel you can abide by that, leave now."

The murmurs of the crowd rose in volume as they considered his words. The villagers could not help but wonder if Radolf would remember the slights done to him and his mother when he became their new Overlord, and make them suffer because of it.

The chance to have larger farms though, and the time to work them, was a great enticement and everyone decided that it was in their own best interest to swear their fealty to Calder.

His knights began the procession and, one by one, the people from the village took turns promising to obey and protect their Overlord. They knelt before Calder, saying the necessary oath and bowing respectfully to Regan before going back down the steps.

Regan's face was flushed with excitement and anticipation. She made a vow to herself that, if her people would give her the chance, she would help them to see how much better their community could be if they worked and got along together. Tears filled her eyes when she watched her father swear his fealty to Calder, then he hugged her and kissed her cheek before walking slowly back down the stairs. She sincerely believed that this could be a new beginning for all of them and prayed it would be so.

*   *   *

The next few months passed quickly and peacefully. Everyone was busy tending their crops or working within the castle. The villagers came to appreciate the value of having Calder's worthy knights to protect them when they dispatched a group of marauding thieves who had been preying on the outlying farms.

Regan had a few tense days when she first decided to assert herself as the Lady of the Manor, but soon she was obeyed as quickly and easily as Calder. No one wanted to risk his wrath or the possibility of losing their position within the Keep, so they determined that they would be as respectful and dutiful toward her as they could manage.

In return for their consideration, Regan tried to do as much as she could for them, with the hope of rebuilding the relationships that she had once had with these people. She surprised them by stopping at the homes of those who had fallen ill, bearing a special broth that Julian made, and bringing flowers to those who had recently given birth.

Initially cold and aloof in response to her kindness, the people gradually began to overlook her past and supposed betrayal of her people. They even began to develop a grudging respect for her, particularly after she met with Iona.

"Julian has need of more help in the kitchens," she stated hesitantly to Iona from the doorway, not having been asked inside. "It pays a farthing more per week than you were making as a servant at the Manor, and Lord Calder and I would be grateful if you would consider coming back to work for him."

Iona had been very bitter toward both of them after Calder fired her from the Manor but, never having liked working the fields, she was grateful for the opportunity to have a job inside once again.

"I would like that, Milady," she answered respectfully, still somewhat reserved, but able now, if not to develop a friendship with Regan, to at least tolerate her and give her the necessary respect.

Regan also sat with Calder at the weekly judicial hearings, remaining quiet unless she felt that she could interject something to aid her people. Calder realized the value of her experience with them and saw that relations were beginning to improve, so he generally conceded to her suggestions.

Radolf had more friends nowadays and several began to join him in the afternoons when Regan instructed him on his lessons. Soon the Hall was filled with the giggles and whispers of children as parents decided to take advantage of the situation and insisted on their own children joining in. It gave Regan a great sense of fulfillment to be able to teach them their letters and numbers.

Radolf had further instruction later in the day, from his father. They spent several hours before dinner learning how to properly shoot a bow and to handle weapons. And, again, some of the older boys, done by that time of day helping their fathers in the fields, came to learn, as well.

Calder eventually had to enlist the aid of some of his knights to help and Draco fashioned additional wooden swords that they used for practice.

*   *   *

Bernia and Garrick returned later in the summer. A tendon had been severed in Garrick's arm during the melee and he had required more of Gideon's care than the others. Bernia cut short her apprenticeship to accompany him back.

The night that Garrick arrived, he sat dismally with Calder and Regan after dinner, drinking tankard after tankard of ale. "I'm useless to you now, Calder. My arm will never have the strength again to wield a sword in battle."

Calder heard the resignation in his voice and his brow furrowed in concern. Garrick was a fearless warrior, but now it seemed as if he felt he had nothing to offer anyone. Calder ignored his words. "You seem to have become quite close with Bernia."

"Before the tourney, I actually considered asking for her hand," he said with a self-depreciating laugh. "Now I am not even good enough for a Saxon wench."

His widening gaze flew to Regan and he quickly added, "My apologies, Milady."

"Your apology is accepted," she answered warmly, realizing the depths of his despondency.

"So, what will you do now?" Calder asked callously. "Drink yourself into oblivion? Curl up into a ball and die?"

Garrick looked at him sharply. "You cannot understand what it feels like to no longer be the man that you once were."

"No, I can't," Calder replied, trying to keep any sympathy or pity from his voice. "But can you not determine now what kind of man you will be? I have need of a Woodward to oversee my forests and lands, to make sure no one is poaching or cutting down what is not theirs. Does a weak arm prevent you from doing that service for me? Does it keep you from loving and being loved by a decent woman? Does it keep you from marrying her and accepting some land from me and building a new and, possibly, even better life? Or will you just give up altogether?"

Garrick looked at him with a glimmer of hope in his eyes. "You would do that for me?"

Calder grinned at him. "How many times have you taken a cut in order to protect me? I need someone like you for this job, someone that I can trust. Of course, I would do it, not for you, but for my own benefit."

"Thank you, Milord." His gratitude was evident by the expression on his face. "I think mayhap it's time that I cleaned up a little and paid a visit to Bernia, if you will excuse me."

"Good e'en to you, Garrick. And good luck."

After he left, Regan took Calder's hand in her own. Her eyes were filled with love and adoration as she gazed at him. "You are such a good man, Calder. It makes me proud to be your wife."

"What did I do?" he asked in confusion. "I spoke nothing but the truth to Garrick."

"Yes, but you did it in such a way as to allow him to keep his pride. Everything is going along so well, isn't it?" she asked, sure that nothing could make her happier than she was at that moment.

"The only thing that could make life better is this little devil arriving soon," he said, placing his hands tenderly over her well-rounded belly. "Then all will be as it should be."

But, he would never have spoken with such eager anticipation if he knew what lay in store for them just a few days hence.

CHAPTER 28

Calder hurried back to the castle with Radolf riding in front of him. Their lessons had gone on longer than usual this day.

"Any fool knows that peacock feathers are no match for goose feathers for fletching arrows, no matter what Aart tells you," Calder was instructing as they arrived at the stables and dismounted.

He insisted that Radolf help in currying down Alerio and preparing his feed, then they walked together into the Hall. Calder was surprised that Regan was not there to greet them, but thought she must be resting before the evening meal.

Sitting down at his table, a cup of ale was placed in front of him almost before he was comfortably settled in. He sighed in satisfaction as he took a healthy draught. Since he began hiring newcomers to work in the castle, service had improved tenfold. Even the original villagers were becoming more courteous and accommodating in their chores. It seemed almost a competition of sorts, with the original villagers trying to outdo the newcomers.

Whatever their motivation, it gave Calder a great deal of satisfaction to see things running so smoothly. Due, in no small part, to Regan. Always polite, but firm and determined at the same time, she ruled over the servants as fairly and reasonably as she could, but accepted no slights, nor insolence on their part. Her self-esteem had risen greatly when she became Lady of the Manor and her assertiveness was a wonder to behold.

Calder frowned in irritation as his thoughts were interrupted by an annoying sound coming from the fireplace.

"What are you doing, Orvyn?" he asked, looking around for Radolf. The boy was nowhere to be seen, having skipped off to the kitchen to steal a snack before dinner.

"Stop it, boy," Calder said a little more firmly, as the dog continued to whine and dig at the base of the fireplace.

"What the hell is your problem?" he asked, his patience wearing thin when the dog continued to ignore him.

Striding angrily over to the mutt and grabbing him by the scruff of the neck, Calder suddenly stopped dead in his tracks and the blood froze in his veins.

Slowly, he bent down and picked up the gold medallion lying in front of the fireplace. Running the chain through his fingers, he felt a tremor of fear run up his spine. Bounding up the stairs, two at a time, he prayed that he was wrong.

He was not. The bedchamber was empty when he slammed the door back against the wall.

Running back downstairs, he began bellowing orders. All of the knights were called to the Hall and Radolf was taken to the kitchen for his dinner. The servants were brought in one after the other, but none had seen Regan since early afternoon.

Calder sent his knights to search the entire castle and grounds, but knew they would not find her. He paced back and forth in front of the fireplace, emotions coursing through him that he had never experienced before. In his image of himself as a man, he had never allowed for the possibility of being so utterly humbled by fear. It was imbedded so deeply that he worried he would not be able to overcome it and think clearly enough to get Regan back.

"Are you sure that she was taken?" Draco asked, his own worry beginning to equal Calder's.

In answer, Calder raised the gold medallion. "I gave this to Regan a long time ago and told her to send it to me should she ever need my help. Since Edgar died, she has never removed it from around her neck. The chain is broken. She tore it free and left it for me to find. Yes, someone has taken her."

"But, the chain could have broken on its own, Milord, and fallen unnoticed."

"Then where is she?" Calder's voice boomed throughout the Hall. Taking a deep breath, realizing that losing control would not help Regan, he continued in a quieter voice. "I find it so ironic, I struggled to get this castle built quickly, to protect us all. Now that it is about done, I have relaxed my guard and allowed people in and out without worrying about their intentions. I have been blind and now someone, most likely that bastard Roderick, has taken Regan from under my very nose."

"We will find her, Milord," Draco promised as he left the castle to help in the search. Calder continued to pace in front of the fireplace, running the chain continuously through his nervous fingers, feeling impotent and useless as he waited for word from his men.

"Will you stop that?" he yelled at Orvyn, as the dog continued to dig frantically at the face of the fireplace.

"Oh, my God," he whispered, as he realized what the dog was doing. "Oh, my God, you wonderful, smelly cur, you."

Grabbing the dog, he gave him a brief hug, grateful for the dog's persistence in trying to get through to such a simple human and explain what had happened.

Unsheathing his sword, he pulled the hidden lever under the mantle and a small door opened silently, leading to one of the secret passageways that went behind the fireplace and down to the river. Calder crept stealthily down the narrow, stone stairs, allowing the large dog to follow behind.

Rounding a sharp bend in the circular stairs, he jumped back as a broadsword was swung directly at him. It barely missed, but clanged loudly against the stone wall next to his head. Calder lost his footing as he hit the wall and was unable to counter when he saw the man preparing his next attack. Orvyn took advantage of the moment while Calder was attempting to regain his balance. The dog leapt at the assassin, the two of them rolling like misfit lovers down the remainder of the stairs.

Calder heard a howl of pain as he hurried to join them and was able to bury his sword in the man's back before the bastard finished off the dog as he had intended.

He removed his tunic and wrapped it around the Orvyn's bleeding belly, stanching the flow of blood from the wound. "Hold on, boy. I'll get you back upstairs and have you taken care of soon. Just hold on a few minutes more."

He ran over to the doorway leading to the river, broadsword at the ready as he slowly pushed it open. The adrenaline coursing through his body turned swiftly to disappointment as he found only footprints leading to the river.

They had gotten her away, and there were no tracks to follow.

With some difficulty, he carried the heavy dog back up into the Hall. Some of his knights had just returned to let him know they had been unable to locate Regan.

"Someone get Bernia, quickly. The dog needs care. Call together the rest of the men. They've taken her by way of the river."

Calder waited impatiently for his orders to be carried out, grinding the blade of his sword with a whetstone until it gleamed with deadly sharpness.

Bernia quickly cleaned and stitched the dog's wound with just minimal help from the knights, who held him still as she did so. "He will survive, Milord. It will just take some time for his wound to heal."

"I am happy for that," Calder replied, looking at the dog with a new sense of respect and gratitude. He ran his hand through his short, black hair, his brow furrowed in worry. "Men, they have taken Regan by way of the river. Whether upstream or down, I do not know. We'll have to split up and search each side, in both directions. It is almost dark now," he said, trying to hide the desperation in his voice, "so we will not be able to track them tonight. We'll wait for first light, I won't risk missing them in the darkness."

It tore his heart out to speak those words and to have to sit idly by while Regan was in the hands of men who only wanted to cause her harm, but he knew there was no other option.

Draco clasped his shoulder. "Tomorrow, Milord, we will find her. And those who took her are spending their last night on this God's earth, have no doubt of that."

Calder placed his hand over Draco's. "Thank you, my friend. Will you help me keep my wits about me while we do this?"

"Aye, Milord," Draco answered, squeezing his shoulder once more before walking away.

*   *   *

After a sleepless night, Calder and his knights filed out of the castle at dawn and halted in amazement at the sight that met their eyes. At least twenty of the village men were standing in the square, some carrying pitchforks, others with makeshift weapons they had been hiding in their homes.

Filbert stepped forward. "We have lived here all of our lives and know these lands better than anyone. We want to help you search for Regan. We are prepared to fight to get her back."

For the first time in his life, Calder had to swallow back tears as he walked down the steps and reached for Filbert's hand. "Thank you." No other words were necessary.

They broke up into groups and were given instructions. By mid-day tracks had been spotted and the men collected together. Quietly, they set out to follow them, Draco and Calder leading the way. They stopped abruptly at the top of hill, spying a large camp down below.

The wagon appeared to be empty, but knights mingled around the fire and a tent of animal hides had been set up to one side.

"Roderick," Calder said balefully, as he watched his nemesis sitting near the fire, laughing and joking with his men.

They pulled back to determine their best course of action. Roderick had double the men that they had and all of his were seasoned knights, not inexperienced farmers, as they had in their group. If they attacked, Roderick would no doubt bring Regan out and use the threat of her life to stop them.

As much as it tore up his insides to do so, Calder decided that they must wait for nightfall before taking any action. "They would not be sitting out in the open that calmly if they were not waiting for us with a plan to repel our attack. I fear Regan's life would be forfeited should we not catch them by surprise."

He brushed his hand through his hair and deep lines of worry etched in his face as he continued. "We will wait until dark, then two men will sneak up to the tent while the others attack from the opposite side of the camp. We must ensure Regan's safety before all else."

Calder and Draco stayed on watch while the others fell back a mile or so to get some food and rest. The day would stretch on interminably waiting for darkness to fall and the fewer they had close to Roderick's camp, the less chance of discovery.

"You should go with them and rest, Calder," Draco said firmly.

"I can't," he replied, staring fixedly down at the camp. "I need to be here."

"As you wish," he replied, shaking his head in disgust at Calder's stubbornness, but also knowing that was why he, himself, had chosen to remain.

It took all of Calder's will power to not rush the camp himself when they brought Regan out of the tent and paraded her before the knights sifting there. Voices and laughter carried on the wind, but he could not hear what they were saying.

He felt the blood in his veins turn to ice as he watched Roderick run his hands over her distended belly and vowed that the man would not live to see another sunrise.

At long last night fell and, with just a quarter moon and heavy cloud cover, they made their way surreptitiously toward the camp. Calder and Kenny would try to get to Regan first as the others approached from the opposite side. When Calder heard Draco's war cry, he quickly sliced through the leather covering Regan's tent and slid through the opening. He stopped abruptly when he saw Roderick with a dagger to her neck.

Sounds of the battle rang loudly outside as Roderick smiled at Calder, sliding his blade along Regan's throat without breaking the skin. "You didn't really think that you could outsmart me, did you, Calder?" he asked, his voice low and filled with smug self-satisfaction.

"Let her go," he replied coldly, as Kenny slipped in beside him.

"Do you know how easy it would be for me to kill her, or your bastard growing in her belly?" he asked, moving the blade down against her extended stomach.

Tears slipped down Regan's cheeks, but she made no sound.

"What would be the point?" Calder asked. "It's me that you want. Why harm them?"

"Because I can. Because you scarred me and now I must make you suffer before you die. What better way to do that than to kill what you hold most dear?"

"Roderick," Calder said in a calm, reasonable voice, "everyone knows what a cowardly bastard you are, but this is a new low for you, murdering an innocent woman because you are not man enough to take me on alone."

"Don't, Calder," Roderick replied softly, his eyes narrowing as he pressed the knife deeper into Regan's stomach. "Don't insult me. I will only make it that much harder on her."

Regan winced in pain and blood started to trickle through the fabric of her kirtle.

"What do you want?" Calder asked, trying to keep the desperation from his voice.

"You dead, her dead, your lands. It's not too much to ask, is it?"

"Well," Calder said, sighing deeply, "you'll just have to kill her then, because that is the only way that you can destroy me. And if you do not destroy me, you will be back in the arms of hell before this night is over, I promise you that."

Roderick changed the position of the dagger in his hand. Regan screamed when she realized that he was about to plunge it into her stomach. Tearing herself out his grip, she stumbled awkwardly and fell to the ground. Hesitating momentarily, worried about Regan's close proximity to Roderick, Calder threw his own dagger. A split-second later it was buried deeply in his nemesis' throat.

Roderick slid to the floor with a wet gurgle, both hands flailing in an attempt to remove the blade. The strength left him quickly, however, and within moments he lay still, gazing out of sightless eyes.

Calder rushed over to Regan and helped her to her feet. "Are you all right?"

Unable to speak, she just nodded as tears flowed down her face.

"Kenny, take her out through the back. I must go help our men. Let no harm come to her," he said quietly, but forcefully.

"Yes, Milord," Kenny replied, as he peered out the opening to make sure the way was clear before helping Regan through.

Calder rushed out the front, his broadsword swinging with reckless abandon, his rage overpowering any concern for his own safety as he struck down Roderick's men one after the other.

Soon the ground was littered with bodies. Most were Roderick's men but, unfortunately, a few villagers had fallen as well. Calder left his knights to take care of the bodies as he helped Regan into the wagon and began their trip back to the castle.

Her contractions started before they were even halfway home and Calder began to sweat profusely in fear and concern. Regan lay in the back, her screams making the hair on the back of his neck stand up as he urged the horses on to greater speeds.

*   *   *

"Milord," Bernia said softly, rousing him from where his head lay on the table. The birds were chirping and life seemed to go on as always, but Bernia gave no indication as to how Regan or the babe fared when she asked him to come with her to the bedchamber.

Anxiety threatened to overwhelm him as he rushed up the stairs. It left him only when he opened the door to find Regan sitting up in bed, smiling tiredly as she rocked a tiny bundle in her arms.

Calder hurried to her side and kissed her forehead, then exhaled deeply, not even been aware that he had been holding his breath.

She turned the bundle around so that he could see the tiny, red, wrinkled face. "Your daughter, Milord."

With an overwhelming sense of delight, Calder ran his finger along the tiny cheek, smiling as the baby tried to suckle it. His smile faltered slightly as he thought of the battles still to come. Although defending King and country was a noble endeavor, the stakes now would be much higher; for he would allow no one, Norman or Saxon, to threaten his family's happiness or security. These were battles that he could not lose.

And with that resolve in his head, he gently lifted his baby and held her close to his heart.

THE END

WHEN THE KNIGHT FALLS
Knights are Forever series Book #2

CHAPTER 1

Wyndymshire, England 1089

Calder woke in a cold sweat, his muscles tensed for battle. Glancing swiftly around the bedchamber, he could detect no danger in the soft shadows thrown by the fading light of the fire.

Regan was murmuring in her sleep, her hand resting lightly on his leg. He brushed a curl from her face, the reflection from the embers making her red hair glow like it was afire. Assured that she remained sleeping peacefully, he slid from under the furs that kept them warm these cool spring nights and donned an undertunic to cover his nakedness.

Calder's heart continued to pound erratically in his chest and he was unable to understand why. He knew that it was not a bad dream that had awoken him, it was something much more than that.

He considered grabbing a candle to help him find his way, but felt more comfortable wandering in the darkness, guided only by the pale moonlight entering through the intermittent window openings.

This was his Keep, the living quarters and stronghold of his castle. Calder knew every inch of it and worried more about a flame giving warning to an intruder than of stumbling through the rooms. He slipped his sword from its nearby scabbard and made his way into the hall.

He paused for a moment but heard nothing untoward, so he continued to his youngest daughter, Lora's, room. Calder walked through the arched doorway and could see that she was sleeping peacefully in her bed. He stood over her for a moment, watching the gentle rise and fall of her chest, letting it soothe him a bit before continuing on.

Stepping quietly back into the hallway he made his way to his oldest daughter's room. Pushing the door open, Calder ignored the small creaking noise it made and sighed in relief when he saw Synne's sleeping form snuggled under the furs. For some unknown reason, his fear seemed to center on her and abated somewhat upon finding her safe in her bed.

Synne's dog slept at the foot of the bed, not by any means a guard dog, the greyhound did, at least, raise its head to be sure no warning bark was in order. Recognizing Calder, it laid its tiny head back down and curled up deeper into the furs.

There was a kak-kak-kak from the falcon over in the corner of the room and Calder was assured that he could at least count on the raptor to signal a warning, should any danger encroach upon his daughter.

Ava, her lady's maid, was asleep on a comfortable pallet in the corner of the room. All was well, so he headed back in the direction that he had come from, continued past his own room and entered the bedchamber belonging to the two younger boys, Beorn and Gwyn.

Beorn's bed was empty, as it had been for the last several years while he trained to become a knight in London. Calder gently pulled the fur up over his youngest, Gwyn, who gave a sleepy moan, turned over and fell back into a deep sleep.

Calder began to question whether or not the alarm he felt upon awakening may have been his imagination, after all. Until he checked the last occupied bedchamber on the floor and found that his oldest son, Radolf, was nowhere to be found.

His feelings of worriment suddenly escalated and he moved faster through the corridors. Poking his sword into the shadowed niches, he swept through the remainder of that floor of the Keep and headed for the stairwell.

Any knight that was not on guard duty would be sleeping off their ale over in the barracks. Calder hesitated and considered having one of the guards call the knights to arms, but he wasn't ready to cause such an undue panic just yet.

Gliding silently down the stairs and into the Great Hall, Calder spied the silhouette of a man against the open window.

"Father, is that you?" Radolf asked, the strong, broad figure of his sire unmistakable, even in the murky darkness.

"It is," Calder replied, some of the tension draining from his body, but his feeling of unease still would not leave him completely. "What are you doing down here in the dark?"

"Something doesn't feel right," Radolf said, shrugging his shoulders. "Why are you awake?"

"Same reason," Calder replied, rubbing his brow. "Something woke me, but I could find naught amiss."

"Nor could I," the young man responded. "Mayhap, it is trouble still to come?"

Calder peered through the shadows, unable to see Radolf's face clearly with the moonlight streaming in behind him. "What do you mean?"

"I do not know," Radolf replied, turning to stare out the open window again. "Mayhap, it is just my imagination playing tricks on me, but I feel something bad is coming our way, and that it will be here soon."

Calder felt a trickle of fear run down his spine, remembering the same feeling that had overwhelmed him years before, and had been true enough that he almost lost his wife and unborn daughter.

Swallowing those unwelcome memories, Calder clasped his son on the shoulder and began to walk with him back to the stairway.

"Should trouble come to us, we will be ready, son. There is no need for you to worry anymore about it this night."

I hope you enjoyed If Not For The Knight. It was the first book that I ever had published and I am very proud of it. I received several requests to do a sequel and I have finally accomplished that.

The second book in the series, When The Knight Falls, will be published in the Fall of 2019. I've included the first section of that novel so you can get a taste of what it's about.

These two books are more of a saga than a series, a continuation of the achievements and events in the lives of one family over two generations. I believe there is at least one more story left to be told about the Wyndyms. I hope you'll join me for that one, as well.

Thank you for accompanying me on this adventure. Please be sure to check out my website so you can get all of the most current information on my books that have been, or will soon be, published.

If you enjoyed the book, I would be very grateful if you would post a review at either amazon.com and/or Goodreads. It can be as brief as you'd like, reviews are not only helpful for the author, but also for other readers who might be interested in the book.

Thanks again and keep on reading!

Debbie Boek
debbieboek.com
debbieboek.blog

www.ingramcontent.com/pod-product-compliance
Lightning Source LLC
Chambersburg PA
CBHW071539110726
47908CB00007B/1939